Lost Time

WINONA KENT

ACKNOWLEDGMENTS

I'd like to thank the following people, without whose assistance this novel would not have been possible:

Brian Richmond, for his continuing inspiration, wonderful story sense and clever suggestions.

Greg Easton, for his insights about rehearsals, touring and trip diaries.

And, of course, my mum Sheila Kent, my sister Stella Kent and my husband Jim Goddard, for their patience and understanding while I indulged in my passion.

Thank you all!

CHAPTER ONE

I was thinking about *Tempo Rubato*.

It's Italian for stolen, or lost, time. Basically, it just means when you're performing a piece of music, you can express your own rhythmic freedom. You can escape from a strict tempo by speeding up or slowing down what you're playing.

I was thinking about it because, for the first time in many years, I was prepping for a tour.

My mum and dad were the founding members of Figgis Green, a folky pop group that was huge in the 1960s and 70s and less huge—but still touring regularly and putting out albums—in the 80s and early 90s. My mum, Mandy Green, was the main singer: long haired, long skirted, a beauty with a voice that could shake the angels. My dad, Tony Figgis—famous for his shaggy moustache and his fondness for brightly coloured silk shirts—shared the vocals and played lead guitar.

Their best-known song was "Roving Minstrel", a catchy thing about a faithless suitor and his careworn lady, tormented hearts, lessons learned and a really fortunate ending. It was the group's anthem, and they always closed their shows with it.

A couple of years earlier, one of the Figs—Mitch Green, my mum's brother, who'd played bass guitar—had floated the idea of a 50th Anniversary Tour. All the old bands were doing them. They'd have guaranteed sell-outs and the merch alone would make it financially worth their while. The Figs' fan base had never really gone away and for years had been vocally advocating—in online groups and on message boards—for just this kind of reunion.

1

For a variety of reasons—notwithstanding the fact that my dad had died in 1995—it didn't happen. But Mitch was still keen, and he kept at it. He eventually got my mum on board, and then my dad's cousin, Roland Black—Rolly—who was the drummer.

He had to work hard to convince Pete Chedwick, though. Pete, who played the fiddle, had joined the band after the original fiddler, Keith Reader, had quit over "philosophical differences". Pete wasn't interested in a reunion. When the Figs had folded, he'd gone on to make quite a good living producing records. So Mitch went calling on Keith. Which also turned out to be a challenge. While he'd been with the band, Keith had constantly been at odds with my dad. A small disagreement about musical influences had escalated into an ongoing feud about the direction the Figs ought to go in.

Neither side was willing to cave in. Keith wanted the band to embrace its folk roots and its dalliances with classical composers, believing that the uniqueness of that mix would propel Figgis Green into the annals of musical history. Dad didn't disagree, but he wasn't the purist that Keith was. Dad's vision was to enhance the traditional instrumentation with electric everything. Jeff Lynne and Roy Wood, who'd infused modern rock and pop with classical violins, cellos, horns and woodwinds when they created ELO in 1970, were my dad's heroes.

By 1989, Keith had finally had enough. He left, Pete took his place, and the rest was history.

But with my dad dead, the main obstacle to Keith's re-joining the band was removed. He agreed to the reunion, much to Mitch's relief.

Besides mum and dad, Mitch, Rolly and Keith, the original line-up had included a rhythm guitar player, Rick Redding. Rick had always been a problem. And when he'd made it known that he fancied my mum, things took a definite turn for the worst. Since my parents were never actually married, I think he must have reckoned that my mum was fair game. He was totally out of order, of course. But he still thought he had a chance, and got into an argument with my dad, which led to a backstage fight and, after the medics had stitched up my dad's chin and my dad called in the coppers and had him charged with ABH, Rick was out.

Rick wasn't welcome on the Lost Time Tour and his replacement, Ben Quigley—a lovely guy who'd continued on as a brilliantly successful solo act for decades after the Figs folded—flat out refused. So Mitch recruited Bob Chaplin, a "friend of the band", to fill his spot.

The reunited Figs were almost complete.

Mitch didn't tell Keith that he'd pencilled me in as my dad's replacement.

I am actually a musician and I do actually play the guitar. Jazz guitar. I have a regular gig at a club in Soho—the Blue Devil—with three mates who join me on tenor sax, organ and drums. I am actually quite good.

And I was familiar with the Figgis Green catalogue—I'd grown up with it.

Mitch knew Keith would be sceptical, so he came down to the Blue Devil and recorded one of my sets on his phone to convince him.

A week or so later, he was back at the club. Mitch is a really nice guy, younger than my mum by two years, with a shock of white hair that always makes me think of Albert Einstein. He's recently taken to wearing spectacles to help him read, and his waistline is somewhat more portly than it was when he was with the Figs. But, like everyone in the group, he's never allowed himself to appear unremarkable. Once a showman, always a showman.

"So that's everyone," he said, as we enjoyed a post-show drink in the upstairs venue that was my musical playroom. It was just past 3 a.m. on a Friday night and the guys in my band had gone home, as had our audience. The club's front doors were locked.

"Even Keith?" I mused.

"Even Keith."

"What did he say?"

"Not a lot. I reminded him that in no way are you remotely the same person as your dad."

It was true. Throughout my life I've made a point of avoiding comparisons, as well as the nepotism that invariably follows along with having well-known musical parents. My professional name is Jason Davey, not Jason Figgis.

"And anyway," said Mitch, "we know we're playing our history. We're not presenting anything new. People will come for the memories. Not for our latest streaming offerings on YouTube."

"I'll do it," I said. "But I will not grow a moustache. And I absolutely will not wear that waistcoat."

The Figs had a colour they used in all their marketing—a really distinctive shade of moss green that showed up on all their album covers, in their stage lighting and even in some of their clothes when they were gigging. My mum had a special floppy velvet Figgis Green hat she popped on in the second half of the show. My dad had a Figgis Green waistcoat.

Both were the height of trendiness in 1974.

"I think we can all agree on that," Mitch said.

#

It had been more than 20 years since the Figs had last appeared together. But, to be fair, none of them had ever really stopped performing. Mitch ran a well-appointed pub in Hampshire and played in a band that offered once-a-week live entertainment to its customers—much of it featuring Figgis Green standards. Keith had been making records of his own, featuring variations on folk tunes, and he'd been touring around festivals for decades. Rolly had moved to the States and had built his own studio and filled it with instruments and had made a second career for himself scoring music for films and TV. And mum had been offering music workshops at her house in the Hertfordshire countryside every summer since 1998.

Mum had hired a manager—Colin Beresford, the son of the guy who'd managed the Figs back in the day—who was well-known in the business and was happy to take the band on. Colin came up with a plan for two tours—one in the fall that would last 35 days and cover 18 stops in southern England and Wales, finishing up in London, and a second one in the spring that would cover Ireland and the north of England. The venues would be a bit smaller than the ones the Figs had filled in their heyday. The average seating was between 700 and 1,500, with one or two in the lower capacities, around 300 or 400. But Colin assured mum we'd have sell-out performances and, he added, he'd arranged for one of the early gigs to be recorded for an album and a DVD, so the band would make extra money on that as well.

I was a bit leery about the idea of recording so close to the start of the tour. There's that old saying about every piece of music having to be learned twice—once in rehearsals and then a second time out in front of an audience. And then once you're playing in front of audiences, it takes a while before you've "settled in" and got to know your voice and your instruments and the band dynamics as a whole.

Nevertheless, we were all professionals—and what we ourselves might immediately spot as a mistake or something that still required work would largely go unnoticed by the audience.

Mum sent around suggestions for set lists and we all contributed our thoughts.

I arranged for a leave of absence from the Blue Devil and found a temporary stand-in to keep my band employed and my post-tour career in safe hands.

And then we all practised hard to bring ourselves up to speed. I literally had to start from scratch, committing my parents' musical legacy to memory as I listened once more to their recordings, watched their performances on YouTube and played their DVD's. Aside from my dad's various guitar parts and singing, I was also going to have to become an expert on the mandolin, bouzouki, banjo, dulcimer and concertina.

I do love a challenge.

#

I was giving mum a lift to Stoneford.

I could tell she was excited. She was waiting for me outside the house, perched on her suitcases like an impatient schoolgirl.

Mum is in her late 70s and her hair is silver-white. I think the specific name of the colour is Shale and Lace. She has essentially the same cut that she did when she was fronting the Figs all those years ago. Except, of course, that her hair is thinner now, and her face is fuller. She's a bit heavier than she was back in the day, too, but that's to be expected as well. She's happily embraced a cushiony comfy grandmotherly look, and it suits her.

"I'm going to buy you a new car," she said, as I loaded her stuff into the back and she got inside. My dad left my mum fairly well-off and the music royalties have never stopped coming in. We had this discussion at least twice a year.

"I love this car," I replied. It's an old, beaten-up silver Volvo V70. It's fast, reliable and tough, and it has room for all my gear. I'd bought it second-hand from the police after a tip from my sister's husband, who's a retired copper.

"Nevertheless. It's embarrassing."

"I don't find it embarrassing," I said. "If you buy me a new car, I'll give it to Dom."

Dominic is my son. He's at college, studying film.

"You're so like your father. He had one of those hippie Volkswagen campervans he absolutely refused to part with. I put my foot down after you were born. I told him it was unsafe for an infant to ride in. He gave it to Mitch."

And I knew Mitch still had it, stashed away in the garden shed at the back of his pub, the rust spots growing more prominent with each passing year. But that was the first time I'd actually been told how it had come into his possession.

Life's full of surprises.

#

Stoneford's a little village in Hampshire, on the south coast of England. At its heart is a triangular-shaped green, with an ancient manor house perched on a hill overlooking its western edge, a venerable old coaching inn at its top end, and a picturesque collection of shops and offices along its two sides and bottom.

The sea, with its stony shingle beach, is a five-minute walk to the south.

And a ten-minute drive to the north is Middlehurst, where our first concert was scheduled for Friday, September 7th.

Figgis Green was born in Stoneford. In the summer of 1965, mum, dad. Mitch, Rolly, Keith and Rick had installed themselves in Stoneford Manor while they came up with 12 songs for their debut album and prepped for their first big tour. After the tour, mum and dad had stayed on in the village and had lived there until just before I was born, when they'd relocated to north London. And when Figgis Green went on subsequent jaunts around England and the rest of the world, Stoneford was where my sister and I spent our childhood holidays, lodged in with Auntie Jo—who was married to Mitch.

It was now Sunday, August 27th, 53 years later.

And it occurred to me, as I drove into the parking lot attached to the inn where we'd be staying, that we were completely off our rockers. Two weeks in which to coax four septuagenarians into shape for 18 concerts in 35 days. Absolute insanity.

#

Centuries in the past, The Dog's Watch Inn had serviced carriages, horses, drivers and passengers. It was situated across from the Village Green, at the top end of a triangle where the High Street met Church Road. There was a single-storied pub made of red brick that had been stuccoed and painted white, and it was attached to a two-storied establishment next door that made up the coaching inn. The inn had square sashed windows with working shutters and a six-foot chimney that was rumoured to have been struck by lightning three times in four years, much to the consternation of those sleeping underneath.

Much to my consternation, too—one thing a lot of people don't know about me is that I have a deep and almost paralysing fear of lightning.

The Dog's Watch was Grade II listed, and it was owned by Arthur Ferryman, a direct descendant of the original innkeeper, Lemuel Ferryman, whose portrait hung on the wall behind the bar in the pub, just above the rack filled with packets of crisps and peanuts.

I love the name Ferryman. It reminds me of that song by Chris de Burgh. I'm tempted not to pay for anything whenever it worms its way into my brain.

Arthur Ferryman was a cousin of Alfred R. Ferryman, Esquire, who'd owned the place in 1965, the last time my mum had a look in.

"He was a real prat," mum said, to Arthur. "Tony and I tried to book a room when we first arrived and he refused because we weren't married. He said he ran a respectable establishment."

"I'm so terribly sorry," Arthur Ferryman replied, as he took us upstairs to the second floor. "Drastically different times."

We learned that his philosophy was nothing like his cousin's—nor indeed was it anything like his cousin's son, Reg Ferryman, who'd run the establishment until 2016, when he'd sold up and moved to Spain.

"I have a background in marketing and hospitality," Arthur added helpfully, showing us to Room 4, which was where mum would be staying. "Our best Superior accommodation, as you can see. Very tranquil, with a hint of the Hampshire countryside. Dusky woods with suggestions of cream and pale gold."

I thought he was talking about the view from the window but then realized he was actually describing the bedspread.

"And of course, the large ensuite facilities, including a full-size bath and shower."

"Very nice," my mum agreed, sitting on the bed to test it. "I'm sure it looks nothing like it did in 1965."

"Nothing like," Arthur Ferryman assured her, again, and then he took me along to Room 6.

It really was lovely—a huge six-foot bed with a grey and white cover, two windows with heavy grey brocade curtains, grey-accented bedside tables and a writing desk with a chair.

"Egyptian cotton, of course," Arthur said, adopting a cosier tone with me as I was 30 years younger than my mum and I hadn't been turned away by his morally-minded cousin in 1965. "Pocket sprung mattress." He illustrated this with a push of his hand. "Extremely nice 32-inch flat-screen TV…" He nodded at the TV up on the wall opposite the bed. "With Freeview."

He took me into the loo.

"Full bath with overhead shower, very nice high-quality towels, and of course, a robe and slippers provided for your ultimate comfort."

"Tea and coffee?" I checked, going back out to the bedroom. I'd be counting on those to ease the transition from night-club hours to early morning rehearsals.

"Earl Grey, Yorkshire and herbal," Arthur replied. "And of course, the pods."

#

Mum and I had dinner in The Dog Watch's dining room with Bob, our rhythm guitar player. Bob was staying in Room 9 (redberry and taupe accents against a buttermilk background).

Rolly and Keith had also checked in, but they'd obviously decided to wait to meet up, and Mitch actually only lived about five minutes away and was going to drive in every day for rehearsals, so overnight accommodations weren't required.

Arthur Ferryman was anxious for us to appreciate the fact that he'd updated the inn's menu at the same time as he'd renovated its rooms. Our first night's dinner was therefore on the house: lamb, or sea bass, or chicken, with a fabulous dessert concocted of chocolate ice cream and lavender shortbread and an unparalleled cheese board that came with chutney and crackers and three kinds of jelly.

"Still apologizing for turning us away in 1965," my mum said, humorously, tucking into the sea bass while I rearranged my chicken for social networking purposes.

"Give his website a 'like'," Bob suggested. "See if he'll extend his gastronomical offer to our entire stay."

"Instagroup?" Mum inquired, as I took a photo with my phone.

"Instagram," I corrected, gently.

I'd decided to create a trip diary consisting entirely of pictures of what I had to eat. Lesser mortals might chat about rehearsal notes, hotel amenities and sound checks, appreciative audiences and backstage visitors. Apparently I'm a bit of an oddity—I'm reliably informed that most men don't bother to document mains and puddings and coffees and confections. According to Katey, my independently faithful girlfriend, and confirmed by Jenn, my grown-up daughter, it's definitely a female thing.

I'd promised them both I'd be an exception to the rule.

When I was at sea, back in 2012, I was obsessed with Twitter. I had a huge online presence—and a commensurate number of followers. My handle was Cold_Fingers, as I was tweeting anonymously from Somewhere in Alaska, and I didn't think my employers at StarSea Cruises would be impressed with my confectionary-related tweets which were, more often than not, tasty invitations to virtual foreplay.

I'm older now and less like a kid in a candy store. I like to think I've matured. And I now have Katey in my life, which removes the need for constant flirtatious reassurances.

I uploaded the inaugural entry to my *Lost Time Culinary Chronicle*, along with an appropriate comment:

Pre-rehearsal dinner with mum and Bob in Stoneford. Roasted chicken breast with bread sauce, stuffing, and oven-browned potatoes.

I was going to add @TheDogsWatch but thought the better of it. I suspected our audiences were mostly going to be made up of senior citizens, but, once a fan, always a fan, and it's never a good idea to publicise where you're staying until after you've checked out.

After dinner I went back to my room, woke up my laptop, found the The Dog Watch's website and wrote a glowing anonymous review of the chocolate ice cream and lavender shortbread. I gave it five stars, then sent my laptop back to sleep and got ready for bed.

It was 11 p.m.

Unheard of.

CHAPTER TWO

I woke up at half past six experiencing mild panic. It was Monday and our start was scheduled for 9 a.m., which meant I had plenty of time to make myself look presentable and have breakfast. And the manor, where we were rehearsing, was only a five-minute walk up the hill from The Dog's Watch.

But I hadn't toured in nearly ten years. The last time I'd gigged around England was 2009, the year Em died. I'd been on the road with my own band, desperate to "make it" playing concerts in pubs and clubs and converted churches and renovated city halls and repurposed corn exchanges. And staging late night turns at so many music festivals I'd lost count.

I really wasn't sure I was up to this.

I made myself a cup of tea with the clever all-in-one device on my writing table and tried to force myself to think past it. I wasn't at all the same person I was back then. I was ten years older. I'd settled. I was far more confident now, and much happier. And "making it" wasn't even in my lexicon anymore. I had "made it"—at the Blue Devil.

This tour was going to be the icing on the cake. And the feeling of apprehension was, I assured myself, temporary. I knew it would pass.

I had a shower and a shave, and then I went downstairs for breakfast.

It was half past seven.

Mum and Bob were already there and had saved me a seat at their table in the dining room.

"'Morning," I said, trying to do my best impression of "awake". It was a challenge.

"Bucks Fizz?" Bob inquired, offering me the menu. "To celebrate our first day on the job?"

"It's a bit early for me," mum said.

"I don't drink," I said. "But a straight-up orange juice would go down nicely."

"Ah," said Bob, in that tone of voice that people revert to when they find they need to express an understanding of alcoholic recovery.

"By choice," I added. "Not any particular adherence to higher powers or staircases."

"Well done," said Bob, acknowledging that my willpower had control over the broken "off-switch" that many of my friends who actually have embraced AA enthusiastically own up to.

The menu offered a fresh fruit salad with berries, or yogurt, or porridge, or cereals. And the ever-popular Full English, which all three of us decided to order. There's nothing like going to work on two free-range eggs, sausage, mushroom, baked beans and a roasted tomato. Even when you're showered and shaved but your brain's still upstairs buried under the pillow.

"I trust you solved your smoking issue?" mum inquired, conversationally, as I took the mandatory photo for Instagram.

"You know me too well."

"I should think so," she said, pouring out a cup of her favourite Yorkshire tea.

"A chuffer?" Bob guessed.

"I'm trying to quit."

"He's always trying to quit," mum replied, humorously, stirring in some milk. "I don't know where he got it from. Neither Tony nor I ever smoked."

"Cigarettes, anyway," I said.

I know it's difficult to imagine a Shale and Lace granny regularly toking up. But when she was younger, she did. And so did my dad. Along with the rest of the band. There's a wonderful ornate hookah from India somewhere in her loft and I can attest to the fact that it was exceptionally well-used.

"I reckon," I said, "that as long as you keep trying, you've never actually thrown in the towel."

Since The Dog's Watch was a non-smoking establishment, last night's bedtime ciggie had forced me to become inventive: take the battery out of the smoke alarm (not an option—it was hard-wired—I checked); open a window and aim the smoke outside (a possibility—if I'd been able to figure out how to unlatch the bloody thing) or retreat into the loo, shut the door and blow it down the—

"Sink drain?" mum guessed.

"I won't tell Arthur if you don't," I said, embracing my first coffee of the day. Very strong. With cream and two sugars.

#

Stoneford Manor has an interesting history. It was built in the early 1800s by a widower, Augustus Duran, who'd arrived in the village after hurriedly abandoning a very draughty chateau in Amiens in the midst of the French Revolution. He'd remarried and set about raising a second family. But it turned out his new wife preferred to live in a far less ostentatious cottage at the bottom of the hill, and so the manor had been sold to the Boswell-Thorpes, who owned three other stately country homes and a townhouse in Eaton Square in London.

A century or so later, in the 1960s, the house and its grounds became notorious for the social events thrown by Giles Jessop, whose mother was Gwendolyn Boswell-Thorpe and whose father was Gilbert Jessop, the 17th Earl of Brighthelmstone. Giles fronted a band called Brighton Peer, and he and his twin sister Arabella were part of The Scene. They attended all of the trendy night spots and all of the important parties. They threw important parties of their own. They wore the latest fashions, drove the fastest cars, and were on first-name terms with everyone who was anyone. If you wanted to meet a pop star, or a photographer, a model, or a gangster, they could arrange it.

It was still party-central until mid-1965, when Arabella ran into some unfortunate dealings with the police, the west wing of the manor caught fire, and Giles, wisely, decamped to the safety of Swinging London. His parents also decamped, had the charred remains restored, and let the house out to discerning clients, provided they paid a damage deposit and promised not to kick holes in the walls or smash the stained-glass windows or trash the antique suits of armour in the downstairs gallery.

Figgis Green had been one of the first bands to rehearse in the manor, and the tradition of being an accessible and desirable haven for musicians had continued for some years. But by the time my sister Angie and I were scrambling through the wild undergrowth at its rear and exploring the crumbling ruins of its derelict stable block, its windows and doors had been boarded up and there were rumours the Boswell-Thorpes had plans to turn it into a bed and breakfast. Which was what it eventually became, until 2016, when it was quietly boarded up again and its premises abandoned. And then, two years later—just in time for our Lost Time tour—it was back in business as a rehearsal space.

We were convening in the library, which was on the second floor in the east wing and was reached by way of an immense central staircase. One of the library's walls was fitted with exquisitely carved oak panels with mantels and twisted spindles and archways and linenfold inserts. In the middle of the wall was a massive fireplace, surrounded by blocks of white stone and protected by a filigreed iron fireguard. The wall opposite the fireplace was decorated with carved oak panels. And the wall opposite the doorway contained three bay windows overlooking the sea.

It was huge but completely appropriate for our purposes. Our crew had been busy—they'd arranged a collection of acoustic screens around the room to baffle the sound. They'd also set up our mikes and instruments and amps and music stands to replicate what they guessed would be our positions onstage.

I went in with mum and Bob and put on my best "new boy" face and manners. Bob was a new boy too, but at least he had a history with the band, subbing in on occasions when Rick, and then Ben, were unavailable. I was still in nappies when Figgis Green was riding the radio charts. Everyone else—even Bob—had spent years together, recording and performing, and they'd built relationships. My interaction had always been peripheral. I was Tony and Mandy's kid. I showed up in photos taken for PR pieces in papers and magazines. I attended Christmas parties and visited backstage during gigs and I was always around when there were band meetings or social events at our house. But I'd never played with them—not formally, anyway. And I was feeling incredibly uncertain as a result.

Mitch and Keith were already there, tuning up and testing out, impatient to start. Rolly, who was still recovering from jet lag and the eight-hour time change between Los Angeles and England, was slumped in an armchair in the corner, quietly snoring.

I'd brought a jar of Kenco Smooth instant coffee as my "housewarming" gift to the group. I'd assumed, a bit naively, that someone else would be taking care of mundane things like a kettle. And mugs.

It turned out there was a kettle, in the kitchen, which was downstairs, and which looked as if it had last been renovated around the same time that Mary Quant had invented the mini-skirt. The kettle was electric and it still worked, though I wasn't at all confident about the plug. And there wasn't any milk.

A blank piece of paper had been tacked to the wall beside the kettle, along with a pencil on a string, and a note from Kato, our runner, explaining that if we needed anything to add it to the shopping list, which he promised he'd check and act upon every morning at 10 a.m. He'd helpfully provided his mobile number at the bottom, along with three smiley faces.

I added "a new kettle" to the list, and "milk", and, after checking the cupboards and drawers, "jammy dodgers", "ginger nuts" and "custard creams". There were two boxes of cubed sugar—I had no idea how old they were, though that sort of thing doesn't really go off, does it. There was a container of that disgusting powdered stuff that passes as coffee whitener, and there was a jar of generic instant coffee to go with it, and a box of teabags.

I was prepared, on that first day of rehearsals, to run through our two set lists, song by song—but it didn't happen. What did happen was a long discussion *about* the set lists, song by song—including how they would be lit and what they ought to sound like, and where and when we were going to stand—and sit—and what we were going to say in between the songs, and how long we were going to take to say it.

I made notes.

I checked my emails.

I uploaded a picture of my breakfast to Instagram.

I dashed off texts to Dom and Jenn. And Katey, who promised to come and rescue me from the doldrums of celibacy as soon as she could manage a day off work.

There was a break at half past ten (during which I dashed outside and smoked two hurried ciggies, one after the other, and made friends with Tejo, our sound guy, who was also a chuffer and who, as it turned out, enjoyed the same brand as me—Benson and Hedges

Gold), and came back to drink one of the worst cups of tea in the history of tea making. Much more of that, I thought, spying a box of chocolate-chip muffins that someone had brought up from the village, and I'd find it necessary to resort to criminal acts.

And Kato still hadn't put in an appearance.

By the time lunch rolled around, I was starving, in desperate need of another cigarette and craving a decently-brewed coffee.

"There's a place on the other side of the Village Green," mum said. "At least there used to be. It was called The Four Eyes back in the day—they had a house band called The Spectacles who shared the pop charts with us for a few weeks."

"It's still there," Mitch said. "Independently owned and operated—not your average Starbucks."

Indeed, it wasn't. Smoking furiously, I trudged down the hill and across the little green and there it was, in a parade of buildings that was home to two firms of solicitors, the *Stoneford News*, a hairdresser's and Oldbutter and Ballcock Funeral Directors. The Four Eyes.

Its glory days had been roundabout 1965. There followed a long, slow decline in popularity and function; in the mid-1970s, when I was spending those long summer days with Auntie Jo while my parents toured, it was sitting empty and forlorn, its place in history on the verge of being forgotten.

I was happy to see someone had decided to rescue it and restore it to its former glory, albeit with a completely up-to-date take on coffee culture. I opened the door and went in.

Inside there was a huge silver Italian espresso machine on the counter and an authentic jukebox from the 1960s in the corner, though I doubted either of them were actually in working order and were largely there for their nostalgic value.

On the walls were photos of the place in its heyday. A little room crowded with earnest-looking teenagers. An exterior shot featuring a painted sign declaring that this was, indeed, The Four Eyes Coffee Bar, its name reinforced with a graphic representation of a pair of black-framed Hank Marvin-style eyeglasses. A smaller sign on the pavement advertising the house band—The Spectacles—and an amateur night when anyone could join them onstage.

Another of the photos showed a view of the counter, with that same espresso machine in use, and the jukebox lighting up the corner. There was also an orange juice dispenser, and a display case containing a few sandwiches and sausage rolls and a large bowl of what looked like spaghetti.

I ordered a coffee and a baguette with grilled veggies and generous slices of cheese, along with a very tasty-looking slice of something smothered in chocolate for dessert.

I'd just arranged it all on my table so I could take a picture for my *Culinary Chronicle* when I was approached by a guy wearing a hand-knitted V-neck sleeveless pullover and a shirt and tie. You don't often see that nowadays. A shirt and a tie and a sleeveless pullover. I'd guess he was probably about my mum's age—early 70s anyway. He had very neat grey hair, combed carefully, and a pink and white face. He was carrying an old-fashioned leather school satchel.

"Hello, Jason," he said.

I was pretty positive I didn't know him. But that happens a lot. I perform. I'm in front of people. I enter their lives, and because of that, there's an assumed familiarity. On their end, anyway.

"Hello," I said, doing my best to convey the impression that I was actually looking forward to an uninterrupted lunch on my own.

"Duncan Stopher," he said, sticking out his hand.

I shook it. "Hello."

I sat down. He remained standing.

"I tried to see you this morning at the manor but your security guard wouldn't let me in. I'm a huge fan of Figgis Green."

Did he want me to sign something? Was he going to tell me all about his extensive record collection? His sister's grandchildren? His dodgy insides? He looked the sort of person who maintained a journal about his bowel movements.

Excellent contribution this morning...

Nothing today. Requires an investigation.

"I wanted to let you know how much I admired you for the way you tracked down Ben Quigley when he disappeared. I know you're good at solving cases involving missing people."

"Ah," I said. "Thanks."

A few years earlier, Ben had travelled to Peace River, Alberta— in northern Canada—to take part in a music festival. He'd never come back and people—my son, in particular—were understandably concerned for his welfare. I'd gone there to look for him. It had taken some work, but I'd found him…rescued might be a better word…and brought him home to England. His story had ended up in all the papers, and my second-string career as a PI had been launched.

"I have something I think you might be interested in. Might I join you…?"

Without waiting for me to reply, he appropriated the chair on the other side of the table.

"It concerns a missing girl," he said. "I've approached the police but they simply aren't interested."

"Why not?" I asked.

"They're of the opinion that the young lady in question is dead."

"Why would they think that?"

"She was declared legally dead by her mother a few years after she disappeared."

"Well," I said. "That more or less closes the book on the case. Really."

"However, they are wrong."

"You think they're wrong or you know they're wrong?"

"I know they're wrong."

He placed the old leather satchel he'd been carrying onto his lap, opened it and proceeded to transfer its contents to the tabletop in neat, perfectly aligned stacks.

"I took a lot of photos of Figgis Green when they were at the peak of their popularity in the mid-1970s," he said.

And there they all were. Some were in colour, some in black and white. Each had a label affixed to the back, with meticulous printing identifying the date and location.

"Fairfield Halls," he said, reading them aloud. "Croydon, October 1, 1973. Brangwyn Hall, Swansea, November 13, 1975. Sheldonian Theatre, Oxford, July 10, 1976—"

"Yes, I understand," I said.

"August 1, 1974. The Wiltshire Folk Festival."

He wanted me to pay special attention to that one. Actually, there was more than one. There were five 5x7 colour photos, taken from where he must have been standing in the middle of a crowded grassy field. A stage at the far end featured Figgis Green. Behind that was a small forest—useful for damping the sound so the neighbours wouldn't complain. The Wiltshire Folk Festival had only lasted a few years but was famous for who it attracted and how well it was organized. *The Old Grey Whistle Test* had done a story about it in 1972.

I glanced at all of the pictures. I didn't have a lot of choice— Duncan was sliding them in front of me, one at a time, helpfully moving the plate with my baguette off to one side to accommodate them.

"I'd forgotten about this roll of film," he said. "I'd put it away in a drawer and then, you know, things…"

He gestured in a way that suggested his unreliable lower colon or his grandchildren's tonsils had interrupted whatever plans he'd had for that particular summer.

"I found it last month while I was having a clear-out, and I sent it off to be developed. I'd labelled the film canister, of course, so I knew it was from the festival. But it's this which captured my attention."

He held the picture up for my benefit.

"Pippa Gladstone."

In the foreground of the photograph were a teenaged boy and girl. They both had long hair: his was dark brown and shoulder-length. Hers was dark blonde and wavy and hanging past her shoulders. The boy was looking away from the camera, but the girl was staring straight at it, and I noted that she had really striking blue-grey eyes. Both the boy and the girl were wearing trendy New York Yankees baseball caps. And they were dressed, like everyone around them, in rumpled Indian cotton shirts and grungy-looking bell-bottomed jeans and they both looked as if they needed a bath, which wasn't surprising as they'd likely been camping in a nearby meadow for the better part of a week.

"Who's Pippa Gladstone?" The name sounded familiar, but I couldn't think why.

"The young lady who disappeared in 1974 and was later declared legally dead by her mother."

"Did she disappear at the folk festival?"

"No, she disappeared while she on holiday with her family in Spain. She was 16 years old at the time and the locals claimed she'd been seen out and about with the son of a local businessman. But when the police questioned the boy he said he'd been to a party with her but he'd given her a lift back to her hotel and had dropped her off outside. He said the last he'd seen of her was when she'd got out of his car. He didn't stay to make sure she was safely inside."

"No CCTV or anything to confirm his statement, I suppose."

"That technology was still evolving at the time. It hadn't evolved as far as that particular hotel in 1974."

"And the police investigated…?"

"The police were unable to unearth any evidence to suggest that the boy had harmed or killed her."

"And that's where it ended?"

"That is indeed where it ended, although there were a number of so-called sightings over the years, and a few claims that her body had been found. All proved to be false."

"So why is this picture relevant?" I asked.

"Because," Duncan replied, "the date I took that photo was August 1, 1974. You can verify when the Wiltshire Folk Festival ran that year. I have all of the details—"

He paused again and removed some more papers from his satchel and laid them out on the table. A set list. A very tattered handbill advertising the festival—signed by my mum and dad.

Some scribbled writing in peacock blue ink on lined paper.

"I made note of which guitars your father chose for the performance," Duncan provided, helpfully. "And where he played misplaced notes in three of the songs."

"And Pippa…?"

"She disappeared on March 23, 1974."

"Five months before that photo was taken."

"Yes. So you can see the problem."

"Are you sure it's her?"

"I'm absolutely positive."

"But you didn't know it was her when you took the picture…?"

"I was taking a picture of Figgis Green and she happened to be in the frame. I didn't actually notice her until I got the film developed and recognized who it was."

There were even more things in the satchel. Pippa Gladstone's last school photo, a colour headshot. And an 8x10 enlargement of the photo from Duncan's camera. I put them side by side. The girl in Duncan's photo was turning to look at him, so her face was visible full-on. It certainly did look like the same person.

"Who's the boy she's with?"

"I don't know his name, alas."

"And you've been to the police with this."

"I have. As I told you, they're not interested. They don't consider it worth their while to re-open her file on the basis of just this one photo. In fact, they were quite dismissive of me."

"And what's your interest in all of this?" I asked.

"I'm a bit of an obsessive," Duncan replied. "I've followed your parents' band faithfully from the beginning. But Figgis Green is not my only passion. I have also been intrigued by Pippa Gladstone's disappearance. There are some who have never quite believed that she is dead. I happen to be one of them. And that photo has, at long last, proved me right. As I said, I know you have a certain amount of notoriety as someone with an ability to track down missing people. I would be very honoured if you would take this case on. I will, of course, make it financially worth your while."

The fact that the photo was taken five months after Pippa was reported missing did stir up a certain inquisitiveness in me. If that really was her.

"Could I borrow these pictures?"

"Of course."

"Can we meet up here tomorrow? Same time? I'll let you know what I've decided. And I'd like to see the negative of the one from the music festival."

"I'll bring it tomorrow." Duncan took his phone out. "Would you mind…?"

A selfie.

Him and me.

I gave him my best smile. He beamed into the lens and refrained from draping his arm over my shoulder, which I appreciated.

"Thank you, Jason. I'll see you here tomorrow."

#

I arrived back at the manor carrying a plastic bag with a carton of milk in it that I'd bought from a little grocery on the High Street, most of my baguette wrapped in paper napkins and Duncan Stopher's photos in an envelope tucked under my arm.

I popped the milk into the fridge and went upstairs to find Rolly, our drummer, fuelled by undiluted caffeine, ranting about a senatorial candidate from his adopted home in California.

"Todd Wolfe," he said. "I don't wish evil upon anyone…but in this moron's case, I'd make an exception. He's a Class A arsehole."

"Does he stand a chance?" I asked.

"More than a chance, son. He's climbed aboard the golden escalator and he's riding it all the way to the top."

I try not to think a lot about American politics these days. It gives me indigestion.

Mum had spent her lunch break with a mug of fishbowl tea and an egg salad sandwich someone—not Kato—had fetched from the bakery at the bottom of the hill.

"And how is The Four Eyes after all these years?" she inquired, saving me from a further earful about sexual harassment complaints, accusations of tax evasion and rumours of unpaid child support from three different relationships.

"Happily nostalgic," I replied. "Pictures on the walls from its glory days. Espresso machine and jukebox lovingly preserved."

"I must go and see for myself," mum said. "I remember in 1965 the walls were decorated with discarded eyeglasses. It was all very clever. If you didn't know better, you'd think you'd stepped into an optician's shop. Did you go downstairs?"

"I didn't know there was a downstairs."

"Oh yes. The cellar. Unfit for human habitation. But that was where it all happened back in the day. That's where the stage was. Where the Spectacles played. And anyone else who wanted to take part in Amateur Night, which was every Friday. Your dad and I decided we'd do a turn. That's where I discovered how much I loved being in front of an audience."

The rest of the band was trickling back in, along with Tejo and our lighting guy, Dr. Sparks, who also had the advantage of being a fully licensed physician (incredibly useful when you're travelling with four senior citizens).

We reassembled for the afternoon like ragtag schoolkids forced back into their classroom on a gloriously sunny day. Our morning had been spent standing around, drinking coffee and tea, listening to technical discussions and making notes. I'd felt useless. And impatient. I wanted to play.

I knew everyone else was feeling the same way. The sentiment wasn't lost on mum.

"Enough of this technical stuff," she said. "Let's have the encore. Everyone up front."

"I Can't Stay Mad at You" was a Gerry Goffin/Carole King country and western/pop crossover that Skeeter Davis had made famous in 1963. It had a catchy beat and throwaway lyrics and it was a song—mum always maintained—which represented a study of unhealthy obsessive love. It was also an inside joke about the starstruck fangirls who used to lust after Ben Quigley and, before he was married, Uncle Mitch.

The Figs did the song *a capella* at the end of every concert, and although they'd never actually made a recording of it, their audiences not only expected it—they demanded it.

Back in the day, mum handled the lead while the guys abandoned their instruments and came down front to gather around a second single mic to do the "shooby dooby doo bops" while she sang. They had a little choreography to go along with it, too, just like the doo-wop bands from the early 1960s. It never failed to break up the audience, especially when they tackled the high notes that the Anita Kerr Singers did on the original Skeeter Davis recording. There was also an instrumental string section three-quarters of the way through that was entirely performed by the guys using just their voices.

I'd spent an entire day mastering that song at home. I joined the line-up beside mum with Keith, Mitch, Rolly and Bob.

Rolly tapped his sticks together to count us all in, and we were away.

It's a tricky piece to get right but after about six attempts, we nailed it. Choreography and all. Including the high female chorus parts which were relegated to me—since I was the youngest and still had the range—and the bit in the middle where we all pretended to be the string section.

It was a grand way to finally start our countdown to the opening night of Figgis Green's Lost Time Tour.

"Henceforth to be known as the Last Time Tour," my mum quipped.

We all agreed it was entirely appropriate.

#

We finished at five.

Dinner at The Dog's Watch was on the house again—Arthur Ferryman had obviously read my thumbs-up on his website and possibly my comments on Instagram.

I arranged my dishes and drink and cutlery to its best advantage and took the mandatory photo: *Spinach and ricotta ravioli with baby gem lettuce, shallots and pine nuts.* Sixteen people loved it immediately, two commented on the food, three asked me to pass on their good wishes to Mitch, four to Keith and one to Rolly. Another four wanted to know what mum had for dinner and one just wanted to reminisce about the time he'd met my dad after a gig in Birmingham, where he'd got his program signed and he still had it and it was too bad my dad had died as he'd have been fantastic on this tour and was going to be sorely missed.

I didn't disagree. I missed him too.

Over the next hour another 214 people recorded their appreciation of my ravioli.

Power to the Figs.

After dinner I went back to my room and sent the smoke from my evening ciggie down the bathroom drain while I had another look through the photos Duncan Stopher had given me.

My gut instinct told me it was very likely a case of mistaken identity. But I had to admit, the girl at the Wiltshire Folk Festival did look almost identical to the 16-year-old in the school pic.

What I really wanted to do was go online and read everything I could about Pippa Gladstone, her family, and the circumstances surrounding her disappearance. But it was getting late and I was tired and we had another 9 a.m. start in the morning.

I popped onto Instagram to check my dinner post. My "likes" had risen to over 600 and there were 231 comments.

I couldn't possibly read them all in one sitting, let alone react or reply.

I settled on wishing everyone good night in a single, very genuine message, and stumbled off to bed.

CHAPTER THREE

The Figs weren't—and never have been—a high-tech act. No lasers or *Live and Let Die* pyros, no huge screen up the rear with rolling cameras on tracks in the pit, no complex light shows and multi-level stages. No need for in-ear assistance, either—we were planning to have wedgies in front of us and amps in the back and Tejo with his trusty mixing board to make the band sound excellent. No multiple trucks filled with rigs and hundreds of rolling flight cases, either. We were going to tour in a comfy bus, with a van for all the equipment following us (driven by Kato, who would also take care of moving our gear on and offstage and setting it all up).

We'd also hired a Tour and Merch manager—Freddie—who'd planned our itinerary and arranged our hotels and was going to be on hand to check us all in and out and, additionally, was going to run the merch table and look after our gigging clothes.

And there were two more people who were going to be essential to our continued wellbeing and good health while we were on the road: a couple of caterers to make sure we all ate properly. Following each show's sound check, dinner would be served promptly at 6 p.m.

#

Day Two of rehearsals—Tuesday—began in much the same way as Day One—me struggling to wake up, breakfast with mum and Bob (I hadn't yet succeeded in convincing Arthur that I required two scrambled eggs, toast and marmalade to be delivered directly to me in my room, despite a generous monetary incentive), and a bracing trudge up Manor Rise, with Bob chatting on his phone with his girlfriend, and mum somewhere ahead of us, putting us both to shame with her agility and her very expensive, very trendy hot pink and purple trainers.

We showed our passes to Security at the front door, and we were admitted.

Kato was still missing—in fact, my shopping list was where I'd left it, tacked next to his note on the wall in the kitchen. We were without a reliable kettle, jammy dodgers and ginger nuts, although someone had left the remnants of a packet of custard creams on the counter and my carton of milk—now half-empty—was still in the fridge.

I went upstairs to join the band.

#

At lunch time, I walked down the hill and across the green to The Four Eyes, where I'd promised to meet Duncan.

He'd already snagged a table next to the big glass window. And he'd bought me the same grilled veggies and cheese baguette that I'd had yesterday, the same chocolate cake thing, and a gigantic coffee in a cardboard cup, onto which he'd popped a plastic lid in order to keep it warm.

"I hope you don't mind," he said. "I've taken the liberty. I put cream in your coffee but I wasn't certain about the sugar so I'm afraid you'll have to add your own."

"Thank you," I said, helping myself to two paper packets, three paper napkins and a wooden stir-stik from the self-serve buffet against the wall.

"Have you decided?" he asked, as I sat down.

"I still think it may be a case of mistaken identity," I replied. "But you've made me curious enough to want to look into it. So yes, I'll do it. Just to put the whole question to bed, one way or the other."

Duncan looked very pleased indeed. "Excellent," he said. "I think you'll find the fee I'm prepared to pay very generous."

He wrote a figure on my paper napkin.

"Very," I agreed.

"I'm so pleased," he said. "And I've brought the negatives."

He presented me with a piece of cellulose wrapped in a protective

25

sleeve of thin, transparent paper.

I held sleeve up to the light. Inside was a 35mm strip of five negatives. All the colours were reversed, making it look weird and surreal and overwhelmingly orange. I couldn't really see the details, but that wasn't going to be a problem.

"I also brought along some of my research," Duncan said. "Anticipating you'd say yes."

He opened his satchel and out came newspaper clippings. Photocopies of newspaper clippings. Printouts of online stories. Words and sentences and entire paragraphs highlighted in pink, yellow, green and blue.

I snapped a quick picture of my lunch and posted it to Instagram while Duncan arranged everything on the table in front of me.

"There you are," he said. "From the first reports of her disappearance until now. Although I must say that these days, it's all just a rehash of earlier stories. The family stopped commenting years ago."

"Can you just sort-of give me a potted history of the case?"

I had no doubts that he would be able to recount every minor fact and detail.

"I'm due back at work in an hour," I added.

"Yes, of course, where would you like me to begin?"

"At the beginning," I said. "Pippa and her family."

"Harry and Susan Gladstone and the two children: Bernard and Philippa. She was the eldest. They lived very near here—in Middlehurst, in fact."

Of course. *That* was why they sounded so familiar. In March 1974, the Figs were touring, and my sister and I were staying with Auntie Jo. The disappearance of Pippa Gladstone had been huge news. I wasn't quite six but I remembered the commotion it had caused, the opinions exchanged in the shops, the horror in my own mind that if someone's daughter could vanish, just like that, it could happen to *me* as well.

"And they went on holiday…"

"Yes, they travelled to Malaga. They arrived on March 10, 1974 for a two week stay. It was a Sunday."

I was making notes. I have a handy mechanical pencil and a little lined notebook with spiral binding that I use for things like this. And I always record the conversations on my phone.

Duncan waited for me to catch up, then continued. "The

complex where they were staying was comprised of the main hotel and some self-contained self-catering villas. The Gladstones had rented one of the villas. It had three bedrooms, a small kitchen and a sitting area. Susan and Harry occupied the first bedroom, a king double, Pippa the second—a single—and Bernard had the third room to himself. It was furnished with twin beds but of course he only occupied one."

"At a time, anyway," I said.

Duncan gave me a blank stare. Subtle humour was obviously not his strong point.

"Their stay was uneventful for two weeks. However, on their last night there, her parents reported—and their son, Bernard, confirmed—that Pippa left the complex for a farewell party with some other teenagers she'd met at the resort. The police identified all of these teenagers and they also confirmed that Pippa had been with them on that evening. As far as the police were able to determine, she left the party at about midnight in the company of a young man named Alvaro Izan. His father, Marcano, was a well-known property owner and businessman in the area. The police took several statements from Alvaro, who swore each time that he had dropped Pippa off at the resort complex at one o'clock in the morning. She'd had a few drinks, he claimed, but she was not at all drunk."

"And she never arrived back at the villa…?"

"The reception area at the complex was staffed 24-hours a day and the staff were interviewed and none could recall seeing Pippa coming back that night. However, it was not necessary to go through the reception area in order to access the villa so their testimony was not deemed helpful. Her parents had stayed up waiting for her to return, and, at 3 a.m., they notified the police. I've given you all of the original newspaper articles containing these details."

I leafed through the collection, which had been presented to me in chronological order, the oldest stories first.

"You must take great care to curate these stories appropriately," Duncan warned. "You know how the British press can be."

"Indeed I do."

"I always think it best to stick to the *Guardian*, the *Telegraph* and *The Times*," he added, confidentially. "There's a little too much…hysteria…attached to the red-tops. And you can never really trust what they're saying to be the truth. At least with the other three, you can more or less have faith in the veracity of their reporting."

He picked out a page from the collection, and leaned forward in earnest.

"Although this particular journal, *Del Sol*, which has its headquarters in Andalusia and is written in English specifically for the ex-pat community of Brits in the region, was particularly excellent in its initial coverage of events. Not," he added, "to be confused with the Spanish-language *Del Sol* which made its debut in Madrid in 1917 and which ceased publication in 1939."

"I'll keep that in mind," I promised. "So she was reported missing. And searches turned up nothing…?"

"Nothing at all. And there were, of course, many of those searches over the next few days. The family delayed its return to England for two weeks and then, reluctantly, went home. You must remind yourself that this was 1974. If it had happened a quarter of a century later, the internet would have been filled with opinion, gossip and theory…but as this all took place before the introduction of the all-seeing web, the only information we were privy to was that which was reported in the papers and on the television and radio."

"We?" I said.

"Yes…my fellow researchers and myself. We convene on the Pippa Gladstone Mystery Forum. There are a number of groups on social media which have fora dedicated to specific cases, which you should, of course, have a look at. But there is only one group which is entirely devoted to Pippa. You would do well to sign up. And then you would have access to the Members Only sections."

"I'm guessing you don't use your real name on the forum."

"I do, in fact," Duncan replied. "I have nothing to hide."

"And is this photo common knowledge on the forum?"

Duncan shook his head. "It is not. I thought it best not to share for now."

"Must be difficult for you to keep it to yourself."

"Very much so. But after the reception I got from the police…I want to be certain about what I have before I share it."

Fair enough, I thought.

"So," I said, "Pippa was missing…the Spanish police investigated…were her parents ever questioned?"

"There's nothing in the newspaper reports to suggest they were ever questioned about anything other than the basic facts. They appear to have been considered above suspicion."

"Usually the parents are the first people the police want to eliminate. What about the young man?"

"Alvaro Izan came from a privileged background and was somewhat arrogant as well as condescending in his attitude towards the police. But he steadfastly maintained his innocence and his story never wavered. He also appeared to be above suspicion."

"So Pippa's family flew home…"

"Yes, and then, two weeks after that, Harry—Pippa's father—was involved in a horrific accident. He fell—some say he was pushed—off the platform at Holborn tube station as a train was approaching and was killed instantly."

"That's in these papers too?" I checked.

"Oh yes, of course. The press loves a tragedy, doesn't it. And a tragedy upon another tragedy—a virtual gold-mine."

"What did the inquest conclude? Pushed or fell?"

"Inconclusive, I'm afraid. Accidental death with no proof of criminal involvement. Plenty of people were questioned but nobody was arrested."

"Did Harry have a history of depression, anything like that?"

"None at all."

"And when did Pippa's mother have her declared legally dead?"

"Seven years after that. 1981."

"Is Mrs. Gladstone still alive?"

"She is. And she still lives in Middlehurst. Coincidentally, where your opening night concert is in two weeks' time."

"You have a front row seat." It wasn't a guess.

"I bought my ticket the moment they went on sale. I hope you'll be available afterwards to sign the memorabilia."

I scribbled a note to remind myself to buy a black indelible marker for the t-shirts, CD's, posters, and souvenir programs Freddie was going to be hawking at the merch table. I had no doubt Duncan would be buying at least one of everything.

"I don't suppose you have Mrs. Gladstone's address."

I needn't have asked.

"Here you are," Duncan said, handing me a sheet of lined paper, upon which was neatly printed, in peacock blue ink, the contact information for Pippa's mum, Susan, and her brother, Bernard, who also still lived nearby.

"Tell me a little about her family. What did her father do for a living?"

"Harry was a professor at Hampshire University. He specialized in the cultural and political history of modern England. His particular interest was World War Two. Of course, that was also the focus of his publications and ongoing research."

I glanced at the clock on my phone.

"I don't suppose you know where I could buy a kettle.".

"I believe there's a Currys in Christchurch."

Christchurch was ten miles to the west along the coast road. Desperate times meant desperate measures.

"Do you have a car?" I asked.

"I do indeed."

I took out my wallet and gave him a wad of cash.

"Buy me a decent electric kettle? If you bring it up to the manor and let the security guy know it's for me, he'll let you in. I'll have a word."

"I would be very honoured, Jason."

"Thanks," I said. I meant it.

Duncan left. I once again wrapped my baguette in paper napkins and, on my way out, stopped to examine the branded wares The Four Eyes was offering for sale. I left with four French presses (yellow, green, red and blue lids), four paper bags of signature blend roasted and ground coffee, a tin box of loose-leafed breakfast tea and the biggest Brown Betty teapot they had. They must have appreciated my custom because the cashier threw in a special Four Eyes bar of fruit and nut chocolate at no extra cost.

"Enjoy," she said, with a pleasant smile.

"Thanks very much."

"And have a good rehearsal," she added.

Of course.

I was not in London anymore.

I'd waived all rights to anonymity.

#

Our finalized set lists had 19 songs—eight in Set One, then a break for the loo, rehydration, a change of clothes, back and leg rest for the elderlies and a smoke for me—then another nine songs in Set Two, plus the two encores. Sometimes bands like to switch things out, especially if they have a huge catalogue and anticipate getting bored with the same nightly setup. Or if they think some tunes might be better appreciated by a particular audience than others. So we had half a dozen songs on standby, just in case.

Our plan was to present a fairly reliable selection of Figs favourites, in no particular order, along with some well-rehearsed banter. Mum's always been good at that. I'm a bit more of a risk-taker—one of the features of my act at the Blue Devil is improvised chat—with my bandmates as well as my audience.

We'd planned to devote that afternoon to "The Whistling Gypsy"—otherwise known as "The Gypsy Rover", composed by Dublin songwriter Leo Maguire in the 1950s. It was the Figs' first release, in October 1965, and it had leaped completely unexpectedly into the charts at a time when record sales were dominated by the Beatles, Manfred Mann and the Rolling Stones.

True to its name, the song involves a spot of whistling. Which was me. A cold opening with a jaunty banjo (also me), with Bob and Mitch providing some musical depth on their guitars in the background. Then mum stepping in with the main vocals. It's a folk tune that's usually sung by a man. But when Figgis Green recorded it, they changed the focus so that it was mum, rather than a male storyteller, relating the tale of how she'd left her father's castle to follow her gypsy lover.

The chorus was simple and featured mum, me, Keith and Mitch harmonizing, then mum changing the focus to winning the heart of *this* lady, rather than *a* lady.

It was really the story of how my mum and dad had originally met—my dad a bit of a rootless rambler with a passion for music and my mum from an upper-class family, posh education, the lot.

We ran through it twice, and then mum had an idea. "Would anyone object if we changed the last few lines so that Jason sings them?"

"I would," Keith said, immediately.

Here we go, I thought.

"I think it would be a nice touch, that's all," mum said. "My son acknowledging the love story between his father and me."

"Change for the sake of change, Mandy?"

"Not at all, Keith. It's a nod to our past as well as our future."

"It's not what our fans expect. Or want. We should stick to what they remember."

"Let's just try it, Keith," my mum said, patiently. "The last two lines again—Jason?"

I sang them, changing the final words to my point of view instead of mum's.

"Turn to look at me," mum suggested.

I sang it again, our eyes meeting as we slowed the tempo down to the end.

"Lovely," mum said. "So much better. We're all in agreement, then?"

"You're the boss," Keith replied. But it was obvious he wasn't happy.

He was still unhappy when Duncan arrived, slightly out of breath, accompanied by our security guy and bearing my new electric kettle from Currys.

"I took the liberty of buying you a top of the line appliance," he said, unpacking it from its box. "Green, of course."

"Duncan Stopher," I said, introducing him to the band.

Duncan was beside himself.

"I'm so very pleased to be given the opportunity to provide this favour," he said, shaking all of their hands in turn. "We have met before, of course, many years in the past. I'm sure you don't remember."

"Ah yes," said Mitch, humouring him. "The Swan Theatre, Worcester…1976, wasn't it?"

"1979," Duncan corrected. "And it was the Philharmonic Hall in Liverpool."

"Of course," said Mitch, ever the showman. "My mistake." He winked at me.

"This is a SMEG," Duncan said, presenting it. "A little bit pricey, but the salesperson assured me it was worth every penny."

I was fairly certain I'd only given him about thirty quid in cash.

This was not a £30 kettle.

I looked it up on my phone. The SMEG KLF03PGUK Jug Kettle in Pastel Green retailed for £129.00.

"Does it have flashing strobes and an indicator thingy that tells you if you're two degrees over your favourite boiling point?" Rolly inquired.

"Alas, no. Boil dry protection is included, however. An LED indicator. And a two-year guarantee."

"Let's plug it in and christen it," mum said. "We've got custard creams in the kitchen. Tea or coffee, Duncan?"

"Oh my goodness. Tea. Please."

And so my contribution from The Four Eyes was put to immediate use—although their biggest teapot was still far too small and we had to use it in shifts.

Down in the kitchen, after seeing Duncan safely out of the building, I crossed "new tea kettle" off the list on the wall and replaced it with "two large teapots".

And then I went back upstairs to tackle "Meryton Townhall"— a 17th century composition by Henry Purcell otherwise known as "The Tythe Pig". You heard it in the Keira Knightley version of *Pride and Prejudice*. The Figs did it first, a wonderful jiggy adaptation that featured Keith on the fiddle, Ben on rhythm guitar and my dad switching to a concertina to play the lead alongside Keith, which made it sound like a sea shanty. Mitch echoed the deep cello parts on the strings of his bass guitar, and mum blew into a *feadóg stain*— an Irish tin whistle—while Rolly banged on a *bodhrán*—a Celtic drum.

It's a very short piece, around 1:15 in total.

The way it was structured, Keith was supposed to play the first 30 seconds and then step back to let me do a solo on dad's little concertina. That was supposed to last about 20 seconds, and then Keith would be up again and everyone would let loose for the last 25 seconds of tumultuous celebration, all the way to the end.

My mum had always hated that concertina solo.

"You know what I'd like to do?" she'd said to me, quietly, over breakfast. And then she'd told me.

I was following her instructions now. I strapped on my Strat and slid it 'round to my back, then picked up the concertina.

Keith leaped into his fiddle intro. Then Mitch and Bob laid down their accompanying rhythm and bass guitar parts and Rolly banged his tipper on the *bodhrán's* skin. Mum joined in with her tin whistle and I stepped in last, tossing the concertina onto a nearby stool and whipping my Strat around and playing the 20-second solo on that instead.

Keith was furious.

"Why did you do that?"

"I thought we might give it a try," I replied, as diplomatically as I could.

"If we're going to reimagine and change up every song in the programme, I may as well go home now. I agreed to this tour because I wanted to bring Figgis Green's music back to the fans.

They're the ones who bought our records. They want what they heard on the radio. They don't want our new and improved versions of anything."

He had a point. But when you can see what you think are flaws in the original piece and you have an idea that fixes those flaws and makes the tune sound better in the process, I don't think it hurts to experiment.

"Possibly time for a band discussion…?" I guessed.

"We should have discussed it before you played it."

"Oh, come on, Keith," mum said, "you know you'd have said no immediately. Anyway, it was my idea. Don't put all the blame on Jason. I think it's very bold and rather good."

"I vote for Jason's version," Mitch added, bravely.

Rolly banged his *bodhrán* in agreement. Which left only Bob.

"I'll go with the consensus," Bob said, falling back on years of band-wisdom.

"You're outnumbered, Keith," mum said. "Sorry."

The concertina was consigned to the back of the room.

The guitar solo stayed.

#

Day Two was finished. Why did it feel like the end of Month Two?

Back in my room at The Dog's Watch, I phoned down to Reception and ordered a plate of scrambled eggs and toast for my dinner, promising to collect it when it was ready.

And then I rang my daughter.

"I've got a project for you," I said. "Can you drive down here and pick up a photo and some negatives? I want to see if you can blow something up."

"Like David Hemmings in that movie?" Jenn inquired, humorously.

"Exactly the same," I said.

It was a good two-hour drive from London, where she lived, to Stoneford. But Jenn had grown up in Canada—Vancouver—and she wasn't fazed by long distances.

"I'll be there tomorrow," she promised. "Lunch time."

While I was waiting for my dinner, I joined the Pippa Gladstone Mystery Forum using my old Twittername, Cold_Fingers. That gave me access to the Members Only section, where I could see all of Duncan Stopher's contributions.

There was an entire section devoted to "The Last Picture?" It was 40 pages long, and nearly a thousand messages.

But the conversations weren't about the photo that Duncan had given me. They were, first of all, lamenting the fact that Pippa's parents had taken absolutely no photos of their daughter at the holiday resort in Malaga—along with an unshakable belief that there *were* photos, but Harry and Susan Gladstone had declined to provide them to both the police and the media. Secondly, the chatter concerned itself with a random photo that someone *else* had taken of Pippa in the pool area at the Spanish resort. I looked at it closely. It certainly did look like her. She had the same long, dark blonde hair as the girl in Duncan's photo. She had the same face. She was walking towards an unoccupied sun lounger and she was wearing denim cut-off shorts with frayed hems and Figgis Green t-shirt. She was carrying a camera.

Duncan himself had last posted on the thread in 2016, expressing his support of Pippa's obvious good taste in music.

I saved the picture to my phone. I went downstairs to pick up my scrambled eggs and then arranged the plate on my writing table, snapped the obligatory photo, and posted it.

Who says you can't have eggs for supper? I wrote. *I've shelled out for worse.*

And then, while I tucked in and waited for the inevitable egg-related puns in response, I got back to work.

I read through all of the printouts and photocopies that Duncan had given me, just to double-check the facts. Age, height, description, what Pippa had been wearing when she was last seen. And then I went online and did a search for myself.

There wasn't a hell of a lot. Duncan was right. If it had been 30 years later, there'd have been a massive archive available from curated news sources. The only information I could find now on the internet were the stories that had been written in retrospect: articles on the 25th anniversary of Pippa's disappearance; occasional follow-ups by curious reporters on a slow news day; a brief flurry of activity after one of those true crime TV shows had done a segment about Pippa and concluded that, even though she was considered legally deceased, there were still unanswered questions about her disappearance.

I have subscriptions to a few paywall sites that give me access to historical newspaper archives. I checked those and found the same articles that Duncan had printed off. And Dom, my son, had given me his student login at his university, which got me access to their library—and from there I could pull up the digital copies of another massive collection of journals and newspapers.

I checked them all.

Duncan's research had been extremely thorough.

There wasn't much he'd missed.

The last thing I did was read through the stories about Harry Gladstone's unfortunate accident at Holborn. I have to admit to a bit of a morbid interest in his death. It's not every day that someone falls under a tube train in London.

Back in 1974, the Underground platforms were busy during rush hour, but not as suffocatingly crammed full of people as they are now.

There were no CCTV cameras back then. It wasn't until 1975 that CCTV began to be used on the Underground and, even then, it was only at a handful of stations. And there were no grizzly photos from peoples' mobiles because, of course, mobiles wouldn't be in general use for another 20 years.

There were press pictures of the outside of the station, with police cars and an ambulance. And eyewitness quotes from passengers who were there when it happened.

And then a few brief stories about the aftermath—the coroner's report that his death was inconclusive, leaning towards a tragic accident exacerbated by a busier-than-usual evening on the tube, train delays and a large crush of people all anxious to get home from work.

Nothing more to see there, then.

Please mind the gap.

CHAPTER FOUR

These early starts were going to be the death of me.

I'd planned to walk over to The Four Eyes on Wednesday morning to sample one of the breakfast sandwiches they had featured on the blackboard menu hanging over their counter. I was quite looking forward to a choice of bacon or ham with an egg filling.

But I'd managed to oversleep.

It was half past eight by the time I stumbled into the shower.

There was still no sign of Kato at the manor, however the shopping list in the kitchen had been replaced by a new blank one, there was an additional carton of milk in the fridge, and a bowl of little packets of M&M's had been put on the counter next to Duncan's SMEG.

Seven custard creams and a handful of peanut M&M's it was for breakfast, then.

Picture duly posted on Instagram.

Delicious, I wrote, *and nutritious. Desperate for a nice big fry up with an immense cup of tea. Any takers? I tip well.*

#

We were on our fifth run through of "Farewell to Nova Scotia".

You know the tune. It's been done over and over by a multitude of singers and bands and it's even popped up recently on the soundtrack of a computer game. It has its roots in "The Soldier's

Adieu", a Scottish folk song from 1791, and it's been in the public domain ever since. The Figs had a rollicking great hit with it in 1981.

"Farewell to Nova Scotia" was one of Keith's contributions. Mum was soothing his ego after yesterday's blow up, so he was front and centre with his fiddle and enjoying every moment—especially as we were presenting the song exactly the same way the Figs had recorded it almost three decades earlier.

Which wasn't as easy as you might think. To begin with, my dad was playing the banjo. He was a great banjo player. I'm not. I had to learn it from scratch during my personal practice time. I was OK with it—far from perfect—but as long as I could bury my picking under the others' contributions, I reckoned I could swing it.

Rolly was back with his *bodhrán* and Bob was still playing his acoustic six-string but Mitch had to switch to a mandolin and my mum was in her element, strapping on an accordion. The accordion is one of her hidden talents. Dad and I always used to joke that she should have put out an album of polka favourites. She'd have given Weird Al Yankovic a run for his money.

I was thankful that, 30 years earlier, a random suggestion that they also incorporate bagpipes had been roundly vetoed.

The Figs' live arrangement of the song was about four minutes longer than the version that ended up being played on the radio. It started out as a rousing instrumental, then dad sang four verses of lyrics and Mitch and Ben joined him for the chorus in between, and then they reverted back to instruments for the remaining bars, because it was just that good.

It was also one of those pieces where mum and dad invited the audience to sing along—though, to be honest, they'd never needed much encouragement. It was ingrained in the Figs' culture, just like the *a capella* "I Can't Stay Mad at You" in the encore.

One more play-through and we nailed it. There were no suggestions for improvement from mum, and Keith must have had a good night's sleep because he couldn't find fault with any of it.

We broke for lunch.

#

I had 148 comments waiting for me on Instagram, fully half of them accompanied by "horrified" emojis, admonishing me about my food choices and providing suggestions to eat more healthfully. Six of my followers gave me thumbs up and agreed that seven custard creams and a packet of peanut M&M's were the showbiz equivalent of Breakfast of Champions. Four wanted to know what my mum thought of my culinary habits and another four had decided it would be a good idea to lecture me about the warning signs of diabetes.

Only one person offered to cater breakfast for me. I had a look at her Instagram page. Frilly lingerie (which was in the process of being removed) followed by a tasty selection of Early Trampoline Headstands, Monoi Oil After the Shower and Getting Ready for Ladder Fun.

Do the sausages come with their own trampoline? I wrote back.

She didn't reply. But with 13.3K followers, I shouldn't have been surprised.

I suspected Duncan might be lying in wait for me at The Four Eyes, hoping to buy me a coffee and my favourite baguette while he engaged me in a discourse about the Figs' appearance on *Top of the Pops* in 1979 and how well my mum had mimed the words to "Roving Minstrel" in spite of a raging temperature and a case of the flu that had sent her to bed for a week immediately afterwards.

So I met Jenn at a café on the seafront instead.

Wellers occupied a rambling old cottage which dated from the end of the 18th century. When my mum and dad had been staying at the manor in 1965, a young couple named Wendy and Toby Weller had just bought the cottage and were desperately trying to turn it into a profitable guest house after years of neglect and dereliction.

Wendy and Toby had long since departed, but the name had stuck. The current owners had dispensed with the overnight accommodations and had opened the place up for banquets and meetings. And they'd created a wonderful restaurant with outdoor seating in their leafy back garden, with a view of the sea.

There were granite-topped tables with comfy wicker chairs arranged under bright blue umbrellas, and the drinks menu featured an amazing collection of fruit juices, an exotic-sounding cream soda and four different concoctions featuring elderflowers and lemonade.

"Wine?" I offered.

"Thanks," Jenn said. "Better not. I'm driving straight back to London."

"No paddling in the sea…?" I asked, with mock disappointment.

"I will if you will."

I smiled. I was still getting used to having a daughter. Jenn was the result of a one-night liaison with a wonderful woman who was—and still is—one of my closest friends. We were both teenagers when Sally moved to Canada with her parents. She had a going-away party, where I drank too much wine and smoked too much weed, and the only thing I remembered afterwards was waking up to a hangover from hell after spending the night on her sofa.

Sal kept her pregnancy a secret from me, and gave her daughter up for adoption after she was born. Thirty years later, Jenn tracked her birth mother down. She travelled from Vancouver to London to meet Sal, and Sal offered me the option of letting myself into her life as well. After I'd recovered from the initial shock, I decided it was absolutely something I very much wanted—and needed—to do.

Jenn has my long, untidy dark brown hair, to which she's introduced subtle, occasional streaks that are just a shade or two lighter than the silver filaments that are infiltrating mine. She has a fringe. My eyes. Sal's nose and her smile. My chin.

"If we eat quickly," I said, "I think we can just about manage a paddle."

Our waitress was young but she knew who Figgis Green was and she knew who I was, without me saying a word. She was probably related to the barista at The Four Eyes. She took our orders—Lager Battered Fish and Chips for Jenn and a Weller Burger for me—and had them delivered to our table in record time.

"So where's this picture and the negs that you want me to look at?" Jenn asked, after I'd taken my mandatory lunch photo and uploaded it to my gastronomically-enthused followers (Getting Ready for Impossible Headstands While Nakedly Enjoying Ladder Fun notwithstanding).

"In here."

I gave her the brown envelope. She looked inside.

"The girl in the picture is Pippa Gladstone," I said. "She went missing in Malaga in March 1974, when she was 16. Her mum had her legally declared dead seven years later. That photo was taken in August 1974. Five months after she disappeared."

"Interesting," Jenn said, studying the 8x10 and then the negative it had come from.

"I want you to have a really good look at the picture, and the negs, and tell me if there's any possibility it could have been photoshopped. I can't see any obvious signs, but I'm not an expert."

"I can't see any either," Jenn said, "but I love a challenge."

Something else we had in common.

"Also," I said, "what kind of camera is she carrying here?"

I showed her the so-called Last Picture on my phone, the one where Pippa was walking beside the hotel pool.

Jenn studied it for a moment.

"I'd say it's an Olympus Pen," she said. "They stopped making them before I was born. Early 1980s, I think. It was a handy little thing. Very lightweight, very small, and it used the standard 35mm film cartridge but it was unique in that it took half-frame pictures instead of full frame. So, you got twice as many negs and twice as many prints."

"Clever," I said.

"The only drawback was that it would also take twice as long to get through the whole roll. So if you loaded the usual cartridge of 24, you ended up with 48 pictures. And 36 would give you 72."

I was old enough to remember SLR cameras that used film. You kept the film in the camera until you'd taken all the pictures, then you wound the film back into its cartridge and sent it off to be developed. This often resulted in random photos near the end of the roll that had only been taken to avoid wasting the film. Or blank frames because you didn't care about wasting the film—you just wanted to see all the pictures you'd taken on holiday.

Wellers' back garden ended where some scrubby sand hills led down to the water. There was a rough trail leading to the beach, which was mostly pebbles, though our waitress had very helpfully advised us that there was sand at low tide. Unfortunately, low tide was around seven that evening.

Jenn was wearing expensive leather sandals and I had on my favourite trainers—also expensive—and getting them wet wasn't an option. Off they came, deposited on the shingles along with the brown paper envelope and Jenn's bag. Jenn gamely tucked the bottom of her flowery summer skirt into the leg holes of her knickers, and I rolled up my jeans. We grasped each other's hands to keep from toppling over and braved the high tide in our bare feet.

"This," my daughter decided, as we stood in the waves up to our knees, gazing out at the Isle of Wight and The Needles, "is…exquisite."

"You'll be hunting for shells and bits of sea glass next," I said.

"Be honest. When was the last time you went paddling in the sea like this?"

"Can't remember," I said, and then I added, "It must have been with Dom. When he was very small. Decades ago."

"What about when you were at sea? Your winter itinerary in the Caribbean?"

"Jaunts to beaches were rare," I said. "And when they did happen, brief. Fitted into a few spare hours between on-board gigs."

"Wish I could have seen you," Jenn said. "I very nearly did, you know. I wanted to go on a cruise to Alaska and it was a tossup between the *Sapphire* and the *Amethyst*. In the end I decided to go on the *Amethyst*. Bigger, glitzier, newer. You know."

"I know," I said, wistfully. My *Sapphire* had been old and creaky— a former ocean liner. But she'd been something very special. And standing like this in the gently-lapping waves with my daughter was something very special too. "I wish you could have seen me as well."

A little boy was trying to launch a red plastic kite with a tail of ribbons just down the beach from us. We watched him run with it and throw it into the air…but there just wasn't enough wind where he was to send it skyward. His mum suggested relocating up on the sandbanks instead. Reluctantly, he left the water's edge. But a few moments later, his kite was dancing above the scrubby hills, a brilliant swirl of colour against the cloudless blue sky.

"I know what we need," I said. "Ice cream."

"In a cone," Jenn agreed.

"I think they sell them at Wellers."

Jenn checked the time. It was nearly half past one. "You'll be late getting back."

"The way to my mum's heart is through a double scoop of Toffee Crunch," I said.

"Mine too," said my daughter.

#

I was, indeed, very late getting back. Not good, when it was only Day Three of rehearsals. And I was still the New Boy, in spite of being the founder's son. And Keith hated me.

I'd had a word with the manager at Wellers—a woman who was probably the mother of our waitress and the aunt of the barista at The Four Eyes—and I'd arranged to buy an entire tub of Toffee Crunch, along with a scoop and a generous supply of cones. I also persuaded her to drive me and Jenn and the enormous tub back to the manor, promising her a couple of free tickets to our opening night in Middlehurst, the possibility of a meet and greet backstage afterwards and a signed poster.

The ice cream went over well, although it transpired Tejo was in a medically-supervised weight loss program and Keith was lactose-intolerant. Jenn stayed long enough to finish her cone and then she left to drive back to London.

We turned our attention to "One Summer Day."

Figgis Green wasn't really known for its original tunes. Both Keith and Rolly had come up with a few numbers they thought the Figs might try, but they weren't as successful as the rest of their hits. The Figs tended to do better with songs that had been written by others, or with straight-up traditional folk music that had very murky origins and was readily available in the public domain.

"One Summer Day" was different: my dad had written it for my mum. He'd sat down with his acoustic guitar and sung it to her while she was clearing up after dinner one night, and the next day they'd gone into the studio and recorded it. There were only two voices: dad and mum. And the basic instrumental track had just dad's guitar. Ben Quigley had come in afterwards to add some colour and texture and his contribution was mixed in to the master. And that was it. No drums. No fiddle. No bass.

Upstairs in the manor's library, we arranged three high stools in a row. I switched out my dad's classic Lake Placid Blue Strat—it's an original from 1965 that he kept in immaculate condition—for my RainSong WS, a lovely lightweight graphite-bodied acoustic with an extra deep cutaway that lets you play well up the fretboard. Bob sat himself on mum's right and I took the seat on her left.

The way dad had written it, the lead and rhythm guitars had a kind of "conversation" with each other which complemented the vocals. I was playing without a plectrum and with nylon strings which allowed me to do some really intricate fingering. Bob was sticking to his pick—and metal strings. He had a tricky intro to deal with, which was repeated three or four times throughout the song.

I'd always loved this one, with Ben (and now Bob) dancing over the strings, my dad (and now me) providing some depth and rhythm and harmony. There was a subtle change during the bridge, a sequence that was optimistic and fanciful, recounting the summer memories of a young couple in love. And then a further changeup as the two lovers voiced their doubts and fears…and then everything was all resolved…they reassured one another that they'd always be true…and the song ended on a wistful, forward-looking sequence of chords: A, D, E and then F#.

It was beautiful. My voice and mum's blended together perfectly. There was silence as we finished and then a burst of absolute applause from Tejo, Dr. Sparks, Mitch, Rolly and even Keith.

"You know what would make it even better," mum said, after a moment.

Oh no, I thought. I glanced at Keith. Wait for it…

"I think we should add a bass line—Mitch—and some very quiet strings—Keith…and we should bring Rolly in on the drums to give it a little beat. All of it very subtle. In the background."

"You sure?" I said, doubtfully.

"We're not naive young things anymore…most of us are bloody grandparents and we know a thing or two about life. Let's reflect that in the song."

"You know how I feel," Keith said, still no doubt miffed that I'd neglected to buy dairy-free ice cream to accommodate his dietary needs.

"Our fans are all bloody grandparents too," mum replied. "They'll appreciate the embellishments."

We ran through it again, this time with Rolly drumming quietly on the snare behind us, then Mitch and Keith joining in after the first verse. When we got to the doubts and fears, Rolly switched to tapping the closed high hat and then added a dramatic couple of kicks on the bass drum. When everything was starting to be all right again, Keith played a beautiful accompaniment on his violin, reverting to something that sounded as if it had been lifted from a symphony, carrying it all the way through to the wistful ending.

Once more, there was applause from Tejo and Dr. Sparks. And I had to admit it really did sound good. My mum's idea was brilliant.

#

Dinner was scrambled eggs—again—and two slices of toast with butter, and a fabulous pot of tea. And my Instagram followers and commenters were growing exponentially. I suspected the majority of them were Figs fans, veterans of another era when gleaning morsels of "inside" information about their favourite band was confined to exclusive interviews in popular mags and papers, the results of the usual PR push that preceded a tour.

I remember very well when the internet arrived in the UK, roundabout 1996. I had friends in the US and Canada who'd already been using it for a year, and they were excitedly telling me all about it. I remember thinking, as I explored the newsgroups and chat forums and, after that, what quickly evolved into Myspace and then Facebook and then Twitter, how, all of a sudden, a performer or a group of performers, were going to be able to connect with their fans on a much more intimate level.

I'd embraced that connectivity from the start.

So had a lot of the people who were now routinely checking into my Instagram feed.

I decided to expand my food observations to include a few random thoughts about how the rehearsals were going and at least one exclusive tidbit about the band that they weren't likely to find anywhere else.

I was telling them all about our new SMEG kettle when my daughter called.

"You're going to love this," Jenn said. "I did a little quick and dirty conversion...I scanned the neg to create a digital image and then reversed it to positive. I'm just sending it to you."

I grabbed the image off my email and loaded it onto my laptop.

"Got it," I said.

"OK," said Jenn. "First off, you can see both kids are wearing baseball caps. But it looks to me like the hats have been added to their heads after the fact. I don't think they were wearing them originally. And those strands of hair around the girl's face...they've definitely been painted in."

"Isn't that difficult to do?" I asked. "I thought hair was one of the most challenging things to replicate."

"Not if you've had lots of practice and you know what you're doing."

"Why paint in hair strands?"

"For the same reason they're wearing hats. If you cut someone out of one picture and paste them into a new picture, it's going to look really obvious unless you can disguise the edges. And hair's a dead giveaway because of all the hundreds of stray strands around the top and sides of your head. So, you pop a hat on. You can get away with hard edges on a hat."

"I'm astounded," I said.

"So am I. Someone's gone to a lot of work to try and make this look authentic. And check out under the girl's chin and down towards the open neck of her shirt."

I looked.

"What do you see?"

It was all dark grey and in shadow.

"What should I be seeing?" I asked.

"A very faint pattern of stripes."

There were some smudges and lines that looked to be a darker grey than the rest of her neck area, but nothing that I could definitely state to be anything that looked like stripes.

"Make it as big as you can," Jenn suggested.

I zoomed in on the jpg.

There they were. Pixelated and distorted. But definitely stripes. And hints of colour.

"I made a copy of the jpg and played with the colours on my computer. I made them outrageous—almost neon. I'm sending that to you now."

I opened her second picture on my laptop.

"You can see the stripes much more easily," Jenn said.

Indeed I could. There were the same horizontal lines, this time leaping out at me, completely visible, completely defined, in brilliant pink and orange.

"What does it all mean?" I asked.

"Well, first of all it proves the photo definitely didn't come from a negative from 1974. It's a constructed jpg using digital technology. The girl's head and neck came from one source, and her body came from another source, and they were stitched together and added to the original photo. But whoever did the editing got lazy. Instead of using a clone brush to copy the shadow from somewhere else and extending it under her chin and down her neck, they just darkened the area. The clone brush would have covered it all up. Darkening it just made what was there darker—it didn't get rid of the stripes."

"So where did the stripes come from?"

"The original photo. The source of her head and neck. A photo where she was wearing a striped top that had a high collar."

I stared at the pictures. It was all so clear. And completely undetectable if you happened to be just glancing at it.

"There's more," Jenn said. "See the guy standing beside the girl?

Where's his right arm?"

Again, I had to look hard. The boy was wearing a rumpled cotton gauze shirt with its sleeves rolled up past his elbows. He was standing on Pippa's right, his left arm hanging straight down between them. On his right, I could see the ruckles and folds where he'd clumsily rolled up the sleeve. But below the sleeve was just a tiny sliver of skin.

"His arm is behind him," I said.

"If that was the case, then you wouldn't see the full sleeve like that. You'd see tension in the fabric and it would be pulled back behind his back."

"Not if the sleeve was loose."

"But it's not loose. Look at his left sleeve. It's tight around his upper arm. There's no wriggle room. Now look at his right sleeve. It looks like there's no arm at all in that sleeve, and someone's smudged in something that's supposed to be his lower arm. It doesn't even have a clear edge like the sleeve does."

She was right.

I blew the picture up on my screen again, and saw that she was even more right.

"So what happened to his arm?"

"I think that guy came from another picture as well, but in his case, I think his entire head and body was used. They just put a baseball cap on his head to disguise the hard edges. And they had to crop his lower arm out, probably because something else from the original picture was in the way. Maybe part of another person, maybe an object. So they dropped him in beside the girl and had to make it look like his arm was behind him."

"Surely they had to make sure the light was right though…"

"Easily done, shadows and light adjusted after both images were in place. It's a cloudy day so they really didn't have to worry about well-defined shadows."

"But the background is real."

"Oh, absolutely, it's genuine. Just like the rest of the negs on the strip. Figgis Green playing on a stage in a field."

"But," I said, "the one with Pippa's right in the middle of the strip. Two genuine pics on one side, two on the other? How do you get a fake negative in the middle of a series of real ones?"

"I really had to think about that. But you know what you do? You make digital pictures from each of the four other photos. Then you get a new roll of film—Kodak and Fuji still make them—and expose that roll to your new pictures—you basically project the digital images onto each frame of the film. One, two. Then you project the fake photo. Then you do the last two images. Simple."

"Then you develop the new roll of film," I said, "and you end up with a row of negatives in the order you want them."

"You got it," said Jenn. "And if anyone gets smart and tries to put the fake photo through analyser software to look for the usual tell-tale signs of digital manipulation…they won't find anything. Because the photo in question has not been digitally altered. The photo in question is a picture of a picture."

"Someone," I said, "has gone to a hell of a lot of trouble to convince me that photo's genuine."

"So, is this going to be a new investigation for you?" Jenn guessed.

"Not anymore," I replied.

CHAPTER FIVE

I had some rather pointed questions I wanted to ask Duncan. His tall tale about discovering the undeveloped roll of film in a forgotten drawer obviously wasn't going to wash anymore. But why had he lied to me?

I put off calling him for a few minutes as I sat in the sun during our morning break on Thursday, chuffing with Tejo. We'd discovered the manor's former kitchen garden, which featured a little stone patio and weather-beaten wicker chairs and gloriously scented wildflowers with masses of industrious bees and the odd hummingbird. It was so beautiful and so peaceful, I didn't want to spoil the moment.

But I had to get back to work.

I rang Duncan with the bad news.

There was silence on the other end of the line. And then:

"I'm really very sorry, Jason."

I waited.

"I feel I owe you an explanation."

"Yes," I said. "I think you do."

"As you know, I've become quite obsessed with this case."

"You'll get no argument from me there."

"And you're correct. I didn't take the photo. In fact, I bought it from someone on the Pippa forum."

"The photo and the entire strip of negatives," I said.

"Yes."

"I had a look at all the postings on the chat group the other day,"

49

I said. "And I didn't see any mention of that picture at all."

"It was all done by private messaging."

"But how did you know the photo even existed?"

"I was approached, again in private. The owner was aware of my interest."

"So he just gave you the photo…?"

"No," said Duncan. "He wanted me to pay for it. Which I did, happily. I thought there might be something in it…so, knowing you would be coming here to rehearse, and also knowing about your talent for solving similar mysteries, I made up my mind to ask for your help."

"But why invent the story that you'd taken the photo yourself?"

"I confess," said Duncan, "that I thought it might act as a sort of…enticement. I thought if you saw the Figgis Green connection…Pippa and her friend actually attending your parents' concert in Wiltshire…and you knew that I was a follower…you would more likely be persuaded."

He paused.

"Are you absolutely certain it's a forgery?"

"I'm absolutely certain," I said.

"Then I've wasted your time, Jason, and for that I'm really very sorry. No hard feelings?"

"No hard feelings," I said. "Whoever created the picture has excellent photoshopping skills."

"Well, he really had me fooled. I shall send him a very stern rebuke."

He paused again.

"I will still see you next Friday evening in Middlehurst…?"

"Opening night," I confirmed. "Backstage. And I'll give you back your pictures and the negatives."

"Thank you, Jason," he said. "I'm your biggest fan."

I had no doubts about that, at all.

#

Our fourth day of rehearsals was going to be cut short because a reporter from the *Stoneford News* was coming over to interview mum and me. Mum had very fond memories of the paper's part in helping to launch Figgis Green back in the day and so, to return the favour, she'd rung them up to offer them an interview.

There would be more interviews scheduled for the following week and also while we were actually on the road—TV, radio, magazines, tabloids and broadsheets—it was apparently a Very Big Thing for the Figs to be reunited and back touring. But, just for today, Stoneford's local paper was going to enjoy an early exclusive.

Before we could get to that, however, we had to tackle "Greensleeves".

The Figs' version of the old English folksong had shot up the charts and stayed at the top for three weeks, largely because of my dad's *twang* and Rolly's driving drums.

I've never heard anything that's come close to my dad's arrangement of that tune, which borders on "surf" and has stonking lead and rhythm guitars and a relentless snare that reminds me of waves hissing over a pebbled beach, and no vocals whatsoever. Instead of singing, my mum played along on an autoharp. And there was no fiddle, so Keith shook some maracas instead.

It was Keith's least-favourite tune, for obvious reasons. And one of my most-favourites. Also for obvious reasons—because I got to show off my fingering skills and a couple of dazzling tech effects on my dad's Strat.

We'd played through it twice that morning, and it had sounded rough. We all knew our parts, but it had literally been decades since the Figs had performed it—and never with me.

I knew Keith was looking for any excuse at all to strike the song from the set list. But mum wasn't ready to give in.

"How about if we slow it down?" she said.

"People will think it's Christmas," Keith argued. "'What Child is This'."

"Slow it down temporarily," mum said, with patience. "Until we've got the sense of it. Then we'll bring up the tempo again."

I knew Keith was bored with his maracas. "How do you feel about adding a bit of fiddle?" I asked.

"There are no strings in your father's arrangement," he answered, pointedly.

"Just play with me during the intro and the chorus. Any way you think will work. And I'll give you two of the solos in the second part of the song. Fiddle for guitar."

I could tell mum wasn't quite on board with that idea. But she was as anxious as I was to keep Keith happy. We ran through it again, slowly, with Keith tagging along and then taking over the two rocking bits that dad usually played, and it didn't sound half-bad.

Three more run-throughs and we had it nearly perfect.

Up to speed and it sounded magnificent.

"Time for some ice cream," mum decided, clearly inspired by yesterday's Toffee Crunch. "And before we break for lunch, Jason's going to run down to the village to get some of that soy lookalike stuff for Keith, isn't he?"

#

The reporter from the *Stoneford News* was a young woman, early twenties, I guessed, probably fresh from a journalism degree and needing some hands-on training before trying her luck at the bigger papers. The *Stoneford News* had been around for generations. It still put out a weekly print copy, but it also had an online presence, like every other news source in the world, that was updated a few times a day. The paper ran only local stories, and was heavily supported by advertising. The editor was quite excited at the prospect of scoring an exclusive interview with my mum.

The rest of the band was dismissed for the afternoon, so it was just mum and me. The reporter—Janice Winstanley—had brought us lunch: ham and cheese sandwiches from the little bakery at the bottom of the hill, and iced coffee.

"She's quite dishy, isn't she," mum said, with a nudge, as we went downstairs to the gallery in the west wing which had been the subject of one of the conditions of rental in the 1960s: Thou Shalt Not Trash the Antique Suits of Armour in This Olde Location.

The gallery itself was set in between what had once been the manor's massive dining room and its rather large, echoey sitting room. It had been lovingly restored to its original state, with a lavish blue, red and gold oriental Axminster carpet and ceiling-to-floor leaded stained-glass windows, and, occupying pride of place, four full sets of armour, completely assembled and ready to do battle.

Sometimes I think my mum still sees me as a teenager, in need of guidance and advice and, of course, mothering. This, in spite of the fact that I've been married and widowed and I've made her a grandmother twice over.

Janice Winstanley's photographer was Dom's age and Janice herself looked to be not much older. She had long honey-coloured hair with a fringe. A little makeup—some shadow and mascara, a little neutral-toned lipstick, the tiniest bit of blush. She was wearing skinny jeans and strappy sandals and a very expensive bright blue t-shirt. If I'd been about 20 years younger, and I didn't have Katey in my life, I'd definitely have followed through on my mum's nudge.

There were three comfy armchairs and a little table in the corner. We sat, and Janice switched on her voice recorder and took out her notebook.

"And what made you decide to do a tour now?" she asked. It was her lead-in question. I wondered, as mum answered, how much she really knew about Figgis Green and its history. And whether, in the end, it was really all that important.

Ten questions later, we were wrapping up the interview. Janice had scribbled notes as we'd chatted to remind herself about thoughts she'd had while we were talking. Her photographer, James, had taken a lot of pictures, most featuring me and mum together, though some were of mum on her own.

"My dad's a fan," he confessed, as he came around to my side and lined up a shot of mum and me, in profile.

Janice, it turned out, had actually done her research, and even though neither of her parents had been particularly fond of the Figs, she at least knew our top-selling songs and what everyone's names were, and she knew that I was subbing for my dad and that I had a regular gig in London at the Blue Devil. And that was good enough for me.

As we got up to go, Janice's mobile rang.

"*Really?*" she said. I watched her face. Her eyes were huge. "What do we know so far?"

She sat down and wrote some hasty words into her notebook.

"OK. We'll get over there. Ten minutes?"

She disconnected.

"Someone's been found dead," she said. "In the little park at the end of Poorhouse Lane. And it doesn't look like natural causes."

Poorhouse Lane was across the road from the Village Green and at the foot of Manor Rise and was named after the house that had once stood there. The lane itself was about eight feet wide and 100 feet long, and it led to a small grassy area with trees and meandering paths, lots of flowering shrubs and a kids' playground. A sign identified it as Emmy Cooper Park.

The police had taped the whole area off but we could see, as we approached their perimeter, that there was very definitely a male body lying on the ground in the long grass next to some hawkweed, gorse and broom.

In an instant, I recognized the man's hand-knitted pullover.

"That's Duncan Stopher," I said, my heart dropping into the pit of my stomach.

#

There were obviously things the police had to do before they could confirm Duncan's identity. The coroner arrived, and a couple of investigators who swept the area for evidence the killer might have left behind. In the end, poor Duncan was packaged for transportation, and the police tape stayed up so that the investigators could continue their work.

"I've never covered a murder before," Janice said, clearly excited by the prospect. "I've never even seen a dead body. What did you say his name was?"

"Duncan Stopher," I said. "He was a big Figs fan. I had lunch with him the other day."

"You don't know anything more about him, I suppose."

I thought it wise not to mention his obsession with Pippa Gladstone. Nor the fact that he'd nearly engaged me to look into her disappearance.

"Not much more, no."

"Well, thanks for the info."

"No problem," I replied. "Thanks for the interview."

#

"There's a turn up for the books," mum said, as we ate dinner. "He seemed such a nice fellow."

"He was," I said.

I wouldn't be telling a lie if I admitted that I'd grown to like him, in spite of all of his obsessions. And I was feeling weirdly unsafe. There was a certain amount of security sitting in the dining room, surrounded by the inn's other guests.

I'd ordered a sirloin steak with fries, a rocket and tomato salad, mushrooms and onion rings.

I was so distracted that I forgot to take a picture for Instagram until I was halfway through eating it, so my entry for Thursday,

August 30th was somewhat underwhelming. It still garnered about 100 likes in the first two minutes—but none from Getting Ready for Ladder Fun Lady.

Fame is so fickle.

In the middle of my meal, I got a call from Janice Winstanley.

"I just thought you should know," she said, "I've been chatting with one of the policemen…he's an old school mate of my dad's. They've ID'd the body. What did you say his name was?"

"Duncan Stopher," I said.

"Strange," said Janice. "That's not what was on his driver's license. Or anything else he had in his wallet. His name's Alistair Watford. Why did you think it was Duncan Stopher?"

"Because that's what he told me his name was," I said. "I suppose that's a positive ID. Someone's come to verify it's him?"

"Yes, his wife. It's definite."

"Thank you," I said.

"Anything else I can do for you, just shout."

"I will."

"See you in Middlehurst next weekend," she added.

"Absolutely."

#

Upstairs, in my room, I rang Jenn.

"Hello," I said. "I've got some news for you."

"I've got news for you too," she said. She sounded upset. "I was just about to call you. Someone's been in my studio. They ransacked the place."

Jenn lived in Primrose Hill. North London. She didn't need somewhere to take photos—most of her work was done on the fly, outside or in peoples' homes or where they worked. But she still occasionally used film—colour and black and white—and she still needed somewhere to develop that, and to make prints—and for that she'd found a little place down the road and around the corner from her flat. She'd invested quite a bit of money to convert it into a professional darkroom: temperature controls, correct lighting, hot and cold running water, equipment and counter space.

"What did they take?" I asked.

I knew she had tanks and driers and a couple of expensive enlargers. I thought she was going to tell me that's what the thieves were after…but no.

"Prints," she said. "Negs. All the Pippa Gladstone stuff."

I truly and literally shivered. "And that's all…?"

"That's all. They left everything else."

"Are you OK?"

"I'm fine. A little shaken. But I've covered wars. It takes a lot more than a break-in and theft to take me down. Though I do feel violated."

"That's normal," I said.

"What news did you have for me?"

I told her. There was silence at the other end. Then:

"Do you think that death is related to my break-in?"

"I'd put money on it," I said.

"It really is like that movie, isn't it? *Blow Up*. Where Vanessa Redgrave tries to get David Hemmings' roll of film and he gives her a fake roll and then someone comes back and steals the real one and all of his prints of the dead body in the shrubs. Isn't that where they found your dead body?"

"Beside a large planting of broom," I confirmed. "Michelangelo Antonioni would have been impressed. All we need now is miming tennis players and Jane Birkin and her friend turning up in their coloured tights."

"And we never do find out who the bad guy is," Jenn said.

"Have you reported the break-in to the police?"

"Doesn't really seem worth it," Jenn said. "Nothing was vandalised…nothing valuable was taken. It's hardly worth their time."

"OK," I said. "Call me if you need to talk."

"I will," Jenn said.

But as I was having my nightly ciggie—I'd figured out how to get the latch to work on one of the windows at last—something rather more ominous occurred to me. How could anyone have known about the photos and Jenn's studio unless they'd observed our meeting in Stoneford and then followed her all the way back to London?

Someone had been watching us.

And it was quite possibly the same someone who had murdered Duncan Stopher…aka Alistair Watford.

CHAPTER SIX

I was still very bothered by Alistair Watford's death. And I was in two minds about whether I ought to talk to the police about what I knew.

My relationship with the police has had its good days and its bad days. My sister's husband, the ex-copper, is one of the nicest blokes you could ever meet—although he tends to take a less-than-generous view of my extracurricular activities. The police in London, I'm sure, would rather I not do any investigating at all. That said, if I run into trouble (as I have done in the past), there's a certain detective named Allan Pappas that I can always count on to help me out.

It was a shame Allan had gone on holiday when I rang him for some advice regarding Duncan.

I decided to wait before I contacted the Hampshire Constabulary. They'd want an interview and a witness statement and all of that would take time. It was Friday and we only had a week until opening night. Rehearsals had to be my priority.

We were working our way through "Viaggio Italiano", which was a jaunty tale based on a vacation that my dad's sister had taken with her husband in the 1970s. Cleo and Stan had returned from their adventure with stories that were a travel agent's nightmare—lost luggage, a driver who had only been hired the day before, who only spoke Walloon...a tour director who spoke five languages, none of which were Walloon...the necessity of the tour director to navigate the driver, who had never been out of Belgium in his life, in German (*links* is German for left and *richtig* for right, by the way)…hotels that weren't expecting us until the following day…roads that were blocked by five-mile-long traffic jams…a non-functioning air conditioner on a bus with windows that didn't open…and the absolute insanity of visiting 13 highly popular tourist destinations in 14 days.

Mum and dad had listened with great interest to Cleo and Stan's tales of woe, and had been inspired to compose "Viaggio Italiano". They wrote the tune in A major and included riffs from the first movement of Mendelssohn's *Italian Symphony*, which gave Keith another chance to shine, as the famous refrain is a brilliantly joyous piece for the violin.

Performed perfectly, "Viaggio Italiano" is the robust and energetic saga of two lovers who embark on a tour not unlike the one Cleo and Stan took. There are a couple of lovely quiet bits, about 15 seconds each, where they wander through piazzas and churches and admire the art and the history—and then it's back on the bus and on to the next city with frenetic madness. Rolly had created an amazing drum beat to go with it and dad, Mitch and Ben had backed Keith on their guitars to make the song really catchy—it's since become one of those tunes you hear in supermarkets but can never quite put a name to.

The original symphony by Mendelssohn's about half an hour long. The first movement, which "Viaggio" is based on, is 12½ minutes, and the Figs' radio version clocked in at 3:39.

We'd tackled "Viaggio" a couple of times during the week, but I felt we'd basically just been going through the motions. It sounded lacklustre. And I knew why—the lead and rhythm guitars on the recording were acoustic, and I felt that even with mics clipped onto our instruments, we were losing some *oomph*.

So, for that morning's run-through, I switched to my favourite Strat.

Keith didn't say anything until we'd finished. And then, all hell broke loose.

"Play it the way it was written or don't play it at all!" Keith shouted, startling us all.

"I am playing it the way it was written," I said.

"It was written for acoustic guitars."

"The song needs some punch, Keith."

"It's got punch. You're backing me. It's *my* piece."

"It's not your piece, Keith," mum said, patiently. "I composed it with Tony. And Felix Mendelssohn, if we're being honest. But Tony and I knew when we wrote it that we had an expert violinist who could do it justice."

"And we can afford to take some risks," I said. "It's not like we're relying on millions of downloads or touring the world for the next ten years to survive. We're reviving the Figs for a limited run while we give the fans a chance to say goodbye."

"You have the spot," my mum added. "Why quibble over the sidelights?"

"And nobody's going to be paying attention to me anyway," I said.

"On the contrary, Jason, everyone is going to pay attention to you," Keith replied. "You're the brilliant progeny of the two founding members. Our fans mourned for weeks when Tony died. And they want you to play it the way your dad did."

"I'm not my dad."

"Yeah, that's fucking obvious."

Keith stormed back to his chair and packed his fiddle into its hard carry-case.

"You can do the tour without me. I'm done."

And with that, he walked out.

There was a moment of silence. Tejo and Dr. Sparks exchanged furtive glances, not even daring a whisper. Rolly, Mitch and Bob looked at me, and then at mum.

Mum ran after him.

Keith was in his late seventies, so I didn't suppose he was going to get very far in those few lost minutes. And mum was pretty agile in her trendy trainers. Zimmer frames were definitely not in her immediate future.

We waited.

"Tea anyone?" Mitch offered.

We all trooped downstairs to the kitchen. Unfortunately, its windows faced the other way, towards the sea.

We could hear shouting outside.

We transferred ourselves to the armoury hall. Its leaded glass windows overlooked the courtyard. And there we stood, like curious children, noses pressed to the panes.

It was all over in five minutes.

Keith got into his Range Rover, slammed the door, and drove

away. I'd like to say that he spun the tires and spewed gravel in his wake, but at his age, all he could really manage was a dodgy skid as he turned the car around and headed down the hill.

Mum saw us at the windows and shook her head. A minute later, she joined us in the hall.

"It's definite. He doesn't want to do the tour."

A nightmare of knock-ons raced through my mind. Travel arrangements, contracts, insurance, merchandise. We'd resurrected the old Figgis Green graphic—six band members in black silhouette, each recognizable by their stance and their instruments. That logo was plastered on everything, including our programmes and advance PR.

"It can't just be me and the arrangements," I said. "There has to be something else going on."

Everyone, except me and Bob, was a senior citizen, and we'd all had to pass medicals for the tour coverage, so I was pretty positive if there was something dodgy with Keith's health, we'd have known.

"There is," mum said. "Lottie's been having some problems with her breathing—COPD—and Keith really doesn't want to leave her."

Lottie was Keith's wife and she was the same age he was.

"She had a flareup last week and had to be admitted to hospital. She's all right but it just made up Keith's mind for him. He'd really rather be at home."

I understood. I think we all did.

"Couldn't he have just told us?" Mitch asked.

"I think he was struggling with it. He didn't want to let us down. He was angry for all sorts of reasons and that's why it came out like this. You know Keith."

"No chance of enticing Pete back, I suppose," Rolly said.

Pete Chedwick had been producing records in Los Angeles for decades. I couldn't see him agreeing to two long tours of small venues in England and Ireland. We didn't even know if he still played the fiddle.

"I don't think so," mum replied. And for the first time since we'd started rehearsing, I could see she was really worried.

#

We couldn't really carry on without a fiddler, so our afternoon session was called off while mum put through an emergency call to

Colin, our manager.

I walked down to the little bakery on the High Street that did fresh sandwiches with local ingredients to take away. I ordered a roasted tomato, mozzarella and pesto panini and a Coke and carried them across to the Village Green. At the top end, across the road from The Dog's Watch, there was a long wooden seat. It was beside a stone bird bath that had a plaque memorializing a certain Mrs. Tamworth—an early women's rights campaigner who, at the age of 35, had donned a pair of her husband's knickerbockers and turned cartwheels on the green, observed by all of her children and most of the villagers. I appropriated the bench and lit up a ciggie—there weren't any signs prohibiting it—took the requisite photo for my followers, and answered my phone.

It was Janice. The reporter from *The Stoneford News.*

"I wanted to give you an update," she said. "The police have spoken to Alistair Watford's wife. And I have as well. I'm working on a story but it won't be published just yet. Alistair was an actor. He lived in Southampton. Quite well known on the radio, apparently. Voices and such."

An actor.

"Interesting," I said.

"Anyway, Jason, the only thing his wife could tell me—and the police—is that Alistair had agreed to take on a small acting job in the days prior to his death. He hadn't discussed any of the details with her, which she thought was odd. It was all arranged over the phone. There was no record of anything on his computer. And his phone wasn't found on or anywhere near his body. It's gone missing."

"So nobody knows what he was hired for," I said.

"It seems that way. You mentioned you'd had lunch with him the other day. No clues there, I suppose."

I was beginning to get a damned good idea, but I wasn't going to share it with her. "Nothing at all, I'm afraid."

"There's one other odd thing, though, Jason. I told his wife that you'd said he was a big fan of Figgis Green, and she seemed surprised. She wasn't aware of that at all."

So, not even a fan of the Figs.

"Have the police released his cause of death yet?"

"No, they're keeping it quiet. Although it looked to me as if he'd been knifed."

"Have they got any leads on who might have killed him?" I

checked.

"If they do, they haven't shared that either. I did tell them that you were with me when Alistair's body was found, and you'd thought his name was Duncan Stopher and that you'd had lunch with him. Have they spoken to you yet?"

"They haven't," I said.

"I'm sure they will. I gave them your number."

"Thanks," I said.

I finished my ciggie, and my lunch, and I was frantically going through my lists of contacts to try and identify anyone who might know a decent fiddler who was available on one day's notice, when my mobile rang again.

It was Detective Sergeant Julie Handsworth from the Hampshire Constabulary. And she was requesting that I attend a voluntary interview at the Middlehurst Police Station at my earliest convenience.

#

The interview room at the station was very much like what you've seen in police procedurals on British TV. Rather grim, in fact, with grey-green walls and a window with frosted glass, a table against a wall, a couple of chairs, the requisite two-way mirror and a machine for recording conversations.

Detective Sergeant Handsworth looked a lot like Sharon Maughan from the Gold Blend coffee adverts in the late 1990s— blonde hair and a fringe, a wide mouth and very white teeth. She sat on one side of the table and I sat on the other. There was another detective in the room, a youngish man with curly black hair and a cocky eyebrow, who reminded me of Richard Greene when he was playing Robin Hood on TV in the 1950s. I couldn't resist remembering the show's opening salvo of trumpets and the *prang-twang* of the arrow shot from the hero's bow into a tree trunk. I suppose it must have made me smile as I looked at the guy, who was leaning against the wall beside the door.

"This interview is being recorded," said DS Handsworth, "and may be given in evidence if this case is brought to trial. We are in the interview room at Middlehurst Police Station. The date is Thursday, August 31, 2018 and the time is 1:05 p.m. I am Detective Sergeant Julie Handsworth. The other police officer present is Detective

Constable Edward Fulton."

She paused to look at me. Her eyes were quite penetrating.

"Please state your full name and date of birth and address."

"Jason David Figgis," I said. "May 11, 1968. Flat 2, 77 Pentonville Road, Islington. London. N1."

"Do you agree that there are no other persons present?"

I nodded.

"Mr. Figgis has nodded his head."

"Sorry," I said. "Yes."

"We are investigating the murder of Alistair Joseph Watford on Thursday, August 30, 2018 in the village of Stoneford, Hampshire. Before the start of this interview, I must remind you that you are entitled to free and independent legal advice either in person or by telephone at any stage. Do you wish to speak to a legal advisor now or have one present during the interview?"

"Not necessary," I said, easily. "Thanks. No."

"I must now ask you why you have not requested legal advice or to consult with a legal representative by telephone."

"I can't think of anything I'd need legal advice for?" I guessed.

"Then I must remind you that you can ask at any time for free legal advice during the course of this interview. If you want legal advice, say so and I will suspend the interview and arrange for legal representation. Do you understand?"

"Yes," I said. She was making me feel uncomfortable. This really wasn't sounding much like a friendly witness chat.

"Are you prepared to continue and answer questions without legal representation at this time?"

"Yes," I said. "I am."

"At the conclusion of this interview, I'll give you a notice explaining what will happen to the tapes and how you and/or your solicitor can get access to them."

"OK," I said.

"You do not have to say anything, but it may harm your defence if you do not mention when questioned something you later rely on in court. Anything you do say may be given in evidence."

Red flag. That was the official police caution. "Hang on," I said. "Am I being arrested?"

"You are not under arrest," DS Julie Handsworth replied. "You are not obliged to remain at the station and you may leave the interview and the station at will."

"What's this all about?" I said.

"The purpose of this voluntary interview is to question you to obtain evidence about your involvement or suspected involvement in the murder of Alistair Joseph Watford. You have a right to obtain information about the offence in question to enable you to understand the nature of this offence and why you may be suspected of committing it."

"I didn't commit it," I said. "And I have no idea why you think that I did."

"When did you first meet Alistair Watford?"

"He approached me on Monday," I said. "I was having lunch in The Four Eyes in Stoneford and he introduced himself and asked me if I'd be interested in having a look into the disappearance of Pippa Gladstone."

Both DC Fulton and DS Handsworth seemed surprised.

"Why would he do that?" DS Handsworth inquired. "You're a musician."

"I am. But I also do some investigative work in my spare time."

"Are you licensed?"

"Not yet."

"But you're aware of the legalities…?"

Indeed I was. And I provided her with the details, which I'm sure she knew, but I felt it important to advise her that I knew them too.

"Thank you." I couldn't tell if DS Handsworth was annoyed that I knew my rights as far as private investigations were concerned or if she was just irritated at having to question someone she considered an interference rather than a help. "And what name did Alistair Watford use when he approached you?"

"He said his name was Duncan Stopher."

"And you had no reason to doubt that was his name?"

"None whatsoever."

"Did you ask for identification?"

I shook my head.

"Mr. Figgis has shaken his head, indicating no." DS Handsworth was looking at me again with those penetrating eyes. "Not a very professional way to begin a relationship with a potential client."

"I realize that now, yes."

"Can you recall the conversation that took place between you and Alistair Watford on Monday, the 27th of August?"

I could, and I recounted it, word for word—or as near as I could manage.

"And what happened after that?" DS Handsworth asked.

"I asked to borrow his photos, he agreed, and I suggested we meet up again the next day—Tuesday—when I'd let him know what I decided about taking on the case. I also asked to see the negative of the photo from the Wiltshire Folk Festival, which he said he'd bring along on Tuesday. And then he took a selfie with me."

"Did you meet up again the following day?"

"We did," I said. "He brought me the negatives and I agreed I would look into Pippa's disappearance. He gave me a package of things…newspaper clippings, copies of articles…he brought me up to speed on Pippa's history, everything that happened when she was on holiday with her family in Spain…"

Again, I recounted our conversation.

"And then," I said, "I gave him some money and sent him to Currys in Christchurch to buy a kettle. Which he delivered to Stoneford Manor. We let him sit in on our rehearsal for a bit and then he left."

"Did you see him again after that?"

"I didn't. I gave the negative and the photo to my daughter. She's a professional photographer. I asked her for her opinion and she told me the picture—and the negative—were very good fakes. Yesterday—Thursday—the 30th—I rang Duncan—Alistair—and gave him the bad news."

"What time was that, do you remember?"

"It was during our morning break," I said. "Probably about twenty to eleven."

"And what was his reaction?"

"He was apologetic and told me he was sorry for wasting my time."

"He didn't react angrily?"

"Not at all."

"We have a witness," said DS Handsworth, "who overheard part of a conversation Alistair had on his mobile at about the time you've indicated. The witness tells us that the conversation was quite heated, and that Alistair had raised his voice and was arguing. The witness recalls the following was said…"

She stopped to consult her notes.

"'I don't care what you think. You fucking owe me.' And then there was a pause, followed by, 'I'll meet you in that little park at the bottom of the hill.' "

DS Handsworth gave me a questioning look.

"That wasn't me," I said. "I didn't owe him anything."

"You sent him to Currys to buy a kettle. What kind of kettle did he buy?"

"It was a SMEG," I said.

"Not an inexpensive item. How much money did you give him?"

"I think I gave him about £30."

"And the kettle he bought...?"

"It was worth about £129.00."

"That's a substantial difference."

"It is. I'd have paid him back...but he obviously didn't want me to."

"You've also mentioned that you borrowed his pictures and his negatives. Had you, perhaps, decided to keep them?"

"No," I said. "I told him I'd return them. He was coming to our opening night in Middlehurst and I said I'd give everything back to him then."

"Not in Emmy Cooper Park later that day."

"No," I said.

"And the fee you'd agreed on, when you also agreed to take on the case?"

"He hadn't paid me anything. Money was discussed. But it never changed hands."

"And where are the pictures and negatives now?"

This was not looking good.

"I don't know," I said. "They were stolen from my daughter's studio."

"When was this?"

"Last night."

"And did your daughter report the theft to the police?"

"No. She didn't think it was worth their time."

DS Handsworth wasn't impressed.

"You can check Alistair's phone records," I said. "You'll be able to see from those who he was arguing with. You'll see my call and the other person's call."

"We're in the process of doing that," DS Handsworth replied. "Were you aware that Alistair was an actor?"

"I wasn't until after he was killed," I said.

"How did you find this out?"

"I was told by a reporter for the *Stoneford News*. Janice Winstanley."

"And what else did Ms. Winstanley tell you?" DS Handsworth asked. She sounded irritated again.

"That she'd spoken to Alistair's wife and the only thing she could tell her was that he'd agreed to take on a small acting job. Which he didn't discuss with her. And there wasn't any information on his computer. The job was arranged over the phone. And she didn't know who hired him, or why. But I think I can tell you why. Somebody wanted me to find out if Pippa Gladstone was dead or alive. And they used Alistair to try and convince me to take on the case."

"And did he convince you?"

"He did. But after I found out the picture was photoshopped, I told him I wasn't interested anymore."

"And he accepted that."

"Yes. He did."

"To the best of our knowledge, Alistair Watford was killed between half past eleven in the morning and twelve noon on Thursday, the 30th of August. Can you account for your whereabouts at that time?"

"I was rehearsing," I said.

"Are you quite certain about that?"

"No," I said. "Hang on. My mum sent me down to the village to buy some ice cream for one of the band members."

"At what time was that?"

"At about half past eleven." Had somebody planned Alistair's death to coincide with my walk down the hill? I already knew I was being watched. This just made everything a thousand times worse.

"Can you tell me where you went?"

"I went to Village Green Treats. I bought the ice cream. And then I walked back up to the manor."

"Can you remember who served you?"

"I don't know her name. But she looked about 16. Short, dark hair."

"So, if I were to show her your picture and ask if she recalled you being in her shop, you're confident she'd be able to identify you?"

"I'd hope so," I said. "I paid for the ice cream with my credit card. I didn't ask for a receipt but there'll be a record of it with Amex, and at the shop."

"And after you bought the ice cream, what did you do?"

"I told you. I walked straight back to my rehearsal."

"We have another witness," said DS Handsworth, "who recognized you—Jason Davey—or Figgis—a member of the band Figgis Green—as being in the vicinity of Emmy Cooper Park at the time of Alistair Watford's murder."

"Well," I said, "that's hardly surprising as the park's at the end of Poorhouse Lane and the ice cream shop's on the corner of Poorhouse Lane and the High Street."

"This witness is certain he saw you with a knife in your hand."

"Is that the murder weapon? A knife?"

"You tell me."

"I can't tell you," I said, "because I don't know. I wasn't there."

I had a thought.

"I also bought a drink. In a tin. It was silver. I was carrying it in my hand as I left the shop. Is it possible your witness has very bad eyesight and mistook my drink for a knife? On top of everything else, I haven't got a motive. I liked the guy."

DS Handsworth wrote something in her file folder.

"Is there anything else you wish to say or add to what has already been said?"

"Yes," I said. "While I was talking to Alistair on my mobile, I was sitting with Tejo, our sound guy. He overheard the entire conversation. Please talk to him."

"Thank you," said DS Handsworth. "We will. Can you give us his last name?"

I shook my head. "No. Sorry. I'll find out for you."

"This interview has now ended. It's 1:57 p.m."

CHAPTER SEVEN

You can report things to the police anonymously, with no fear of recrimination. A made-up recollection of a phone conversation that never happened…an eyewitness claim about a knife that didn't exist. The Crimestoppers website is filled with details about what happens to your information once it's received, with dire warnings about "malicious intent".

The phone call could have been genuine. Alistair might indeed have been arguing with someone. It just wasn't me.

As for the alleged knife…I might have generously supposed that it was someone with bad eyesight. Someone jumping to conclusions, having heard about a murder in the vicinity.

I was more inclined to believe it was someone—two someones—who had "malicious intent" in mind when they'd provided their anonymous eyewitness accounts to the police. I was more inclined to believe that I was being fitted up.

But they had to know their claims wouldn't hold water. They had to know the evidence against me was dodgy at best.

The real reason I was being fitted up was because someone was trying to scare me off.

And I'd got the message, loud and clear.

But if they thought that would convince me to stay the hell away from finding out what had really happened to Pippa Gladstone, they had another thing coming. I'd been ready to abandon the investigation after I'd found out the photo of Pippa had been faked. But Alistair's death changed everything. I was angry.

I rang through to the Middlehurst Constabulary and gave them our sound guy's full name and contact information, with instructions to pass it all along to DS Handsworth. She could check with Tejo herself to find out what he'd overheard while I was chatting with Alistair.

I logged onto Amex and did a screenshot of my transaction at Village Green Treats and emailed that to the police as well.

And then I went onto the Pippa Gladstone Mystery Forum and sent a private message to Duncan Stopher.

Hello, I wrote. *I wonder if I could have a quick word with you. Someone got in touch with me claiming to be you. I have my doubts. Can you message me back?*

I sent it off. I wasn't optimistic about getting a reply. For all I knew, Alistair had been masquerading as Duncan Stopher for years, not days—in spite of what his wife had told the police.

But I had to find out.

And then I consulted the handwritten notes Alistair had given me. I located the contact information for Pippa Gladstone's brother, Bernard. I gave him a call.

After I'd told him who I was and what I wanted, I asked if I could pop round to have a little chat.

#

Middlehurst was a ten-minute drive north of Stoneford along a country road that cut through copses and woods and golf courses and farmers' fields, and ended just inside the southern edge of the New Forest.

Bernard Gladstone lived in a tidy, semi-detached house situated on the outskirts of the town, on a street that had probably been developed just prior to World War Two, and had since undergone successive improvements.

There were brilliant blue hydrangeas and beautifully-scented pink roses nodding over a low brick wall in the front garden, and there was a pebbled path leading up to a glossy black front door with a polished brass knocker.

Bernard himself had a surprising thatch of greyish-blond hair that was combed untidily off his face. He had the same striking blue-grey eyes as his sister. He was wearing an open-necked shirt and khaki-coloured trousers.

"Bernie," he said, shaking my hand. "Let's go upstairs."

He took me up to a bedroom that had probably once belonged to one of his children, but which he'd since made over into a private study for himself.

There was a desk with a computer and a laser printer, and an extremely nice ergonomically-correct office chair—black leather—and a little armchair, and a lot of shelves crammed with books.

"I work from home," he said. "Management consultant. Much handier than having to commute into London and I'm retiring in a couple of years anyway."

"More time for the garden," I said, checking the view from the window: a nice green patch of lawn that had been landscaped to include a little water feature at the bottom, with rocks and ferns and mossy things, and a very large ceramic frog.

"And the grand-children," he agreed. "My daughter's a single mum now and can use all the help my wife and I can give her."

He invited me to sit in the armchair, while he wheeled the leather one around from his desk so that he was facing me.

"The police have been in touch," he said. "They told me about the murder in Stoneford and how they thought it may have been related in some way to Pippa's disappearance. They said the victim had asked a private investigator to look into her case. They mentioned your name but I told them I'd never heard of you. Which, of course, I hadn't. Until you rang."

"I'm the one who told the police about Alistair's connection to Pippa," I said. "Interesting that they're pursuing that line of inquiry. What did they ask you?"

Bernie shrugged. "They just wanted to know if I was aware of the renewed interest in my sister's disappearance and if I could provide any further information. I said I wasn't, and I couldn't. Pippa's story tends to come up for scrutiny every few years. If it's not someone pursuing yet another outlandish conspiracy theory, it's someone else determined to try and unmask her possible killer. I mean, honestly, it was 44 years ago. There can't possibly be any more stones to turn over, can there?"

"Perhaps one or two of those stones might actually warrant a second look," I said. I brought up Alistair's folk festival photo on my phone. "Have you seen this?"

Bernie looked at it, very carefully.

"I haven't," he said. "Where did you get it?"

"From someone on the Pippa Gladstone Mystery Forum."

"Oh," said Bernie. "*That* place. When was it taken?"

"I don't know," I lied. "I thought perhaps you might be able to shed some light on it."

Bernie shook his head. "Sorry."

"But it is Pippa?"

"It is, yes."

"Do you know who the boy is?"

"I'm afraid I don't." He paused. "Could you send me a copy of that? I'd love to show it to my mother."

I got his email address and forwarded it over.

"How about this one?" I asked, showing him the anonymously-snapped photo of Pippa beside the pool in Malaga.

"Yes, I recognize that one. Also from the chat group. Obviously."

"Is it Pippa too?"

"It is. The police contacted my mother after the picture surfaced…months after my sister disappeared. My mother confirmed it was her."

"Can you tell me what she wearing the night she went missing?"

"Whatever was reported in the papers. My parents provided a full description."

"A pale blue shirt, dark blue denim jeans," I said, remembering what I'd read in the notes, "and a red nylon windbreaker."

"That's my recollection," said Bernie.

"So what do you think happened to her?" I asked.

"I think," said Bernie, "that she went off to a party with a group of boys and girls she'd met while we were on holiday. And I think that, unfortunately, she drank more than was good for her, and that Alvaro Izan, the young man who was interviewed and eventually arrested and then let go by the police was, one way or another, responsible for her death. But there was never enough proof to bring him to trial and there never will be. I've always believed he's the one person who truly knows what happened to my sister."

"Alvaro Izan was very well-connected," I agreed.

"His father was a prominent businessman who owned several hotels in Malaga. He was not without influence. We've always believed the police were bought off. There was a brief media circus after my sister's disappearance, which the young man seemed to revel in. He enjoyed the attention. But he had no real alibi. In our eyes, he remained—remains—the primary suspect."

"I'm sure the police asked whether there were any problems between your parents and your sister."

"Of course they did. When children disappear, it's always the family that's investigated first, isn't it? Pippa was at an awkward time in her life. Growing pains, as my mother used to say. But she wasn't at all rebellious. She was well-behaved compared to some of the girls at her school."

"But she wasn't shy about staying out late with the locals."

"She wasn't out drinking with them every night, if that's what you think. She'd met some boys and girls who were her own age and she wanted to pal around with them. My parents weren't all that keen, but they allowed it. She was their eldest child. You learn with the eldest, don't you? The ones that come along later have a much easier time of it."

"So it doesn't sound feasible to you that she drank too much on her last night there and Alvaro dropped her off at the hotel and that was the last he saw of her?"

"It sounds entirely feasible that she drank too much. And if she was incapacitated, it was very likely because Alvaro had encouraged it. However, we've never believed that he dropped her off at the hotel. Something happened, either deliberately or by accident, and she died. Alvaro knows the truth."

"And she hadn't had an argument or a fight or anything like that with your parents prior to going out?"

"She hadn't," Bernie said. "I was there. My father told her what time he expected her back, and she agreed to it. We were leaving to fly home very early the next day."

"And she'd never run away, or disappeared, or anything like that, previously."

"Never. She never went anywhere without telling them first. I remember people saying that she always seemed much younger than 16."

"Emotionally, you mean."

"And socially."

"So perhaps the holiday in Malaga was something of an eye-opener for her…?"

"As in, what she might have got up to with Alvaro Izan?"

"Yes. Did she have any boyfriends?"

"None. She never seemed that interested. It did occur to us that perhaps she'd indicated an interest in Alvaro…a willingness…but she'd changed her mind and he'd reacted badly. It was never mentioned in the papers—why would it be?—but she got her period when we were there. Two days before we were due to come home. Pippa was very irregular—her periods were completely unpredictable."

"Surely if she'd told Alvaro that was the reason, he'd have accepted it."

"You and I would, of course. But an arrogant teenager used to getting his own way? Fuelled by alcohol and possibly drugs. And who knows whether Pippa would even have said that was why. Back then we weren't quite so comfortable talking about things like that, were we?"

"I was only six in 1974," I said. "I didn't even know what periods were until 1980."

For some reason, Bernie found that humorous. "Pippa hadn't packed any tampons so our mother had to rush out and buy something for her. It turned into quite an adventure and she ended up coming back with a huge package of pads with everything written in Spanish. No emergency tampons to be had anywhere, as it turned out."

"I'm surprised you'd remember that."

"Because I was a 13-year-old boy, you mean? I remember it precisely because I was 13 years old and a total bastard and I took great pleasure in teasing her about it, even to the point of helping myself to a couple of the items in question and fashioning a pair of slippers out of them. My creative efforts were not well received."

I smiled. I had a similar recollection—except it was my sister, Angie, who'd got creative, and it was a pair of rabbit ears, and she'd stuck them on my head. "Can you just confirm a couple of other details for me? Her hair was dark blonde—as it is in the photo. Did she have any scars or anything else that might help identify her?"

"Nothing at all," Bernie said.

"And she was how tall when she disappeared?"

"Five foot two."

"She looks taller than that in the photo. The same height as the boy."

"Yes, that photo's a bit deceptive."

Bernie got up from his leather chair.

"I have a little video of Pippa performing. Would you like to see it?"

"I would," I said.

He rummaged through a box full of flash drives and CD's on one of the shelves.

"Here we are. I think you'll like this. Pippa was quite the actress. And she loved Figgis Green, by the way. Her school, Mewbury, was putting on a Christmas show and she came up with the idea of miming to one of your songs. I can't remember the name of it…it's by that American girl."

"'I Can't Stay Mad at You'?" I guessed. "Skeeter Davis?"

"That's the one. I obviously don't have your encyclopaedic knowledge of singers and songs."

I wouldn't have called my knowledge encyclopaedic, but yes, I did have a lexicon of music stored somewhere in my brain. I'm a whiz at trivia when it comes to who sang what and when. I'm in high demand for pub quizzes.

"Pippa liked your version. But she loved the original. So she got together with two of her friends and they arranged a little performance involving singing and dancing. It was a bit controversial because the argument was made that it wasn't really performing if you were just miming…but Pippa stood her ground and they allowed her to do it. She claimed what was good enough for *Top of the Pops* ought to be good enough for Mewbury."

I liked Pippa's attitude.

Bernie played the video and I watched it with him on his computer screen.

It's one thing to see photos of someone. It's another thing entirely to watch them move and breathe and to see their facial expressions, their gestures, their interactions with others.

There was Pippa, with her long wavy dark blonde hair, parted in the middle, wearing black trousers and trainers and a white long-sleeved shirt and a black satin waistcoat. And her two schoolmates, each of them in a black satin waistcoat and black trousers well. It was obviously a rehearsal, or perhaps just a private show for her family.

They were performing in front of a fireplace that had a marble surround and a mantle that showed off a clock, several vases, and some miniature copper milk jugs.

I watched, fascinated.

Pippa reminded me of my first serious girlfriend. We were both

16 and her name was Sophie. I was born in 1968, so it would have been about 1984. A decade later than Pippa's performance, but the similarities were striking. One of the things I loved about Sophie was that she never went along with what everyone else was wearing or doing. So in the middle of big hair, big shoulders and shiny eyes, cheeks and lips, she wore her hair long and straight, and her clothes were throwbacks to Annie Hall, and if she wore makeup, I never noticed. I loved her passionately. We lost our virginities to each other. I've never forgotten Sophie, and I think that's what made me want to find out whatever happened to Pippa even more keenly.

"Who filmed this?" I asked. It was definitely film—video cams for personal use hadn't been invented yet. It had that slightly scratchy, slightly out of focus, slightly jerky removed-from-reality quality that you got with 8mm home movies.

"Our father," said Bernie. "He had one of those Super-8 cameras and apparently it was quite innovative because it allowed for sound. Most of the cameras back then were silent. I was worried the film would deteriorate over time, so I had it digitized a few years ago. It's one of my favourite memories of my sister—and of my father, too, because we're watching it all through his eyes."

Pippa's performance was wonderful. She and her mates had choreographed the song, borrowing most of the moves that our band was famous for when they sang it during the encore.

"Where was this done?" I asked, curiously.

"That's the fireplace in the drawing room of the house where we grew up. Those copper jugs on the mantle are my father's souvenirs from his field trips to Jersey. The film was made a few months before we went to Spain, so it's really a last look at her before she disappeared."

"Do you know the names of her two friends?" I asked.

"I might have at one point," Bernie said. "But it's all left me now. We were at different schools. Pippa was at Mewbury. I went to Shorebridge. They merged together roundabout 1990 but back in 1974 they were completely separate."

I waited 'til the film had finished. I'd enjoyed that.

"Can you make me a copy?" I asked.

"Of course. I'd be happy to."

#

My stomach let me know it was almost time for dinner as I drove back to Stoneford.

I went for a walk, to see if I could find somewhere decent to eat that wasn't the dining room at The Dog's Watch.

My exploration of the village took me to a perfect little Italian place on the High Street that looked as if it had once been someone's house. The main floor had been gutted to accommodate the restaurant, and the back garden—which I made a bee-line for—had been paved over to create a wonderful courtyard furnished with wicker chairs and aluminum-and-glass-topped tables, candles in glasses and subdued floodlights hiding behind potted greenery.

I stayed 'til it was dark, enjoying my table-for-one and my little side dishes of hummus and marinated olives, a starter of button mushrooms marinated with paprika, garlic, cream and white wine, and a linguine tossed with tiger prawns, spinach, lemon, cherry tomatoes and tarragon.

I posted the photos to Instagram, along with a very sly comment regarding the need to *"fiddle about with our stage presence"*.

No response from Getting Ready for Ladder Fun Lady. Typical.

The rest of my Instagram followers were appreciative of my dinner entry, helpfully informing me that if my career as a musician ever came to an abrupt end, I would very definitely be able to make it as an influential food critic. None of them caught on to my cryptic riddle about our new fiddler.

And if any of my fellow diners knew who I was, they didn't let on…though I caught one or two eyeing me and whispering to each other, and a couple sitting in the far corner having a passionate conversation about something while the female half kept copping furtive glances in my direction. I hoped they had a black Sharpie with them for whatever they were going to ask me to sign. Likely a paper napkin. Unless they had a copy of a Figs' CD with them. Or, God forbid, a cassette tape.

By the time I got back to my room, it was about 9 p.m.

I plugged in the flash drive that Bernie had given me, and watched the little video of Pippa all over again.

There she was, full of life, teasing her audience with a clearly tongue-in-cheek rendition of the song, every move and facial expression exaggerated and full of cheekiness.

Pippa's two friends were definitely her foils. One of them, with long hair pulled up into bunches and tied with a pair of those bright thick wool ropes that were popular in the 1970s, rolled her eyes to the ceiling every time Pippa declared her undying love for her undeserving boyfriend. The other, with a mass of long, completely unruly blonde hair, pooh-poohed her idiotic obsession with brush-off gestures and exaggerated head shakes.

They must have rehearsed it for hours: her two friends were exactly in synch with her, their arms, legs, hands and feet completely coordinated.

I was impressed.

On the other hand, I hadn't reached any conclusions about Bernie.

When a child disappears under suspicious circumstances, the first suspects are always the parents and whoever else happens to have close connections to the household. Bernie seemed very friendly and very accommodating. He'd only been a couple of years younger than Pippa, so I doubted he could actually have been involved in her death—though it certainly wouldn't have been the first time a sibling was suspected of killing a brother or sister.

It also bothered me that Pippa's parents had so quickly been discounted as suspects. Pippa's father was a respected university professor. The family, in the eyes of the Spanish police—and no doubt Scotland Yard as well—was obviously above suspicion.

Still, someone had hired Alistair to approach me. To my mind it didn't matter that the photo was a fake. The point of the exercise was to convince me to start asking questions. And quite possibly, to unearth her killer.

And Alistair had ended up dead for it.

The last thing I did before I went to bed was check the Pippa Gladstone Mystery Forum.

There was a message waiting for me.

Greetings from Montego Bay. I am a gentleman of leisure these days, having retired on a comfortable pension some years ago. I really only check the chat group every month or two. I find I've quite lost interest in Pippa. But I look in out of idle curiosity. A few individuals have claimed to be me over the years. I assure you they are not. Best wishes, Duncan Stopher.

CHAPTER EIGHT

I t was Saturday, and I would have enjoyed the luxury of a late lie-in, but I hadn't slept well and once I'd actually managed to drop off, it hadn't lasted. I was awake with the birds.

I got up and checked the Pippa forum to see if Duncan Stopher had answered the follow-up message I'd sent before going to bed.

My name is Jason Figgis. I'm a private investigator. The guy who was impersonating you has died. His name was Alistair Watford. He asked me to have a look into Pippa Gladstone's disappearance. I was wondering if you knew who he was.

I'd waited for him for half an hour, lighting an impatient cigarette and blowing the smoke out of the window. I'd even looked up what time it was in Jamaica. Six hours behind England, in case you ever need to know.

But he wasn't there.

He was now.

I'm not familiar with the name Alistair Watford, he wrote. *How did he die?*

He was murdered, I said.

That is indeed shocking news. You must be careful.

Why? I said.

If you look through all the postings on the website, you'll see that several people have pretended to be me over the years. I am something of an expert on the entire case. They impersonate me to try and convince people of certain theories. Sometimes they'll downplay compelling arguments. Alistair Watford may have wandered too close to the truth about Pippa.

79

What is the truth about Pippa? I asked.

I waited.

Was he going to vanish again?

No. It was merely a momentary absence.

You're a musician, he said.

Wikipedia is our friend, I agreed. If anybody googles "Jason Figgis", they're automatically directed to results that include my stage name Jason Davey. I'm not difficult to find.

You should consider a rhythm that really counts. And after you've done that, look for the golden rings.

Sorry…? I said.

But he'd gone silent again.

I waited.

Nothing.

What the fuck did that mean?

I should consider a rhythm that really counts?

What? 3/4 time? A waltz?

And what the hell did that and golden rings have to do with Pippa's disappearance?

#

I went downstairs for breakfast.

Mum and Bob were waiting for me at our favourite table.

"We may have a solution to the dilemma," mum said, as I sat down.

I forced my still half-asleep mind to switch from Pippa Gladstone to Figgis Green, and our urgent vacancy.

"We thought we'd run it past you before consulting Rolly and Mitch," Bob added.

"Thanks," I said, surprised. I'd have thought Rolly and Mitch merited a greater priority than me, but perhaps it was just my timing. I was having breakfast with mum and Bob. They weren't.

"The thing is," Bob said, a little hesitantly, "my girlfriend plays the violin. She's done folk, rock, country, classical…weddings. Commercial functions. Studio sessions."

"And she's available," mum added.

"I talked to her last night and she's willing to rearrange her schedule."

"Does she have any formal training?" I asked. Not that it was compulsory or even recommended. Keith was the only one of the Figs who'd had any kind of lessons and look where that had got us.

I was just curious.

"Royal College of Music."

"Impressive."

"She knows we're opening in a week's time," mum said, "and she's able to join us this afternoon. If Mitch and Rolly agree."

"Her name's Beth," Bob said. "Homewood."

I didn't honestly see that we had much choice. In the absence of any other courageous—or foolhardy—violinists, we either went with Beth, or we cancelled the tour. Rearranging every piece in our set lists to account for the lack of a fiddler wasn't an option.

"You absolutely have my vote of confidence," I said.

#

Rolly and Mitch were both in agreement but it really hadn't taken much to convince them. A quick call to our manager lent immediate weight to Bob and mum's suggestion. Mum absented herself from the library to ring Beth with the good news, and then we reconvened and explored a few songs from the Figs' catalogue which didn't feature much in the way of strings. Because it didn't matter how brilliant Beth was—the fact remained that she was going to have to acquaint herself with two set lists' worth of tunes in about six days, and the easier we could make that monumental task for her, the better.

It also meant I was going to have to learn a couple of new songs on the fly.

One of them was a fairly faithful rendition of Malvina Reynolds' "What Have They Done to the Rain?". It was one of the Figs' lesser-known chart entries. I'd always fondly remembered it as "What Have They Done to the Train?" because my dad had sung it, very loudly, and with appropriately altered lyrics, while he and I were waiting on a platform for a very-delayed connection at a long-forgotten station when I was about eight.

I found a good recording of it on YouTube and Tejo ran it through his mixing board to isolate, as best he could, my dad's lead guitar. I sat with my Strat and played along a couple of times until I had it down. And then, because Bob, mum, Mitch and Rolly had to reacquaint themselves with the song as well, Tejo routed the full recording through the speakers and we all played and sang along. It was a quick and dirty way to bring ourselves up to speed—but it worked.

Our lunch break was late. I'd looked at The Four Eyes menu on my phone. I was all set for their turkey and basil pesto panini, but by the time I got there, they were sold out and I had to settle for a roasted ham, Swiss and egg.

Remembering my last meeting with Alistair, I snagged my favourite table by the window and quietly toasted him with my mug of coffee. I posted a picture of my sandwich to my followers.

What? someone answered immediately. *No breakfast? No custard creams and ciggie on your break? You're falling behind! Do keep up!*

Many apologies, I wrote back. *We've hit a little snag. But we've been pulling some strings. Back to normal soon, I promise.*

And then, while I ate my sandwich, I applied my brain to Duncan's riddle.

I typed the entire phrase about rhythm into Google on my phone.

Google was exceedingly helpful…but didn't provide me with any answers…only more questions.

How do you count hard rhythms?

How do you count different rhythms?

What is an 8-beat rhythm?

What counts as a beat?

I cursed Duncan Stopher as I keyed in more search terms.

I shortened the phrase to *a rhythm that really counts* and tried that.

I got the same series of responses.

Except that seven or eight entries down there was a piece of music— "Jersey Bounce" by Tommy Dorsey.

I listened to the tune. It was an instrumental.

But someone had attached lyrics to it, and one line of the lyrics referenced "a rhythm that really counts".

Duncan Stopher obviously knew his stuff.

But why "Jersey Bounce"?

I remembered something Bernie had told me yesterday. I gave him a call.

"I was just curious," I said, "about the copper jugs on the mantle over the fireplace in your dad's film. I think you mentioned Jersey?"

"Ah," said Bernie. "Yes. As you may know, my father was a professor of history at Hampshire University. And each year he took his students to Jersey on a field trip to explore first-hand the effects of the German occupation during World War Two."

"And the jugs were souvenirs of those trips?"

"That's right. He brought back a new one every year."

"I don't suppose you can remember the name or the number of the course that he taught."

Bernie laughed. "No clue," he said. "Sorry. Wasn't even on my radar when I was 13."

"Thanks anyway," I said.

"Anytime," Bernie replied.

I looked on the Hampshire University website, which listed some historical course information, but only going back as far as the 1990s.

I tried ringing the uni's admin office, but, since it was Saturday, they were closed. In any case, I suspected their only solution would be for me to pay a visit to their library and have a look through their old printed course directories.

I briefly considered recruiting Dom to drive there and do the legwork.

There had to be an easier way.

I tried googling every word combination I could think of that might bring up a course name, a subject, a list of students, anything.

But there was nothing. It was too long ago. We're so used to being able to search online for instant answers that when we encounter something that requires good old-fashioned manual hunting—the way it used to be, in the days of microfiche readers in claustrophobic libraries, card catalogues in banks of tiny wooden drawers and huge bound volumes of Periodical Indexes—we're stumped.

Lesser mortals would have been stumped, anyway.

I had an idea.

After Jenn and I had found one another and DNA tests had absolutely confirmed our father-daughter relationship, we'd taken it one step further and done a second set of less-official DNA tests that would enable us to track down our cousins and uncles and aunts and ancestors going back to whenever records started to be kept about such things.

I'd discovered—and subscribed to—a family research website that contained no end of squirrelled-away memorabilia from our near and far relatives: photos and certificates, passenger lists, visas and entry cards and newspaper clippings.

I logged onto the site where all my fifth-to-eighth cousins were dangling off tree branches, guessing that someone in Harry's family might have curated his life and provided some documentation to verify it.

I was in luck. Harry had a sister named Barbara who'd created a profile for him and made some entries. And because he was dead, that profile was open for anyone to explore.

Harry Gladstone had been born in 1933 in the little village of Cann, Dorset. There were some photos—Harry as a child, in short trousers and a little white shirt and a knitted sleeveless pullover—very similar to the sort of pullover Alistair had been wearing. The photo had been taken in 1939, just prior to the outbreak of World War Two. Another photo—his wedding to Susan in 1956. She was wearing a long white dress; he was in a suit. Flowers in buttonholes, a modest bouquet, mums and dads and the vicar posing on the front steps of the church, back in the days before weddings began to rival major Hollywood productions.

Barbara had added pages for Susan and Bernie as well—at least, I assumed that's who the entries were for. I couldn't see their details or even their names, because they were both still alive and their files were marked *Private*.

But I could see what she'd added about Pippa, because Pippa, like her father, was dead.

On both of their pages Barbara had archived all of the newspaper articles about Pippa's disappearance and Harry's death. And she'd included some other stories as well…pieces that had been written about Harry's teaching career at Hampshire University…including a curious collection of articles clipped and scanned from the university's newspaper: reports written by Harry's students about their field trips to Jersey. They were just short pieces, focusing on the tunnels the Germans had dug through the island, the highlight of which was a visit to several of the actual caverns. Each story included a photo of Harry and his students—a different bunch each year, obviously— all named, all posing in front of the entrance to one of the tunnels. The course number was HIST2601 and the course name was "World War Two German Occupation of the Channel Islands".

Snap.

I'd found the Jersey reference. But what else had Duncan wanted?

After you've done that, look for the golden rings.

There were no golden rings in any of the pictures, not even through the lobes of Harry's student's ears, and if anyone was wearing rings on their fingers, the resolution certainly wasn't good enough to show them.

Once again, I resorted to Google.

And there, after numerous suggestions about a song featuring Tammy Wynette and George Jones and endless jpgs of jewellery suitable for engagements, weddings and overly-generous gifting, I landed on *The Twelve Days of Christmas.*

Which, of course, featured five golden rings.

Did Duncan want me to consider the rings themselves?

I couldn't see how they might be connected to Pippa at all.

I got myself another cup of coffee and had a think.

Perhaps it wasn't the rings themselves that I was meant to be looking at.

Perhaps it was how many rings there were.

Five.

There were five copper jugs on the mantle.

Harry had made five trips to Jersey.

Was it the last one that Duncan wanted me to know about?

I had to get back to the manor, but before I left, I sent a message to Duncan letting him know what I'd discovered.

Harry Gladstone's field trip to Jersey, I wrote. *February 1974. A month before Pippa disappeared.*

Congratulations, Duncan wrote back, in less than a minute.

How is the field trip important? I asked.

Be studious, Jason. Cast your fate to the wind.

Not another fucking riddle.

Anyway, I knew that one off the top of my head. No googling necessary. Their hit version was in 1965, the same year Figgis Green burst onto the charts.

Sounds Orchestral, I said. *And…?*

Silence.

#

I got back from lunch to discover that Beth had arrived. She had long, light brown, wavy hair, which she'd plaited loosely behind her head. I'd say she was in her mid-40s, a good 20 years younger than Bob, but I reckoned that made her old enough to have perfected her craft and to have dealt with nearly every situation that could possibly arise when you were performing in front of an audience.

Mum had sent Beth mp3's of all of the songs on our two set lists, plus the two encores, so that she could listen to them as she drove from Bristol—where she lived—to Stoneford. It was 80 miles. She'd have got to the encores just as she was motoring up Manor Rise.

A few more calls had been made in my absence. Papers had been delivered virtually and signed digitally. And mum was on the phone with Freddie, our Tour Manager, who was going to have to deal with the hotel reservations, the PR and merch sales and the print run for the programmes.

While we waited for mum to finish her call, Beth, Mitch, Rolly, Bob and I listened to another of our lesser-known tunes, "Rise Again" on the speakers. The song, which has its roots in Nova Scotia, was written by Leon Dubinsky and made famous by the Rankin Family, Anne Murray and Rita MacNeil. And Figgis Green. I'd always felt the Figs' version was under-rated and under-valued. The band had never released it as a single, and they'd put it on their last-ever album almost as an afterthought. But it was now one of the songs we were adding into the show to make life easier for Beth. And I was actually secretly pleased it was going to be given a chance to shine.

Beth had brought two different instruments—a traditional acoustic violin, similar to Keith's—and an electric one—something Keith wouldn't have touched in a million years. She chose the acoustic for the play-along, and when mum came back into the room and took her place in front of the mic, we added in the vocals.

I have to say, it gave me shivers.

The opening bars had mum on her tin whistle and Beth on the violin, and then they both stopped playing and sang instead. Having two female voices together in the band was something really new and unusual and exciting. If Keith hadn't walked out earlier, he almost certainly would have self-destructed.

Mitch, Bob and I played along on our guitars, while Rolly kept a quiet beat behind us.

And then we all joined in for the chorus, in unison, separating briefly for some simple harmony, then falling silent again while mum and Beth took turns with the verses that followed.

But as I was singing, I found myself becoming—inexplicably—emotional.

I was confounded. What was it? Why?

Perhaps, I realized, it was because "Rise Again" was the last song that had been recorded on the band's last album…and it was the last time my dad had gone into the studio to play for the Figs. He'd been contemplating doing something different after that…a new musical direction, me and him, a duo. He was 54 years old and I was 27 and we'd come up with an amazing act, a collection of fabulous songs—both self-penned and borrowed from others—and we'd even played at a couple of small gigs, just to get the feel of it, to see if we could make it work. It was going to be our time.

There was such potential there. So much left to dream, so much left to explore…and then it had all ended. My dad died. Not from a disease, not in a traffic accident, not from any of the usual things that take you out when you're still relatively young and nowhere near the age when you collect your pension and qualify for your free bus pass. He died from something so utterly ridiculous that it still makes me shake my head in disbelief.

Just like the six-foot chimney at The Dog's Watch, he was struck by lightning.

On a golf course.

In the middle of England, a mile or two from the house where he lived with my mum.

And the stupid thing was that he didn't even play golf. He hated it. He'd only gone because a friend of his had just come back from five years working overseas and had invited him along for a healthy walk and the promise of a great meal and a few drinks in the clubhouse afterwards.

My dad had offered to carry his clubs.

There was no rain in the forecast, nothing, clear skies…and then it suddenly clouded over. There was a spatter of rain…not even enough to make dad and Evan hunt for cover…and then…

A gigantic bolt of lightning.

It hit dad. It knocked Evan off his feet.

Evan recalled the percussion from the flash, the sensation that he'd been punched in the chest by a giant battering ram…but no thunder. He didn't hear any thunder, unlike everyone else on the course that day, because you don't when you're at the centre of the strike.

My dad was killed instantly.

Without going into a lot of detail, his jean legs were shredded, along with a sock, and the sole of one of his trainers melted. He had fern-like burns all over his chest and arms. The pathologist determined he'd died very quickly from cardiac arrest, which was a blessing—if there is a blessing—because he also reckoned that if dad had survived, his injuries would have left him permanently disabled and struggling to deal with an unfathomable array of neurological impairments.

It left my mum without her partner of 32 years. And me terrified of lightning.

We finished the song. There was a moment of silence, and then loud applause from Dr. Sparks and Tejo.

"That was truly lovely," Beth said.

"It was," mum agreed, looking at me.

I gave her a thumbs up.

I couldn't summon the words.

#

Mum had planned a Welcome Aboard dinner for Beth that evening at an Indian restaurant called Curried Flavours in Middlehurst. "I expect you all to be there in two hours' time," she said. "No excuses."

Back at The Dog's Watch, I showered and changed. I had a few moments free before I had to drive to the restaurant, so I tried to sort out the answer to *Cast Your Fate to the Wind*.

I'd already suggested Sounds Orchestral but my guess had been summarily dismissed.

That obviously wasn't the right answer.

I went back to Wikipedia to look up the song.

If it wasn't the artist it had to be the composer. Vince Guaraldi. Who'd actually released the original version of the piece in 1962, three years before Sounds Orchestral.

And then what?

Be studious, Duncan had said.

Studious.

Students.

Harry's students?

I'd saved the clipping from the February 1974 Hampshire University newspaper to my phone.

All of the students in the story and the accompanying photo were named.

None of them were called Vince. Or Guaraldi.

OK then. What else had Guaraldi written?

Not a lot, because he'd died very young—even younger than my dad—at age 47.

Jazz impressions…Latin…Charlie Brown.

Aside from "Cast Your Fate to the Wind" the most famous pieces of music Vince Guaraldi was known for were his scores for the animated adaptations of the *Peanuts* comic strips.

But there were no students called Brown, Charlie or Charles among the dozen or so young men and women gathered in front of the tunnel entrance in Jersey in February 1974.

I looked at all of their names.

Amelia Black. A colour. A possibility.

Ken Leyton. Cordelia Dryden. William Taylor. Agbeki Bonu. Gurbani Dasam. Cherry Zhao. Jing Soong. Mark Nisbett. Linus Montrose.

Richard Almond. Not Peanut. But…another possibility?

Edwina Hofman.

I stared at the names.

The most well-known piece from the "Charlie Brown" cartoons was not the title tune, which was slow and lazy and meandering, but a catchy piano score called "Linus and Lucy' that everyone mistook for the main theme.

Linus van Pelt was the smart little kid with the blue security blanket who was always sucking his thumb and getting beaten up by his sister, Lucy.

And there *was* a Linus in the photo. Linus Montrose.

I did a search for his name online. Nothing. Absolutely nothing. No tweets, no LinkedIn entries, no Facebook pages, miscellaneous affiliations or personal websites. It was as if he'd never existed.

Linus Montrose? I said to Duncan.

Congratulations yet again. You are indeed a genius.

How is Linus Montrose connected to Pippa's disappearance?

Find the undecided wave, Duncan replied. *Go. And then come.*

I was ready to throttle him.

But I was out of time. I was due in Middlehurst in 15 minutes for my Chicken Biryani and I knew my mum would make my life a living hell for the rest of the week if I was late.

#

"Welcome to the Figs," mum said, pouring herself—and Beth—another glass of Cabernet Sauvignon. "And once again, many apologies for the short notice."

"Thank you," Beth replied, "and no worries. If I fuck it up, I'm sure I can improvise and get myself—and you—out of the mess. I didn't have a chance to ask—what about stage clothes? Is there some kind of sartorial Figs code? Are we all supposed to be wearing the same outfits, like Paul Revere and the Raiders?"

There was laughter round the table. I think Mitch and Rolly were impressed that she knew who Paul Revere and the Raiders actually were.

"What a clever idea!" mum replied, and for one dreadful moment I thought she was seriously considering it. The entire band in colonial costumes and tricorn hats. But no, it was just another one of her moments. "Wear whatever takes your fancy, my love. I shall have support stockings on underneath my best Stevie Nicks gypsy skirt."

More laughter.

"Just go and buy something that'll do for every performance," I said. "Get three of everything so one can be dry-cleaned while you're wearing the other, and you'll always have the third as a spare in case of emergencies."

"Like lost luggage?" Beth guessed. "You speak from experience?"

"It's been a long time since I last toured," I said. "But…oh yes."

"The stories Jason could tell you about his misplaced bags," mum said, "and having to shop for underwear and socks while the rest of his band went to watch a live sex show in Paris."

"That's the last time I share road stories with you," I said. I could feel my face actually turning red.

"I'll have a word with Freddie about your wardrobe reimbursement," mum said to Beth, ignoring me. "And the per diems. Have you got an appointment for the medical for the tour insurance?"

"Lunch time Monday," Beth replied. "But I promise, no worries, I'm fit."

She certainly looked fit.

"As you're now officially the youngest member of the band," I said, "I think you and I bring the average age down to something like 65.376 years. I'm sure there'll be a hefty discount on our policy."

While everyone tucked into their Lamb Tikka and Salee Boti, I posted a very tastefully-arranged display of my Chicken Biryani to Instagram.

I love chicken, I wrote. *Not many animals provide two different food options and a dance routine.*

And then I added a photo of the group sitting around the table.

Introducing the newest member of our band, Beth Homewood. Excellent fiddler. Able to sing all the high notes. Makes all her own clothes and does The Times crosswords in her spare time. Partial to custard creams—which definitely puts her in good company. Also knows all the Chicken Dance moves.

I knew there would be inevitable questions about Keith's whereabouts. And the story behind his departure.

But I decided to leave it at that and wait for Freddie's press release.

I usually hate it when people start consulting their phones in the middle of a social event like dinner, but I couldn't stop myself. I really needed to try and decipher Duncan's last clue.

Find the undecided wave.

Go. And then come.

Were they lyrics to something?

I gave Google a shot, eliminating words and adding quotation marks until I found it.

Those weren't the exact lyrics. And they weren't even in the correct language.

The correct language was French, and the song was "Je T'aime...Moi Non Plus." Originally written for Brigitte Bardot by Serge Gainsbourg. Not released until much later, after Gainsbourg had re-recorded it with Jane Birkin. Deemed too risqué for American airwaves. Completely banned from the radio in Spain, Sweden, Brazil, the UK, Italy, and Portugal. Banned before 11 p.m. in France. And denounced by the Vatican.

Whoever Duncan Stopher was, he had quite the gift of musical knowledge.

But what the fuck, literally, did "Je T'aime" have to do with Pippa Gladstone?

Other than Jane Birkin also appearing in *Blow Up*, which, to my mind, was a really grimly weird coincidence.

Go. And then come.

Travel? Yes. I knew that. Harry went. To Jersey. He went and he came back again. Five times.

I had another look at the newspaper story while Beth told the rest of the band about a gig she'd once played in a theatre that had a trap door in the stage. The trap door had opened as she'd stepped back after doing a solo and she'd tumbled into it and landed on top of a grand piano, several feet down. After a slight delay (during which she was retrieved and returned to the stage) she finished the gig, but had to go to the hospital afterwards with three cracked ribs and a badly sprained ankle.

Who was the best person to help me out with a travel-related question?

Katey. My girlfriend. Corporate travel consultant *extraordinaire*.

I went outside for a cigarette and gave her a ring.

"Jason!" she said. "I was just about to call you. I can't manage any days off next week at all, I'm afraid. But I was thinking about driving up to your concert in Leeds."

"That would be perfect," I said. "Promise me you won't write any scathing reviews on social media."

"As if," she said.

"I'm trying to solve a riddle."

"OK."

"I'm trying to sort out what's missing. A university professor takes some students on a field trip to Jersey in 1974. One of the students is important. I know the student's name. I don't know why he's important, just that he's connected somehow with the university professor's daughter disappearing a month later. I've been given a song…you know that one by Jane Birkin and Serge Gainsbourg."

"The French one," Katey said. "With all the breathy sex."

"That's it. The song is a clue."

"Is this a pub quiz?"

"Not quite. It's something I'm trying to solve. A case I've taken on."

"What kind of clue is the song supposed to give you?"

"That's what I don't know."

"Where did they stay?"

"I have no idea."

"Because that would be my first question after arranging their flights."

"I don't think there are any hotel names in the lyrics. They're pretty basic…"

"The Gainsbourg," Katey said. "It's a guest house on Jersey. St. Aubin's Bay. I booked a room there last year for one of my clients who fancied a week away somewhere quiet."

"You," I said, "are brilliant."

"I know," Katey said. "Does that get me a free ticket for Leeds?"

"And a backstage pass and an autographed tea towel."

"No wild fucks in a bunk on the tour bus…?"

"There will be no wild fucks on our bus. Or bunks. We're respectable. And old. We'll be sleeping in proper accommodations. I'll let the management at our hotel know that I require an extra-large bed."

"Shall I bring my Zimmer frame?"

"Bring whatever sex toys you wish," I replied. "See you in Leeds."

CHAPTER NINE

We were down to six days before we opened.

After last night's dinner in Middlehurst, Beth had come back to The Dog's Watch and practised until about 1 a.m. I know because she had the room next to mine.

I'd needed an extra cup of tea to get me going that morning.

In the library, we ran through all of the songs from our two revised set lists.

I loved working with Beth. I really welcomed the change she was bringing to the band, and after we'd played "Viaggio Italiano"—with Beth's new-fangled electric fiddle—for the third time, I was verging on ecstatic. Figgis Green was about to embrace the 21st century.

We still had a handful of songs that we hadn't quite got right. One of them was "I'll Be Good"—a 1965 chart-topper by The Spectacles that the Figs had successfully covered six years later, in 1971. The Spectacles, of course, were the house band at The Four Eyes when mum and dad were putting Figgis Green together. Their lead singer was Terry Wiggins.

"Why don't we give Terry a call," Mitch said. "He lives about ten minutes away from me. I'm always bumping into him at Tesco. He'd leap at the chance to join us onstage."

"For the entire tour?" mum asked, her voice betraying a tinge of worry.

"A one-off. Middlehurst. Our surprise guest for opening night."

"It would give us a good mental kick," I said.

"And," said Mitch, "it'll help us keep the song lively and fresh-

94

sounding for the rest of the tour."

Mum and Mitch went off to make the call.

They were back ten minutes later, with Mitch signalling a thumbs up.

"Terry's joining us this afternoon," mum said. "Which leaves the rest of the morning free for 'The Trots'."

Beth looked at me, confused.

"'High Meadows'," I said.

It was actually the theme from a kids' TV show about horses. Mum and dad had always called it "The Trots" because they couldn't stand the series—although the song they wrote to go with the show was actually pretty good.

My sister, Angie, had fallen in love with both the song and the show. I supposed it was because, like a lot of girls at that age, she was besotted with horses.

The show had been created along the same lines as *Black Beauty* and *Follyfoot*, with teenagers as the main human characters and storylines featuring dastardly evil-doers who were always set to rights by the intervention of a clever horse that embodied the best anthropomorphic traits of Trigger, Lassie and Flipper.

Figgis Green had been riding high in the charts when mum and dad had been approached to compose the theme. But they were given an impossible deadline, so instead of coming up with something original, they'd decided to adapt another song they'd been working on. The result had very little to do with the TV series and was more the rambling tale of a wealthy landowner who'd come to grief at the hands of a feared highwayman in the late-1700s. Mum and dad had given it their trademark Celtic sound and the producers had loved it.

It was a cracker of a tune to play—and sing. The musical bed always reminded me of a couple of horses galloping along a deserted beach at low tide, with gently-lapping waves and thunderheads on the horizon and baddies lurking in the long grasses behind the dunes. The lyrics were jaunty and rousing, and Beth's contribution—on her electric fiddle—made it come totally alive.

We actually finished with an audible *whoop* that wasn't scripted or planned for—but which we decided to keep for the performances. There was that much energy.

I was still feeling energetic when I went outside for our morning break, during which I rang Susan Gladstone, Pippa's mother.

A youngish-sounding woman with a lovely Irish accent answered the phone.

I explained who I was, and she explained who she was—a private care nurse—and she told me her name: Moira.

I asked whether I might drop by at lunch time.

"Yes, of course," Moira said, after she'd checked with Susan. "But I ought to warn you, her memory's not at all what it was. She'll remember a fragment of something and then, like a butterfly…off it goes, fluttering away."

#

The house where Pippa had grown up was called The Old Vicarage, and it was situated on a tree-lined lane beside a church near the centre of Middlehurst. I drove through an open wrought-iron gate to a gravelled courtyard which was bordered on two sides by small brick outbuildings that I guessed was the property's original coach house and stable. The house itself was built of red brick, with four chimneys, and the red brick was decorated with blue brick bands all the way around at the top and in the middle.

I finished the sandwich and Coke that I'd grabbed for lunch, then got out of my car and walked 'round to the white front door, and let the knocker drop onto its plate.

The door was answered by the young woman I assumed to be Moira, wearing a sensible navy-blue summer dress and sturdy shoes.

"Hello," I said. "Jason Figgis. We spoke on the phone."

"Yes, of course," she replied. "You found the house easily, then."

"I did." I followed her inside. "Do you live here permanently with Mrs. Gladstone?"

"I do," she confirmed. "I'm more of a paid companion, really. With the added bonus of medical training so I'm able to provide care for her if necessary. Come through."

The front door opened onto a narrow hallway with a turned staircase that led up to the first floor. At the end of the hallway were four doors, one of which took us into the drawing room.

I hate it when people who occupy beautiful old houses take it upon themselves to "update" their surroundings, replacing fireplaces with stoves, painting the walls to look like peacocks on drugs and installing furniture from some high-end shop whose sales associates believe history began the year they were born.

Susan Gladstone was not, thankfully, one of those people. The drawing room walls were beige, and were hung with pictures and paintings reminiscent of the era in which the house had been constructed. The curtains matched the walls—beige, with an olive green and brown floral pattern. There was a comfy padded sofa with matching armchairs—a sort of burnished brown colour—and a lot of cushions, and there was a blue and brown rug on the varnished pine board floor.

And there was the fireplace from Bernie's video, virtually unchanged, right down to the clock, the vases, and the collection of copper jugs.

"Here you are, Susan," Moira said, to a little woman who was sitting in one of the armchairs, with a brown blanket over her legs. "Here's your visitor. His name is Jason Figgis and he's come to talk to you about Pippa."

"Oh yes," said the little woman, with a nod. She had a lot of white hair, which had been styled very modernly with a fringe, and it ended in a blunt cut just below her ears. Her face was quite pink. And I could see where Bernie and Pippa had got their blue-grey eyes from.

"Have a seat," Moira said, to me. "I'll fetch the tea."

She disappeared.

I sat on the sofa beside the armchair.

"Have the police been in touch with you about Pippa?" I asked.

"Pippa is dead," Susan said, the expression on her face unchanged. "I had her declared dead quite a long time ago."

"Yes," I said. "I know. In 1981."

Moira came back into the drawing room with a teapot, milk, sugar and three cups on a tray. And biscuits, of course. Chocolate digestive. She placed the tray on the antique table. "The police did ring," she said, having obviously overheard my question from the kitchen. "But they spoke to me, as they know Susan doesn't really take in much anymore. Nothing 'sticks'. I referred them to Bernie. He's the one who handles all of the inquiries now."

She poured out the tea.

"Do you remember the night Pippa disappeared?" I asked Susan.

"She went off to a party," Susan replied, "with a group of boys and girls that she met while we were on holiday in Spain. And we never saw her again."

I supposed she'd repeated the story so many times, it was automatic.

"And what do you believe happened at that party?"

"That awful boy did something to her," Susan said. "We stayed in Spain for another two weeks because my husband believed she might still be found alive. We wanted to try and help the police and continue the search for her. But, in the end, we had to come home. We couldn't stay there indefinitely. We didn't have the money. And Harry had to go back to work and Bernie had to go back to school."

"What did you do with Pippa's things?"

"We brought her suitcase back with us, and I put everything away in her room."

"It's turned into a bit of a shrine," Moira said, confidentially, to me. "She likes to look in, every now and then. I believe it's always been a great comfort to her."

"What do you think happened to Pippa?" I asked.

"I think," said Moira, "that there are far too many theories swirling about. Peoples' minds are filled with fantasies. They haven't any proof of anything, other than what was in the papers, and so off they go on excursions and flights of fancy, imagining what *could* be the case, but which very probably isn't."

I opened the photo of Pippa beside the swimming pool on my phone and showed it to Susan.

"Do you recognize this?" I asked.

"Oh yes," Susan said. "That was Pippa's favourite t-shirt. I didn't want her to pack it, but she would insist. And those awful shorts."

I smiled. Posh resort. People with money. God forbid a 16-year-old should turn up in a slightly worse-for-wear, washed-out Figs t shirt and frayed denim.

I flipped over to the picture of Pippa at the folk festival.

"How about this? I spoke to Bernie on Friday and let him have a copy. Is this Pippa as well?"

Moira came around with her cup and saucer and had a look.

"It is Pippa," Susan replied, without hesitation.

"Yes," said Moira. "I believe it is."

"Do you know the name of the boy she's with?"

"I'm afraid I've no idea," said Susan. "I've never seen that picture before."

"Nor me," said Moira.

"Do you recall your husband making a little film in this room? It was Pippa and two of her friends rehearsing for a Christmas show at her school. The girls were standing just over there." I indicated the fireplace.

"Oh yes," Susan said. "It was just before Christmas in 1973, wasn't it? And the girls were singing. And dancing."

"That's right."

Susan smiled as she remembered.

"I don't suppose you remember the names of Pippa's two friends?" I asked.

"I'm afraid I don't."

I nodded at the collection of copper jugs on the mantle.

"Those are interesting," I said. "And they're in the film."

"They're my husband's souvenirs from Jersey," Susan said.

"They're Susan's favourite reminders of Harry," Moira said. "That's why we've kept them there. Pride of place."

"Do you remember anything else about your husband's yearly visits to Jersey?"

Susan shook her head. "I'm so very sorry," she said. "But it was all so long ago."

She seemed very sure about that. It was odd how some details were so clear in her mind…and how other details had become permanently lost. But I have a wonderful aunt who's in her mid-90s, and her memory is in much the same state as Susan's was. I was prepared to give her the benefit of doubt.

"I wonder if I might ask a favour. Would it be possible to see Pippa's bedroom?"

Moira looked a little uncertain, but Susan's face was wreathed in smiles. "I don't mind at all. Moira will show you."

#

There were four bedrooms upstairs, and just as many bathrooms. I was pretty certain the house hadn't been built that way originally. In old places like that, there was usually only one bathroom which, typical for its day, would have contained only a bath and a sink, and no toilet. The original toilet was in its own little hideaway, quite literally a water closet, up a step and situated between two of the bedrooms.

Pippa's room was the second-largest, and was across from the one her parents had occupied. And it had its own ensuite toilet and bath.

Pippa's bedroom walls were painted cream, and there was a little alcove between two built-in cupboards, into which the bed had been placed, head first. On the left of the bed was a wide window, through which I could see the garden, brilliantly lit by the noon sun. The curtains reminded me of perfume packaging, pale pinks and pale greens. A door-sized poster of David Cassidy, in a cotton pullover, jeans and trainers, had been tacked on the wall opposite the bed, and a second poster, this one a head and shoulders shot of a young Donny Osmond, all hair and teeth, was on the wall beside it.

There was a tall, standalone wardrobe and a dressing table, scattered with necklaces and bracelets and hair slides. And tacked to the wall beside the dressing table…a glorious colour poster of mum, dad, Mitch, Rolly, Keith and Ben Quigley. The Figs in 1973.

"As you can see, Susan has kept it just as Pippa left it," Moira said, "although the cleaners do come in once a week to dust it all off when they do the rest of the house."

"I'll try not to disturb anything," I said.

Moira watched as I walked around, trying to pick up a sense of the young woman Pippa had once been. I opened the drawers in her dressing table, saw neatly-folded knickers and bras, tights and socks and shorts and a two-piece swimsuit.

I looked inside the wardrobe. School uniforms, dresses, skirts, jeans, shirts and t-shirts. I checked them all.

"Everything's there," Moira said, helpfully. "Except, of course, the clothes she was wearing when she disappeared."

"Of course," I said.

I went into the bathroom, which had a glassed-in shower stall, a toilet, a sink and a little counter with a mirror. Lucky Pippa. Growing up in the 1970s, my sister and I had never merited our very own loos. I checked the cupboard under the counter.

"Thanks," I said. "You've been very helpful. I'll just go downstairs and say goodbye to Susan."

CHAPTER TEN

I was ten minutes late getting back to rehearsals. I bolted up to the library, arriving just as mum and Mitch were introducing Terry Wiggins around the room.

He was probably the same age as the three original Figs—late 70s, with a full head of grey hair which was long and slightly unkempt. He was tall and not at all prone to excess weight, and was wearing a white shirt and jeans and black leather boots.

"My late son, Jason," mum said, acknowledging my unnecessarily noisy entrance.

I shook Terry's hand. "Sorry."

"We have met," Terry replied. "I'm sure you don't remember. You were probably about two. Your mum and dad had popped down to the seaside to visit me and Jilly. I think they were showing you off. It definitely gave Jilly ideas. We got our own family started roundabout that time."

"Glad to have made myself useful," I said, humorously. "Did any of them follow you into the business?"

"Alas no. All three ended up with tremendously boring jobs. Complete and utter letdowns. The eldest will be around in a bit. Trish. She's bringing Battenburg cake."

"Excellent," I said. "I can see my influence stuck."

I picked up my Strat and checked the scribbled notes I'd made the last time we'd played through "I'll Be Good".

"You stand here," mum said, placing Terry in between herself and me. "Perfect."

"I haven't sung this bloody thing in years," Terry said. "I may require an excessive amount of vintage red later in order to adequately recover."

#

The original "I'll Be Good" was based on a working men's song that had become an unofficial anthem of the French revolution, "Ça Ira", which, when roughly translated, means "It'll Be Fine."

The lyrics for English version—The Spectacles' "A" side—had absolutely nothing to do with the lyrics for the "B" side, which was the French original. In fact, the only thing the two songs had in common at all was the melody, which was an improvised surf sound accomplished by the drums and three guitars that were pretty much standard in all the Brit-beat bands from that era.

Mum and dad had taken out the surf and altered the beat, adding in a penny whistle and a fiddle. Then they'd combined both sides of The Spectacles' record, doing the verses in English and the chorus in French. The result was a rousing number that always got the audience on their feet dancing and clapping and, of course, singing along.

Terry was right. It had been a good few years since he'd belted out his hit song, and he'd never sung our version at all. It took a lot of work to bring him up to speed. But Terry was, like the rest of us, a professional. And it helped greatly that his daughter, Trish, arrived just in time for our afternoon break with the promised Battenburg and a crateful of bottles of artisan ginger ale.

Trish's boring job, as it turned out, was in the Reception office at Shorebridge School in Middlehurst—Bernie Gladstone's old school. And she'd been there for decades.

"Come outside for a chat," I suggested, after she'd cut up the cake and shared it around and we'd all helped ourselves to the ginger ale.

Sitting in the afternoon sun in the manor's old kitchen garden, as we both lit up ciggies, I told her about my investigation.

"Pippa Gladstone," Trish said, thoughtfully. "I do recall the name, yes."

"I'm not wrong, am I? Pippa's school—Mewbury—merged with Shorebridge roundabout 1990?"

"1991, yes."

"So, would all of Mewbury's records have been transferred over to Shorebridge with the merger?"

"I should think so," Trish said. "We wouldn't have destroyed anything. What is it you're looking for?"

"Some information about these girls," I said. I played Bernie's film for her on my phone. "Pippa's the one miming the song."

"They're quite good, aren't they?" Trish mused, watching the performance.

"They're very enthusiastic," I agreed. "They were getting ready for Mewbury's 1973 Christmas show. I was hoping to find out more about the other two girls. Their names, anything."

"I'm sure we've got Mewbury's old Christmas show programmes stored somewhere," Trish said. "I'll have a little dig when I go back to the office tomorrow. We're still officially on summer hols, so it's quiet. Though it'll be chaos on Tuesday when our Autumn Term begins."

#

The Battenburg and ginger ale must have done the trick. Three more run-throughs, and Terry had "I'll Be Good" aced.

"I shall see you all on Friday," he promised, as we abandoned the library to walk down the hill for a post-rehearsal drink at The Dog's Watch. "Grandkids in tow. Though I'm not sure they'll be at all impressed."

"I think we must share the same grandchildren," Rolly agreed.

"What about your two kids?" Beth said, to me. "How do they feel about your music?"

"My son exercises great patience when it comes to my jazz residency at the Blue Devil," I said. "Though I don't dare ask him about the Figs. My daughter claims to love everything I do."

"They're both very fine diplomats," mum added. "They take after their father."

"And their grandmother," I said.

I stayed for one drink in the pub and then I escaped upstairs. I went straight to my laptop.

What I'd found most interesting about Pippa's bedroom and the attached bathroom was Moira's comment that Susan had kept it "just as Pippa left it."

I remembered Angie's dressing table when we were in our teens and getting ready to go on holiday. It was absolutely bare. All of the things she thought she'd need were packed away in her suitcase: hairbrush, comb, makeup, jewellery, scent.

And from the bathroom: shampoo, conditioner, shower things. Tampons.

If, as Susan had claimed, she'd brought back everything in Pippa's luggage and returned it to its rightful place, then there were, in fact, a few crucial items missing. Obviously, as Moira had pointed out, the clothes she'd been wearing when she disappeared. That was a given. But I'd looked for the Figgis Green t-shirt she'd had on in the pool photo. It wasn't there. And there were six empty hangers in the wardrobe. There was no toothbrush in her little bathroom and there were no tubes of toothpaste. No hairbrushes or combs—and they weren't on her dressing table, either.

There was a half-empty box of tampons in the cupboard under the sink, definitely made in England—the ones she'd forgotten to take to Spain with her.

But there was no emergency package of sanitary towels with everything written in Spanish.

If anyone were to ask me, at that moment, what I thought had happened to Pippa, I'd have guessed that she'd packed a little bag of necessities—her favourite t-shirt, a few extra clothes and toiletries—and she'd deliberately run off.

I was, in fact, now entertaining a distinct possibility that Pippa Gladstone wasn't dead at all. And that Alistair really had been hired to find her. The photo from the folk festival in Wiltshire may have been a fake, but it was a well-done one, designed to convince me to take on the case.

So who might have wanted to locate Pippa that badly? And why now?

Bernie and Susan came first to mind, of course. But why the subterfuge? Surely if they wanted to try and find Pippa, they'd have just done a straightforward hire—a licensed PI with a long and successful track record at locating lost people, and with a much higher profile than mine. And. more importantly, why would they change their minds now, nearly 40 years after having her declared legally dead? And why stick to their guns and tell me that they still considered her dead?

It wasn't Bernie or Susan.

On top of which, someone else was making it abundantly clear that they *didn't* want me to find Pippa.

Was that someone else actually Pippa herself…?

I wasn't quite prepared to accept that Pippa would resort to murder to keep her location a secret. Making my life difficult, yes. But not killing Alistair Watford.

#

"Oh!" said Moira, opening the front door. "I wasn't expecting to see you again so soon. You ought to have rung ahead."

"I'm sorry," I said. "I was driving in the neighbourhood and I just had a few more questions."

It was a lie. I'd made the trip deliberately. But I wanted to catch them off-guard. I didn't want to give them time to prepare.

"If Susan doesn't mind," I added.

"I'll just check if she's able to see you."

I waited outside for about a minute, and then Moira came back.

"I'm just making Susan's meal. But she says to come in."

Whatever she was cooking in the kitchen smelled delicious, and reminded me that I hadn't had my own dinner yet. Beef stew, I guessed.

Moira took me into the sitting room and stayed as I sat down in the armchair.

"The thing is," I said, to Susan, "when I was upstairs in Pippa's room today, I noticed a few things were missing. And I remembered that you'd said you'd packed all her things up and brought them back to England with you."

Susan didn't say anything. She looked at me questioningly. And then at Moira.

"For instance," I said, "her camera. I know she had one. You can see her carrying it in this photo by the pool."

I showed her the picture on my phone.

"It's an Olympus Pen," I said. "I was wondering what had happened to it."

"Pippa must have taken it with her when she went to the party," Susan replied. "It must have been in her handbag."

"OK," I said. "How about the t-shirt she's wearing?"

"That old thing. I threw it away."

"You threw away Pippa's favourite t-shirt? What if she'd turned up, safe and sound? What if she'd come back and discovered what you'd done with it?"

"I waited," Susan said, a little defensively. "I waited for years."

"And when she didn't come home," Moira said, "you put it into the rubbish, didn't you, Susan?"

"Oh yes," said Susan. "Yes. I did."

"Because it was such a painful reminder."

"Yes," said Susan. "That's right."

"I also saw half a dozen empty hangers in Pippa's wardrobe," I said.

"She'd outgrown some skirts and tops. I gave them away to a charity in the town before we went on holiday."

"Fair enough. But then I had a look in the bathroom. I didn't see Pippa's toothbrush. Or toothpaste. Bottles of scent, deodorant…makeup…"

"You can't expect Susan to remember about all those things," Moira said, leaping to her defence. "And what would be the point of keeping them all these years, anyway? The toothpaste would go all hard. The perfume would dry up."

"I suppose they would," I said. "But my own feeling is that if you're going to create a shrine to someone that has everything 'just as she left it'…you keep the mundane, everyday things alongside everything that was special. Because you're remembering the whole person, aren't you? Not just what was conveniently returned in their luggage."

"You may believe," Moira replied, "what you wish."

"Just one more question, then," I said. "I know this may be a bit…delicate. Bernie mentioned to me that Pippa got her period while you were on holiday. And that Susan had to go out hunting for emergency supplies. She came back with a big package of sanitary towels. I didn't see those in the bathroom cupboard either."

"Surely you can't be serious." Moira was now sounding distinctly irritated. "Why should she keep something like that? It was more than 40 years ago!"

"She kept everything else," I said. "A half-empty box of tampons."

"The package of sanitary towels was too large," Susan replied. "And it wouldn't fit into the suitcase. So I had to leave it behind."

"There," said Moira. "A simple explanation. Are you satisfied now?"

I knew I was on the verge of being shown the door.

"Is it possible Pippa could have deliberately run away?" I asked.

"No," said Susan. "It's not possible." She looked upset. I could see the corners of her mouth turning down. "The police discussed it with us at the time and we told them the same thing. I don't know why you're asking me all these questions again. Why must I answer them?"

"I think you'd better leave, Mr. Figgis."

Moira was on her feet. I'd outstayed my welcome.

"If you have anything further to ask, I think you'd best consult Bernie. Susan's very fragile, as you can see. I won't allow you to bother her again."

"Understood," I replied. "Thank you. I'll see myself out."

#

I didn't believe a word of it.

Susan may have been suffering from the early stages of dementia, but she was a good deal more cognizant than she was letting on. And Moira was her efficient assistant. There were two stories about Pippa's disappearance: the official one, the one her mother had told the police and the press…and the one she was keeping to herself.

I had my mobile on the passenger seat beside me as I drove back to Stoneford. It rang just as I approached the outskirts of the village. I parked in the lot behind The Dog's Watch and then listened to the message that Trish Wiggins had just left.

I called her back immediately.

"You got me so intrigued," she said, "that I went over to the school this afternoon." I could hear the excitement in her voice. "I had a good rummage 'round in the boxes in the archives. And I found something! A programme from the 1973 Christmas show! All three girls are mentioned. Pippa Gladstone, Belinda Smith-Trevynne and Elizabeth Foster."

"Excellent," I said. "Thank you. Can you spell Belinda's last name for me?"

I typed the names into my phone before I forgot them.

"I hope this helps."

"Indeed it does," I said.

"If there's anything else I can do…"

"I don't suppose you know of any kind of newsletter or chat group where the former students from Mewbury stay in touch with one another…?"

"I think there may be something on Facebook. Of course, we didn't have the internet in 1991, when the two schools merged. But in the years since then, all sorts of groups have popped up. I belong to one for my old school."

"Thank you," I said, again. "You've been incredibly helpful. Are you coming along to see your dad perform with us on Friday night?"

"The entire family's turning up," Trish said, humorously. "We wouldn't miss it for the world."

#

Back in my room, I went online and did a general search for Mewbury School in Middlehurst, just to see what Google would throw back at me. Lots of references to Shorebridge and the merger…and a few old photos on Pinterest and Flickr. A dedicated page on Middlehurst's Heritage Society website.

But nothing else that was really of much use to me.

Then I took Trish's advice and tried Facebook. She was right—there was a group that someone had set up for Mewbury's former students. And it wasn't private, so I spent about half an hour scrolling through the discussions and the photos.

I had a look at their membership list, but nobody looked or sounded familiar. And neither Belinda Smith-Trevynne or Elizabeth Foster were there.

But people always knew other people. Friends stayed in touch by other means. And names could be changed through marriage.

I created a legitimate-looking Facebook profile using the name Paula McIntyre. I added a few pictures and postings to the home page supporting the 57-year-old grandmother I was purporting to be. Then I popped back over to the Mewbury Old Girls and asked to join the group so I could post messages.

Fortunately there was a moderator on duty and my request was approved within about ten minutes.

Hello, I wrote. *My name's Paula McIntyre and I'd love to reconnect with some old schoolmates I've lost touch with…Belinda Smith-Trevynne and Elizabeth Foster. Last heard from in 1973. Can anyone help?*

And then I went downstairs for dinner.

CHAPTER ELEVEN

I never sleep through thunderstorms, and there was one in the night.

I was wide awake with the first distant rumble of thunder. Even if it's faint, even if the thunder blows away without ever coming near me, I can't go back to sleep until it's gone. Until I'm sure.

This one didn't blow away. It rolled up and parked itself overhead. It came with pounding rain—big heavy angry drops that sounded like hail. I didn't check. I stay away from windows when there's lightning—and there was a lot of that. I stay away from phones, too, and if it's daytime, I switch off my computer and the TV.

If the storm comes during the day, I try to find somewhere safe. If I'm outside, I go indoors. Quickly. I'm OK in a large store, the bigger the better. I'm less OK in houses. I've been known to flee to the stairs, where I've spent the entire storm huddled on a step halfway up, heart pounding. Stairs are good. They're not usually near windows and sometimes you can close all the doors to the rooms nearby and make the lightning invisible. You can still hear the thunder, though. And when it's close by, things shake.

If the storm comes during the night, I stay in bed. I pull the duvet over my head and I lie there, paralysed, experiencing near suffocation. I know you're no safer in bed than in any other part of the house—or flat, or hotel room. But the bed feels safe. It's something left over from childhood.

The overnight storm raged and flashed and each roll of thunder sounded like a load of giant bricks tumbling onto the roof. And then it wandered off. The rain eased. I came up for air and smelled freshly-washed trees and soaking wet earth, because I'd left all the windows open.

I always think of my dad during those storms. Sometimes, I suspect it's actually him, raging with anger at how his life had been taken so suddenly.

Even though I'm terrified, I can feel him nearby.

And it's comforting, in a way. It helps me deal with the fear.

I fell back asleep, exhausted.

I woke up in the morning to the familiar chirps of my favourite birds.

I looked at my phone and confirmed that it was, indeed, Monday.

I made myself a cup of tea and sat down with my laptop. There was a private message waiting for me on Paula McIntyre's Facebook page, and it was from Elizabeth Foster. Whose married name was Pritchard.

Hello, she'd written. *I don't remember anyone called Paula McIntyre at Mewbury. Have you mistaken me for someone else?*

I answered her back immediately.

Apologies. My real name is Jason Figgis and I'm doing some research into Pippa Gladstone's disappearance in 1974. I've been in touch with Pippa's brother, Bernie, and he gave me a video of a rehearsal of a performance you did with Pippa and Belinda for your school's Christmas show in 1973. I was wondering if we could have a chat.

There was a very long silence, during which I wondered if she was going to report me to Facebook for policy violations—or block me.

And then:

Yes, I'm happy to chat with you.

Can we meet? I wrote back, and then, realizing the stupidity of my assumption that she still lived in the vicinity of Middlehurst, I added: *I'm in Stoneford. Where are you?*

You're in luck, she said. *I live in Lymington.*

Lymington was a ten-minute drive to the east.

Can we meet up? I can come to you.

I'll come to you, Elizabeth replied. *I haven't visited Stoneford in years. It'll be nice to see it again. What time and when?*

The Dog's Watch? I suggested. *Eight o'clock this evening?*

Perfect. How will I know who you are?

Someone who wasn't on top of the Figgis Green tour and didn't know what I looked like. That was a refreshing change. I took a quick selfie—pre-shower and pre-shave, the "tousled rock star who's just rolled out of bed" look that my daughter had expertly captured one day when she'd made me sit for a portrait—and sent it to her. She responded with a photo of herself—much better coiffed than me and already made up for the day—and we were set.

#

I've found that when musicians do tour diaries, they tend to spend a lot of time talking about the venues and the audiences and how their performances stacked up compared to previous nights, and what's wrong with their hotel rooms and who popped by backstage to say hello. They don't seem to include much about the rehearsals leading up to the tour…I guess because they don't think fans would be interested in reading about all the hard work that goes into them. Or, perhaps, it's their egos, not wanting to admit that they screw up the notes, sing the wrong lyrics or forget their cues.

If it was me writing an online journal for Figgis Green's Lost Time Tour (and not just the photographic record of all my culinary adventures), I'd have most definitely begun with our rehearsals. The feeling of being stuck forever in the room where you sleep, because it isn't your bedroom at home. The fact that you have to remind yourself what day it is when you wake up, because you've completely lost track of the calendar. The steady diet of breakfast, lunch and dinner from restaurants and coffee shops—I was really looking forward to getting on the road, if only because the meals before each gig were going to be catered to our specifications. Those were the downsides to rehearsing. But there were positives, too. The new friendships that I'd established and the old relationships that I'd rekindled. The comradery. The absolute understanding that what we were creating now, in the manor's library, was an experience that would never, ever be repeated.

This would be Figgis Green's final tour.

And, by God, we were going to make it sound—and look—phenomenal.

First up that morning was a neat little jazz piece that my dad had composed, never in a million years guessing that it would grow to be my favourite, and that it would become the basis of my own musical career decades later.

It was called "Jay-Jay"—after me— and it was kind of a lazy, slow shuffle, the sort of tune that always made me think of my dad meandering along a meadowy path in the sunshine, straw hat perched on top of his head, the bottoms of his trousers rolled up and his hands in his pockets. The original recording had Rolly brushing his snare drum and Mitch tickling his bass guitar and Ben Quigley nursing the rhythm, while dad played the main melody on his Strat and Keith provided an innovative counter-line on his fiddle. Dad had originally considered that line for a bass clarinet—but he'd quickly realized it would be more or less impossible to reproduce onstage, unless he expanded the Figs' line-up to include woodwinds.

It was one of the few tunes they'd recorded that didn't have a part for mum. But it gave her a chance to sit down, out of the spotlight, and have a little drink of water and get her breath back.

We ran through "Jay-Jay" three times, after which we broke for our mid-morning tea and coffee and custard creams, and I grabbed the opportunity to send off a message to Duncan Stopher.

Find the undecided wave, I wrote, throwing the clue back at him. *Go. And then come. "Je T'aime". Serge Gainsbourg. And Gainsbourg's the name of the guest house where Harry Gladstone stayed on his last trip to Jersey in 1974. What do I win?*

Duncan wasn't long in answering.

You win my esteem and my heartiest congratulations. You are correct, yet again.

Why is all this important? And for fuck's sake stop sending me riddles.

I'm assuming you know your jazz chords.

You assume correctly, I said.

Consider the major and minor 6th, 7th, 9th, 11th and 13th harmonies.

Of WHAT?? I said.

And the choruses voiced as four- and five-part vocal harmonies, Duncan added.

What song are you talking about???

Rose and Valerie, Duncan replied.

The Beatles? "Maxwell's Silver Hammer"? That doesn't have any jazz chords or five-part vocal harmonies. Trust me.

You've missed it, Duncan replied. *Check the papers.*

Fucking hell.

I could grow to hate you, I thought.

What papers? I wrote.

But he'd gone.

I lit a ciggie and had a think.

Maxwell. Maxwell.

If it wasn't the Beatles…who?

Check the papers.

Robert Maxwell? The newspaper magnate? Who'd once owned the Mirror group?

If it was, I still didn't see a connection.

I resorted to Wikipedia. And discovered that Robert Maxwell's real name was Ján Ludvík Hyman Binyamin Hoch. And that he was Czech.

And Czech sounded like Check.

OK, I was right, it was Robert Maxwell.

But then…what did this mean? *You've missed it…*

Back to Robert Maxwell, who had once unsuccessfully tried to buy a leading UK Sunday paper, the *News of the World*. In other words, he'd missed it.

Was it another musical clue? *News of the World?* Queen's sixth album, released in October 1977?

Where was the jazz harmony in that?

I hunted down samples from the album and clicked through all of the tracks.

"We Are the Champions."

It had to be.

I messaged Duncan.

Silence.

I finished my ciggie and drank the rest of my coffee and tried to figure out what the fuck Duncan wanted me to know.

I came up empty.

So I called the Gainsbourg Guest House in Jersey.

The phone was answered by a pleasant-sounding woman, probably in her early 50s, I guessed. I told her who I was and she told me who she was. Her name was Ellie Hammond. A few more questions, and I had the answers to the rest of Duncan's clues. Ellie's mum and dad were running the guest house in 1974 when Harry Gladstone and his students had come to stay. And Ellie's parents' last names were Champion.

#

I thought about asking mum for that afternoon off. But after I checked the airline schedules and the flying time to Jersey from Southampton, I knew I'd need most of the day to get there and back again. And I'd already committed to meeting Elizabeth Foster that evening. It would have to be tomorrow.

Meanwhile, after our break, we were playing through "Lost Time"—another iconic entry in the Figs' catalogue, so much so that we'd decided to name our tour after it.

I took my place beside my mum, and Beth led in with the haunting fiddle intro. The song's about a young woman who's abandoned her lover without any warning, leaving him to lament his loss. And then, after a few rounds of verses and pre-hooks and hooks and a bridge, his lost love reappears, older and wiser, having travelled the world. The young man—also now older and wiser— has remained unattached and now risks everything to ask the young woman to marry him and make up for lost time. Mum and dad never did reveal her answer when they wrote the song, but it ends with a series of optimistic notes—much like "One Summer Day" (which they'd unabashedly borrowed from)—so I always reckoned it was safe to assume she'd said yes.

The recorded version was three minutes and 24 seconds and dad had written it so he could sing lead and mum could provide the harmony, and then in the last half of the song, they switched and mum took over the lead vocals. It was composed in Bb minor and it had a really solid drum, guitar and fiddle bed, and it was lovely.

We'd placed it next to last in the second set list, just before our closing number, "Rise Again", and then our two-song encore.

I couldn't wait to get onstage to perform it.

#

That evening, at the appointed hour, I sat myself at a small round table in The Dog Watch's pub with a posh fizzy water, and waited for Elizabeth Foster. I spotted her immediately as she came through the door: short, dark brown hair and big red spectacles. She saw me immediately too—how did we manage before selfies were invented?—and joined me at my table.

"Hello."

"Hello," I said. "Thank you for agreeing to meet. Drink?"

"White wine, thanks."

I went to the bar and bought her a glass of New Zealand Sauvignon Blanc and brought it back to the table.

"Pippa and I were really good friends," Elizabeth said, as I sat down again. "And it was all so ridiculous, the way she just disappeared and no one could find out what happened to her. The Spanish police were useless."

"So what do you think happened to her?" I asked.

"I don't know," said Elizabeth, "but I'm positive it had something to do with her dad. I mean, here the police always look at family first, don't they? But over there, in Spain, the police were just bloody incompetent. There's no other word for it. They were running around in circles, chasing different theories…and her parents were almost untouchable. And between you and me, I always thought Pippa's mum and dad were very very good at muddying the waters."

"How do you mean?"

"Covering their tracks," Elizabeth said. "Making sure her body was never found."

"So you think they killed her?"

"I never liked her dad. He made me feel…uncomfortable."

"What kind of uncomfortable? How?"

"He had a temper. And I'd seen it erupt. It was enough to make me want to get out of his way, quickly. I avoided going to Pippa's house as much as I could but sometimes I couldn't. That rehearsal was one of the few times I went over there."

"I've spoken to Bernie," I said, "and I've spoken with Susan, and nobody's ever mentioned Harry's temper to me."

"Well," said Elizabeth, "they wouldn't, would they? Susan was married to him—she was his enabler and his apologist and every time he erupted, she'd try to smooth things over because her marriage and her family depended on her keeping things together. But I bet if you asked Bernie about his dad's temper, he'd tell you. He was younger, so he wasn't so much in the way of it. But Pippa…"

Elizabeth shook her head.

"So you think he got angry with Pippa the night before they were due to fly home and she ended up dead?"

"That's exactly what I think. There was no DNA tracking back then, so the police couldn't look for that. And they didn't find any blood stains in the villa, but it had a tiled stone floor and you can wash the blood off that, can't you? Out of the grouting and everything."

"You'd need to find cleaning supplies fairly quickly though," I said. "There wasn't much of a window of opportunity. We know when Pippa was last seen at the party, and if Alvaro Izan's word can be believed, we know when he dropped her back at the resort. And we know when her parents notified the police and when the police showed up at the villa. It's really only a matter of a few hours."

"Toilet paper's good for cleaning up blood. So are a few other things you can generally find in the bathroom." She looked at me. "You know."

I suspected I did.

"And something like after-shave would do a really final tidy-up after a thorough scrub."

"Scent," I supposed.

"Or toothpaste," Elizabeth said.

"Really?"

"Look it up. It's a great grout-cleaner."

I made a note to do just that.

"Anyway, Pippa went out to the party, she came home late, and her dad lost it. The end."

"Were you interviewed by the British police?" I asked.

"Very superficially. A WPC collecting background information about Pippa. Who her friends were, that sort of thing."

"Did you mention Harry's temper?"

"Of course I did. But as you can see, nothing ever came of it."

"Or," I said, "it was noted, but nothing could be proven. And there is another possibility. Perhaps Pippa just decided to run away."

"In Spain?" Elizabeth looked sceptical. "If she was going to leave, she'd have waited 'til she got home. And she'd have talked about it. To me. To her other friends. She wouldn't have kept it to herself. She wouldn't have chosen a foreign country where she didn't speak the language and she didn't know anyone—other than the kids she was partying with. And she didn't have any money. The police looked into her bank account."

"She didn't take any cash out for the holiday?"

"Well, yes, I'm sure she did. But she didn't have nearly enough to live on by herself. And on top of everything else, she left her passport behind. If you're going to run away in a foreign country, you'd never forget that. Would you?"

"No," I said. "You wouldn't. How do you know she left it behind?"

"Because I talked to her mum when they came back from Spain. I had a lot of conversations with her, actually. You know how you go over everything, the last day you had together, the details. She told me she'd brought all of Pippa's things back with her, all her clothes…and she mentioned she had Pippa's passport."

"Thank you," I said. I made a note about the passport, too, and then I took out my phone and showed her Bernie's rehearsal video.

"Wow," Elizabeth said, watching it with me. "I remember that so well. It's Pippa's drawing room. The day before the Christmas show. Bernie was there, and Pippa's mum, and her dad was filming it with his little movie camera. Bernie gave this to you?"

"He did. He had the film digitized. For posterity. Which one is you?"

I had to ask, because to be perfectly honest, I couldn't tell. I knew who Pippa was because Bernie'd pointed her out to me. But neither of the two girls was wearing glasses, and the film was too blurry to focus in on their facial features.

"That's me," Elizabeth said, pointing to the girl with her hair in bunches, tied up with the colourful wool ropes. "Can I have a copy?"

"Of course. I'll send it to you."

"Thanks."

"Do you happen to know how I might get in touch with Belinda Smith-Trevynne?"

A shadow fell over Elizabeth's face. "She's dead, I'm afraid. Cancer. Five years ago."

"I'm so sorry," I said.

"Me too," Elizabeth said. "We were the best of friends. Right up 'til the end."

I brought up the photo of Pippa from the music festival and showed it to her.

"Would you have any idea who the boy is?"

Elizabeth thought for a moment, then shook her head. "Not a clue."

"You don't remember any boyfriends she might have had, anything like that?"

"There was nobody special," Elizabeth said. "We were all a bit behind in that department, to be honest. More interested in Keith Partridge than the boy next door. David Cassidy appearing naked on the cover of *Rolling Stone* in 1972 notwithstanding."

She gave me a twinkle-eyed, completely out-of-character laugh, and finished drinking her wine.

#

After I was back in my room, I gave Bernie a call.

"Do you happen to remember," I said, "what happened to Pippa's passport?"

"My mother brought it back with her from Spain," he replied, without hesitation.

"The thing is," I said, "I didn't see it in her bedroom. Anywhere."

"I'm sure she wouldn't want to leave something like that lying around."

"Where do you keep your passport?" I asked. "Mine's usually on a shelf in my bedroom next to *The History of Jazz* by Ted Gioia. When I'm not on tour."

"Mine's in a locked safe in my study," Bernie replied, without any hint of humour. "Anything else?"

I might almost have suspected that Susan and Moira had been on the phone to Bernie to complain about the direction my last set of questions had taken.

"Nothing else," I said. "Thank you."

I disconnected and rang Moira.

"I'm really sorry to bother you again," I said, "but I was wondering about Pippa's passport. I've spoken to Bernie and he tells me Susan brought it back with her from Spain. I was wondering where she kept it."

"Just a moment," Moira replied.

She put the phone down and I could hear her talking to Susan, though I couldn't quite make out what they were saying.

Moira came back to the phone.

"Susan says she returned it to the Passport Office in 1981."

"After she'd had Pippa declared legally dead?"

"Yes."

"And she didn't ask them to send the cancelled passport back to her?"

"Evidently not."

Something else that had obviously held too many evocative memories to bear keeping, I thought, somewhat unkindly.

"OK," I said. "Thanks for the clarification."

I disconnected, and rang my mum.

"Do you absolutely need me tomorrow?"

There was silence on the other end of the line.

"I know we're not rehearsing in the morning because you have an interview scheduled first thing with the BBC," I said.

"Yes I do," said my mum, "and I was rather hoping you'd be joining me."

"Ask Beth," I said. "She'll be perfect. Female fiddler as a last-minute replacement for the lately departed and not much lamented Keith. It's a great angle. Lots of drama."

"You do know it's Tuesday tomorrow. And our first concert's on Friday."

"I know," I said.

"Are you out of your mind, Jason?"

"We're good," I said. "We'll be ready for Friday. I really need to take tomorrow off."

"I suppose I should know better than to ask why."

"I wouldn't tell you even if you did."

"It's to do with that Duncan Stopher person, isn't it? The one who was killed?"

I thought it best not to answer.

"Promise me you'll be available for our production rehearsals on Wednesday and Thursday."

"I promise. And if we run into any problems I'll stay after school to work them through."

"It's not you I'm concerned about," mum said. "See you for breakfast?"

"I don't think so," I replied. "I've got an early appointment in Southampton."

I didn't tell her the appointment was at the Airport and it involved a 50-minute flight on a twin-engine turboprop leaving at 8:40 a.m.

"Good night," I said, pleasantly.

"Do be careful," mum replied, just as pleasantly.

CHAPTER TWELVE

It was 5 a.m. Back in London, I'd have been unlocking my front door after a late night at the Blue Devil. And getting ready to fall into bed. Not struggling to wake up.

The bloody sun wasn't even up yet. And wouldn't be for another hour. I stood under the shower, hoping one of the clever water-pulse settings would pummel my brain into some semblance of functionality. And I reminded myself that reserving a seat on a plane at unreasonable-o'clock had been my choice, and nobody else's.

I skipped breakfast and drove straight to Southampton Airport. I left my car in the short-term lot and arrived at the check-in with an hour and a half to spare.

I've got a friend who's OCD about being late and consistently appears two hours before he's actually required to be anywhere. I'm actually the opposite. People have complained about my lack of punctuality. I'll always try to be on time for a rehearsal or a gig…but for other things, they have a valid point. The only reason I had an hour and a half to spare on that morning was because I'd had no realistic idea how long it would take me to drive there from Stoneford, allowing for roadworks, traffic volume and the inevitable breakdowns and accidents.

Southampton was tiny compared to some airports I know. And it didn't have that frantic must-be-at-Gate-52-on-the-other-side-of-the-terminal-in-less-than-two-minutes vibe that you get at chaotic hubs like Heathrow. I'd checked in and got my electronic boarding pass ahead of time, so, after confirming when I needed to be at the gate, I looked for somewhere to have breakfast.

And, while I was enjoying my Full English (deliberately not posted to Instagram because I wanted to keep the details of what I was up to that day as private as I could), I was able to confirm that someone was following me. Two someones, in fact.

They'd picked me up as I'd driven out of my parking spot at The Dog's Watch. I reckoned they didn't think I'd notice. I'll readily admit I don't have the benefit of years of experience and training. But, in spite of not being a licensed PI, I have done the courses. And John Le Carré and Len Deighton are two of my favourite writers.

My followers had been in two separate cars, spelling each other off, all the way from Stoneford.

I opened my camera app on my phone and flipped it around, pretending to take a selfie. I could see the first guy sitting a couple of tables away, behind me. He was about forty, shaved head, wearing a black windbreaker and jeans. I hate shaved heads. I know it's all very fashionable but it does nothing for most men and in fact makes them look like bootboys who'd kick your face in for a few minutes' merriment on a Saturday night. There's nothing benign about a hairless male head unless you're eighty and nature's done it to you on purpose.

The other guy was a bit younger and had a full head of hair and a beard and he was wearing a navy-blue pullover and khaki trousers. He was standing outside the café, pretending to read a printed copy of *The Guardian*. He looked a lot less threatening.

I took my time finishing my breakfast and deliberately delayed going to the gate until the very last minute. I wondered if they were going to follow me onto the plane.

Apparently not. They abandoned me at Security.

A transfer bus took us from the terminal to a twin-prop ATR72-500, which was parked out on the tarmac. I made sure I got onto the bus first, so I could get a good look at all of my fellow passengers. Just in case the first two had friends who were taking over the second shift.

On board the plane, my seat was near the front, on the left-hand side, just ahead of the engine with its spidery six-bladed prop. I paid attention to the pre-flight chat and studied the safety card tucked into the back pocket of the seat ahead of me as we taxied out to the runway. I always do that, for the same reason that I always count the rows to the nearest exit. And then the rows to the next-nearest exit.

I'd learned that from Katey. And I always keep my seatbelt fastened, even when the sign's switched off.

It was a very quick flight. But it gave me the opportunity to try and guess who considered me important enough to track like that. I hadn't told anyone I was going to Jersey, not even my mum. I'd conducted my travel-related transactions over the internet…but other than that, I hadn't given out any clues at all. So, either someone was monitoring my mobile and online activities—was I an inherent danger to national security? was I on some Secret Service watch list?—or those two had been keeping an eye on me all along, following my every move, and I'd only just copped onto them.

Perhaps they were the same villains who'd broken into Jenn's studio and stolen the negs and prints.

The same ones who'd tried to fit me up for Alistair's murder. I hadn't heard back from DS Handsworth so I had to assume her follow-up inquiries had put me in the clear.

The same ones who'd killed Alistair.

That was a sobering thought.

Who were they working for? The person or persons who wanted me to find Pippa? Or the ones who didn't?

We flew in over Guernsey and dropped down onto the little runway at Jersey Airport and in what seemed like moments, I was picking up the silver Hyundai i10 car rental I'd arranged the night before. I'd put my phone on Airplane Mode as I'd boarded in Southampton, and I decided to leave it like that. Anyone trying to track me on Jersey was going to have to do it the old-fashioned way. I popped into the back of the car and found the spare tire kit and took out the wheel brace and carried it into the front with me. Just in case.

If you don't know much about Jersey (and I'll admit I didn't, until I invested some time researching it), it's a British Crown dependency located in the English Channel, off the French coast. It had once been part of the Duchy of Normandy, whose dukes went on to become kings of England from 1066. After Normandy was lost by those kings in the 13th century, the ducal title was surrendered to France. However, Jersey and the other Channel Islands remained attached to the English crown. The island itself isn't a part of the UK, and it has an international identity separate from the UK, but the UK is constitutionally responsible for its defence.

You can still see Jersey's French history everywhere—there's a local form of the ancient Norman language, Jèrriais, and the island is absolutely embedded with French or Norman names. But English is the main language and the UK pound is still its primary currency, the cars drive on the left, the school curriculum follows the English school curriculum, and everyone apparently loves cricket.

All that said, Jersey is incredibly tiny—only about 45 square miles—and the top speed limit all over the island is 40 mph. Its roads can be tiny too, and narrow and twisty, which actually made me happy, as I'd decided to take the most circuitous route I could find, along the most challenging little lanes, in order to further circumvent any further attempts to follow me.

Those attempts turned out to be utterly futile.

A man and a woman—again, in two different cars—started tracking me shortly after I left the airport. Although I have to say, they were having a tough time trying to maintain a constant distance behind me.

I decided I'd had enough just before I reached St. Aubin.

I turned off one narrow little lane into another that was even narrower—with no room at all for two cars to pass each other. I slowed down to 15 mph and located a spot where I could safely stop. Wheel brace in hand, I got out of my car and walked briskly back to the guy who'd pulled over about 20 feet behind me and was now, not very convincingly, consulting a paper road map.

"Who the fuck are you?" I shouted, "and what the fuck do you want?"

The guy looked spooked. He said something—not to me, but to the woman in the car about 30 feet behind him—they were in touch with earbuds and mikes. I could see the bloody device hanging off the guy's face.

The woman put her car into reverse and screeched away.

The guy did the same thing.

I ran back to my Hyundai, threw it into gear and sped off, violating the posted limit three times over but ensuring I logged some serious distance between me and them. I took a couple more detours and when I was certain I'd lost them, I finally drove into St. Aubin.

I parked as inconspicuously as I could in a scenic little lot overlooking a mirror-watered harbour filled with sailboats and launches. It was a good 1/4 of a mile away from the Gainsbourg Guest House.

I got out and walked.

The hotel's Reception was just inside its main door.

Ellie Hammond wasn't expecting me. I'd planned it that way.

"Oh!" she said, after I'd introduced myself. "Hello! Welcome to Jersey!"

"Thank you," I said. "Is there somewhere private we can chat?"

#

The original Gainsbourg house dated from around 1715, when St. Aubin was just a quiet fishing village. Over the centuries, its owners had undertaken modernizations and restorations, and had eventually joined the house to its next-door neighbour in order to construct a far more spacious facility.

We were sitting in the Breakfast Room which, I could see, had been created out of two smaller main floor rooms after a connecting wall had been knocked through. There were friendly signs on the walls reminding guests to keep their keys with them at all times, since Reception was only open for limited hours during the day. A display of tourist brochures and leaflets had been installed in what had once been an immense stone fireplace. There were rattan and wicker tables and chairs and a very well-stocked self-serve coffee and tea bar. And there were souvenirs for sale: art prints and cookbooks, postcards and knick-knacks and lots of copper milk jugs in assorted sizes, just like the kind Susan Gladstone had on her mantle.

"They're very popular," Ellie said, fetching one over so I could have a good look at it. "Handmade locally. They put out a new collection every year."

She showed me the back of the jug, which had a little *2018* stamped on it.

"They're meant to be replicas of the real thing. Well, historically the real thing. To go along with our world-famous cows."

"How long have they been making these jugs?"

"God knows. I remember mum and dad selling them when I was small, so at least 50 years."

"Are your parents still alive?" I had my little notebook out, and my pencil, and I was making notes as well as recording our conversation on my phone.

"Mum is. But she has Alzheimer's. She lives in a care home nearby. Dad died a long time ago."

She put the little jug back on its shelf and came back to the table.

"So you think Pippa Gladstone's disappearance in 1974 is somehow linked to this guest house?" she said.

"I'm working on that assumption," I replied. "Do you remember anything about her dad, Harry Gladstone, staying here? It would have been in February 1974."

"I do, actually. I was just a little girl but I remember he came with his students and his family."

"His family?" I asked, surprised.

"Yes, he brought his wife along, and his two children. Pippa and her brother. I can't remember his name."

"Bernie," I said. "I didn't know they'd come along as well."

"I don't remember the first three years but I do recall the last two. My dad made a big fuss of them. Because it was February, which isn't the height of the tourist season, as you know. But they booked all of our rooms for a week, so they were always very welcome."

"So do you actually remember seeing Pippa?"

"I do, yes. She went along on the field trips to explore the German tunnels. Her mum and her brother did something else. I think they went to the beaches. Sightseeing. I don't think they were that interested in the history, to be honest. Pippa was, though. Oh— and there was something else. A conversation."

"What kind of conversation?"

"I overheard something my dad and one of Harry's students said. It wasn't in February, when they were staying with us. It was afterwards—after she went missing and there were all those news reports."

"She disappeared in March. In Spain."

"Yes. And it was April when I overheard the conversation."

"Sorry," I said. "You mean one of Harry's students came back here in April, after Pippa disappeared?"

"Yes."

"Do you remember who it was?"

Ellie shook her head. "'Afraid not. In fact, I don't even think he stayed with us. He just…popped in."

"And he had a conversation with your dad?"

"Yes. I was standing over there—"

She indicated the Reception area beyond the Breakfast Room.

"—and I saw dad and this student sitting at a table very near to where we are now. They were drinking coffee and smoking cigarettes—I remember that because we didn't allow our guests to smoke in the Breakfast Room and yet there they both were, breaking all the rules."

"And you're sure it was April?"

"Yes, positive. It was the day before my birthday—April 23rd."

I brought up the old Hampshire University newspaper story about the 1974 field trip on my phone.

"Would you recognize the student from this?"

I made the picture as large as I could without it defaulting it to a mass of unintelligible grey, black and white dots.

Ellie looked closely.

"Him," she said, at last. "Very definitely that one."

I consulted the caption under the picture, matching up the names, left to right, with the students.

Linus Montrose.

"Do you remember what the conversation was about?" I asked.

"It was really just a few words. I mean, I probably overheard more, but the only thing that stuck was that the student—him—" She nodded at my phone. "—told my dad something about Pippa…I honestly don't remember what…and then he said something about a photo."

"A photo…?"

"Yes…a photo…or a picture. I think he—the student—was telling my dad that it couldn't be found, or it had gone missing, or something like that. And I remember my dad asking, 'What about the girl?' and the student saying something like, 'She's gone.'"

"'She's gone.'"

"Yes."

"Not, she's disappeared, or she's dead, or she's missing…"

"She's gone. I remember that very distinctly."

"Do you remember anything else?"

Ellie shook her head again. "At that point my dad saw me standing in the doorway and gave me one of his looks. You know, when someone wants you to make yourself scarce. They don't put it into words. But you know it from their eyes. So I thought it best to leave."

"And that's all you overheard."

"That's all. I know it's not much. And I don't know if it's helpful to you."

"It is," I said. "Thank you. Did you speak to anyone about any of this?"

"Absolutely not. Because I was told afterwards, on no uncertain terms, to forget what I'd seen and heard."

"By your dad?"

Ellie nodded. "And you know, when you're only seven years old, and your dad says something like that to you, you pay attention, don't you?"

"Can you remember if anyone came to question your dad about Pippa's disappearance or Harry's death?"

"Anyone like the police, you mean? I don't recall seeing anyone in a uniform, no. Though there were a few men I didn't know or recognize who came and went in those few months after it all happened. Dad would always take them somewhere private to chat. I'm really sorry."

"No worries," I said. I looked around me, trying to picture the Breakfast Room the way it had been four decades earlier. Trying to picture Ellie's dad and Linus Montrose deep in conversation.

And wondering why Linus had found it necessary to come back to Jersey a month after Pippa's disappearance to talk to Ellie's father.

"Do you mind if I wander around and take some pictures?" I asked.

"Not at all. I've got to get back to work but I'll tell you what. I'll have a think later on—try and jog my memory—and if anything at all comes back to me, I'll give you a ring. All right?"

#

I bought myself a takeaway lunch of fish and chips with mushy peas from a café across the road and carried it back to the Gainsbourg's enclosed patio, which was a little walled garden attached to the Breakfast Room, with tubs of flowering, fragrant shrubs and hanging baskets of geraniums and outside chairs and umbrellas to provide shade from the afternoon sun.

A few things were beginning to make sense. Whoever Linus Montrose was, I was willing to bet he was the one who'd hired Alistair Watford to convince me to try and find out if Pippa was alive or dead. And now I was even more certain it was Pippa herself who was trying to discourage me from pursuing that investigation.

But the question was still why?

And why now?

I was pretty sure Duncan Stopher knew why. And it had to do with that photo—the one that Ellie had overheard was missing. But trying to get a straight answer out of Duncan was impossible.

I risked taking my phone off Airplane Mode and logged into my private messages on the Mystery Forum to see if he'd offered up any further clues.

Nothing.

Paging Rose and Valerie, I wrote. *Bang bang Maxwell. News of the World. Je T'aime Edward Champion. Gainsbourg Guest House in Jersey. A conversation in the Breakfast Room about Pippa. Your turn.*

#

Not knowing how long I'd need in Jersey after speaking with Ellie, I'd booked my flight home for that evening. It was too late to change my reservation—the next earliest flight was at 1:40 p.m. and it had just gone one and I wasn't prepared to break the sound barrier (and every posted speed limit) to try and get to the airport before the boarding gate closed.

So, after making my phone invisible again, I drove up towards St. Helier and spent the rest of the afternoon exploring the Jersey War Tunnels—the modern museum that had been created out of one of the landmarks that Harry Gladstone had taken his students to see four decades earlier. In 1974, Harry would have required special permission to visit some of the other tunnels, but Höhlgangsanlage 8, or Ho8, would have been open to him, restored as a museum, though not nearly as complete and interactive as it was now.

Ho8 was originally excavated as a bombproof artillery barracks and ammunition store, where an entire army division could be protected from sea or air assault. The complex had taken three and a half years to build using skilled paid workers as well as forced and slave labourers who'd been brought to the island from Poland, France, Russia and Spain.

It was never completed, and ended up being converted into a casualty receiving station and hospital (including a fully equipped operating theatre) in the weeks leading up to D-Day. Unfinished tunnels were sealed off and air-conditioning and central heating systems were installed behind massive gas-proof doors.

A year after the occupying forces in the Channel Islands surrendered on 9 May 1945, Ho8 was opened to the public. Fifteen years after that, the Royal Court ruled that the subterranean complex belonged to the private owners of the land above it, and Ho8 came under private ownership. The complex was restored with a collection of wartime memorabilia, a museum and a memorial.

It was amazing and moving. I walked through the reconstructed operating theatre, doctors and nurses' quarters, wards, offices and stores. I watched wartime archive films, and saw first-hand how the people of Jersey had been forced to live under the Occupation.

I finished up in the museum's café with a cup of tea and a slice of chocolate cake and a book about the tunnels that I'd bought in the adjacent shop.

I hadn't noticed whether my two biggest fans had managed to locate and follow me. If they had, I hoped they'd found the afternoon educational.

I drove back to the airport feeling that I'd learned a lot more about Jersey, and a little more about Pippa, who'd always accompanied her dad to the tunnels—unlike Susan and Bernie, who'd preferred to engage in sunnier pursuits.

CHAPTER THIRTEEN

I knew I was in trouble as soon as I unlocked the door to my room. You know how you can sense someone's there. Even if it's dark and the lights are off. Even if you can't see them. You can smell what they're wearing and what they're breathing out. You can feel their presence. You *know*.

I knew it a fraction of a second before he throttled me and because of that I dodged the full weight of his fist and instead of slugging me full in the stomach he landed a punch off to my side. Which slammed me into the wall. Sideways. Before he could hit me again I swung back, and I think I must have cracked his jaw because I heard a crunch, which might have been teeth, followed by a groan and a "*Fuck!*"

I don't know which of us had the advantage. Me, because I'd been staying there for the better part of two weeks and I knew the room's layout by heart. Or him, because he'd had God knows how much time to acquaint himself with the place while he waited for the telltale sound of my car's engine in the parking area below the window.

I swung at him again but he was quicker than me and ready for it this time, so my fist hit nothing and I staggered forward and that was when he kneed me in the lower back and sent me sprawling to the floor. He'd have kicked me in the head, too, if I hadn't rolled away and scrambled to my feet. I knew where the toilet was and I gambled that he didn't so that's where I headed, thinking I'd barricade myself in. I got there and grabbed the door and swung it in the bastard's face, which bought me two seconds. But the fucking handle had no lock. And he was nearly on top of me.

I flipped on the light and grabbed my antiperspirant—Right Guard Total Defence 5—off the sink counter and sprayed it straight into his eyes. He crumpled, swearing. I hauled the cistern lid off the toilet and smashed it over his head. He collapsed to the floor. Where I kicked him for good measure. Twice. In the balls. And twice more into his middle and once more in the side of his head, though he was unconscious by that time and it wasn't completely necessary.

And then I rang my sister and told her I wanted to speak to Tom, her husband, the ex-copper.

#

Half an hour later, a man and a woman arrived at The Dog's Watch. I'd taken Tom's advice and relocated to the pub downstairs, where I was surrounded by other people and I could stay highly visible. The woman came immediately to my table. The man paused in the doorway, long enough for me to notice him, and then left.

"Andy Escott," the woman said, briefly. "My colleague is Les Partridge. He's gone up to your room. He'll take care of tidying up."

"By himself?" I said, doubtfully. I was in serious pain. My stomach hurt, and my lower back, and my knuckles were grazed and bleeding. I must have looked a complete mess. If I hadn't been a registered guest, I'm sure Arthur Ferryman would have had me thrown out of the pub for being an undesirable influence. But I was in much better shape than my attacker.

"We have additional resources. You won't have seen them arrive. And you won't see them leave. Are you all right? Do you need medical attention?"

A job for Dr. Sparks. I wondered if patient confidentiality extended as far as not telling my mum what had just happened to me. Best not.

"Do you think you could give me a lift to the nearest A&E...?"

"No need," Andy replied. She made a quick call, which consisted of no more than five words, and then put her mobile away.

"What happens now?" I said, unhappily. "Am I going to be arrested for GBH?"

"Nothing will happen to you."

"You're certain about that? The Middlehurst police already have

131

me on their radar. They'll be turning cartwheels when they hear about this."

"Trust me, Jason. Nobody will know about the incident."

"I broke a cistern lid over the guy's head."

"The cistern lid will be replaced. And anything else that was damaged will be made right. Let's go for a little ride in my car."

She must have sensed my hesitation. Which may have been bordering on terror.

"Just to the doctor's office. Unless you'd rather walk."

I shook my head. I wasn't sure I could actually walk. And I was shaking. Possibly from shock. And rage. I was really, really angry.

"My car's just outside," Andy said, taking my arm to steady me as I got to my feet. "Try and relax, Jason. Take your mind off what's just happened. Tell me a little bit about yourself. I understand you play a very good jazz guitar."

#

The doctor was about ten minutes away, in a terraced house that was indistinguishable from its neighbours. His front garden was dripping with roses, and their scent overwhelmed me as Andy helped me through the gate and up the little path to the front door, which was painted bright blue.

I was surprised he was willing to look at me at that hour, but once inside, I was taken straight into a room that seemed to be kitted out like a miniature field hospital. I'm not sure if it was the adrenaline or the shock or just my general sense that things were decidedly weird. It all felt surreal. I took off my shirt and laid back on the bed. I was examined and rolled over, gently prodded and assessed. Ice packs were applied to the bruises that were already in the process of turning into a brilliantly speckled display of red, purple, green and grey. My grazed knuckles were cleansed and antibiotic ointment applied, along with gauze bandages.

This is going to take some explaining tomorrow, I thought. At least it was my right hand and not my left. I reckoned I could still hold a plectrum OK and as long as I didn't have to do any complicated finger strumming, I'd make it through tomorrow's production rehearsal. My wrist was aching though. I'd really jarred it.

The doctor finished up with an injection guaranteed to kill all pain for at least 12 hours, a supply of tablets for when the effects of the shot wore off, and something else he advised would allow me to sleep, should I require assistance. He added that the injection might result in some feelings of "disorientation" and that I ought not to drive (or operate any heavy machinery) while I was under the influence.

I left feeling vaguely like I was about to embark on the sort of journey Jeff Bridges had experienced in *The Big Lebowski*. I really hoped The Dog's Watch wasn't harbouring any dancing women with bowling pin head-dresses or nasty men in red leotards wielding giant-sized scissors. Though I honestly wouldn't have minded floating down a bowling alley on my back enjoying the same view as The Dude.

Andy drove me back to the pub. Her colleague, Les Partridge, was sitting alone at the table we'd vacated an hour earlier.

"I think you'll find everything is in order now," he said.

"Did I kill him?" I asked.

"Fortunately not. He was wide awake, the last time I checked. And not well pleased to have woken up to find his hands and feet trussed to the radiator with electrical leads. Good work."

"Thanks," I said. "Who is he?"

"You've never seen him before."

I shook my head. He very definitely wasn't one of the people who'd followed me to the airport, or who'd continued the pursuit once I landed.

"That wasn't a question," Andy advised. "Nod your head to indicate you understand."

I nodded.

"Time we were going," Les said, standing up

"Have a nice evening," Andy added. "Careful on the stairs."

I watched them leave.

I stayed at the table for another 20 minutes.

And then I limped up to my room.

Just as they'd promised, they'd tidied up. There was no trace of damage. The lamps were back where they belonged, as were the electrical leads. The cistern lid had been replaced. How they'd arranged that on short notice, I couldn't imagine.

I didn't feel very safe. I felt violated. And I was still angry.

I rang Angie back.

"I wanted to thank Tom," I said.

"For what?"

"Passing the word along to whoever he spoke to."

"He rang Allan Pappas."

"I thought Allan Pappas was on holiday."

"He is. Tom had to leave a message on his machine. Allan hasn't rung us back yet. I was just going to call you to give you an update."

A chill literally ran down my spine.

"Tom told me to wait downstairs in the pub," I said.

"Yes, for your own safety. That was just common sense. Are you still there?"

"No. I'm back in my room."

"Is that wise?"

"What did you tell Allan in the message?"

"Nothing at all, Jason. Just to ring Tom back as he had a question about something that had happened to you."

"No details?"

"Nothing else. Why?"

"Someone's come," I said. "Everything's been taken care of."

"But how could they possibly have known?"

Indeed. How could they possibly have known?

I felt it best not to speculate.

#

I'd completely lost track of the time. I'd thought it was only about 9 p.m., but it turned out to be closer to midnight. I found a pizza place in Middlehurst that was still open and bribed them to drive to Stoneford with something that was loaded with hot chilli chicken and roasted peppers, garlic, tomato and mozzarella cheese. I waited 'til they called me to tell me they were outside, and then I limped downstairs to collect it, throwing in an absurdly big tip for the delivery guy to persuade him to stay put until I let him know I was safely upstairs again and back in my room.

After I'd eaten I tried to sleep, but I couldn't. No way was I going to switch off the lights.

I had the tablets the doctor had given me but I really didn't want to take them.

I got up and went online and logged into the Mystery Forum but there was still nothing from Duncan Stopher.

I composed another message.

Who the fuck are you? I wrote. *How the fuck do you know so much? And what the fuck do you want?*

Concise and to the point.

I sent it off.

And then I went looking for more information about Linus Montrose.

There really wasn't much. And most of what I found was by searching the family tree website for public documents that were freely available to subscribers.

His full name was Linus Patterson Montrose. He was born to Garry Hillier Montrose and his wife Lorna on May 1, 1953 in Portland, Oregon. Garry and Lorna had divorced in 1959.

Gary and Linus were listed as passengers aboard the Home Lines passenger ship *Homeric* on July 14, 1960, sailing from Montreal to Southampton. On the Passenger Manifest, Gary's occupation was shown as "Professor". His country of citizenship was England. Also on the manifest was the address where they planned to stay while they were in England. And both Gary and Linus's birth dates. And the intended length of their stay (6 months) and the purpose of their journey (visitor).

It looked to me as though Linus and his father had remained in the UK permanently. I couldn't find their names on any passenger manifests going back the same way. Garry was obviously travelling on a British passport and didn't need any special permissions or accommodations. In fact, most of his family was easily trackable, since they all appeared to have come from Bedfordshire and very few of them—aside from Garry himself—had ventured much further away.

Linus, on the other hand, was a complete mystery. He didn't appear on any voters' lists. He hadn't got married. I couldn't tell if he'd been added to any of Garry's relatives' family trees. If he had, his information was listed as "Private"— which at least would have told me one thing: he was still alive.

There was nothing about him anywhere else online, either. It was as if he'd tumbled off the planet.

Meanwhile, Garry Montrose couldn't have landed closer to Pippa Gladstone if he'd tried. It turned out he was a colleague of Pippa's dad, a fellow professor of History at Hampshire University. And there was no shortage of verifiable information about him on the family tree website. Up until 1974, anyway— when everything suddenly stopped and Garry Hillier Montrose also vanished from the face of the earth.

I scoured the internet for news—anything.

But aside from a few historic entries about papers he'd authored or co-authored, all information about him had ceased in March 1974.

CHAPTER FOURTEEN

I woke up in a panic. My alarm hadn't gone off and it was nearly 10 a.m. Why hadn't anybody rung me? Tejo? *Mum?*

I rolled out of bed and checked my phone and realized that it was Wednesday. Production rehearsal. Late start.

Groaning, I fell back onto the mattress and stared at the ceiling. I'd spent the better part of two hours last night searching for information about Linus Montrose, only giving up in the end because my brain had gone numb.

I was exhausted. And my body was aching for sleep. I must have nodded off in the chair because when I next opened my eyes, it was just getting light outside and my friends the birds were chirping cautious good mornings to each other.

I'd looked at the time and then I'd tried to think up a story about my bruised knuckles and my aching middle that would convince my mum I'd got up to absolutely nothing of consequence during my last-minute absence.

And then I'd crawled into bed.

It was now fifteen minutes past ten and I was in serious pain. The injection's effects had begun to wear off at just about the same time that the sparrow outside my window had got itself into an argument with a crow and had—wisely—relocated to a bush with denser leaves and safer branches.

I made myself a very strong cup of tea, swallowed one of the tablets the doctor had given me, and sat down to see if Duncan had sent me any messages.

Of course not.

For one insane moment I wondered whether he'd been paid a surprise visit as well and had been frightened into silence.

I hadn't been thinking very straight last night, but by the cold light of day, I was well aware that I was treading in dangerous territory. My conversation with Ellie had suggested it and the attention paid to me by Andy Escott and Les Partridge had confirmed it: I was sticking my nose into something I ought not to.

I was meant to stop.

Now.

Unfortunately for those with a vested interest in having me cease and desist, I wasn't in a mood to pay much attention. I was still angry. No—I was furious. Verging on incandescent. There was something very very wrong with Pippa's disappearance. And if I stopped looking for her, and it turned out I could have been instrumental in righting that wrong, I would quite possibly regret it for the rest of my life.

A notice flashed up on my screen: a private message was waiting for Paula McIntyre on Facebook.

I went to have a look.

Hello Paula. My name is Lisa Matthews. My mum was Belinda Smith-Trevynne. I saw your posting on the Mewbury Old Girls Group. I'm sorry to tell you that mum died in 2013 but I'm happy to chat with you about her if you're still interested.

I wrote back to her immediately, but the little green dot that indicated when someone was online wasn't there.

I hobbled into the shower and gently ran the water over my bruises, which had turned into brilliant technicolour fireworks overnight. I washed my hair and shaved, towelled off and employed my hairdryer, and came back to my computer to discover another message.

Hello Jason, Lisa had written. *I'm not sure how much information I can give you, as it all happened well before I was born! But I do know Mum was very upset when Pippa disappeared. She and Liz and Pippa were really good pals. And Mum was always talking about that Christmas show!*

She was online. I sent her a reply. *Thank you! I'd love to have a chat with you about your mum. In the meantime, I have a little film which features your mum, Elizabeth Foster and Pippa, miming to a song. It's a rehearsal for the Christmas show. Would you like to see it?*

Lisa answered right away: *Yes please!*

I sent the video off and made myself another cup of tea while I waited for her to watch it.

Lisa was back with me inside five minutes.

Something's not right with this, she said.

With the film? I asked.

With Mum. With her leg.

I don't understand, I said.

Mum contracted polio when she was six. In 1965. She was one of the 55 unlucky people in England to get it that year. Her left leg was quite a bit shorter than her right leg. She wore a brace when she was at school and for the rest of her life. It was really noticeable. There's nothing wrong with any of the girls' legs in this film.

Hang on, I said.

I got the video up on my laptop and had a look.

You're absolutely right, I said.

And something else. Mum wasn't very tall. She was the bridesmaid at Liz Foster's wedding. I've seen her photos. Liz was much taller than Mum. All three of the girls in that film are the same height. So that film can't be authentic. Where did it come from?

I seriously debated what I was going to say next.

First there was the bogus photo of Pippa at the folk festival. Now there was a bogus film purporting to show Pippa and her two friends rehearsing.

It was given to me, I said, *to help with my investigation.*

Well, said Lisa, *it clearly won't help at all.*

It's very strange, I said, *that Liz Foster didn't mention your mum's limp or the height discrepancy to me when I spoke to her the other day and showed her the same film.*

It's very strange, Lisa wrote back, immediately, *that you spoke to Liz Foster at all, as she's been dead since 2015.*

#

There was no point even attempting to walk from The Dog's Watch to the manor. I was in too much pain. I drove my car and left it parked next to Tejo's Saab in the lot at the top of the hill.

It was a challenge to get up the stairs to the library, too. I took my time, relying heavily on the mahogany railing and expressing my silent thanks to whatever gods looked after dead 19th century architects for allowing them the wisdom to create wide steps with shallow treads for easier climbing.

Tacked to the library door was a note directing me across to the manor's old ballroom—or, as it had been called in the day, the Great Reception Hall.

When Angie and I had spent our holidays in Stoneford, the manor had been empty and abandoned, with padlocks on the doors and everything boarded up. There were, however, several windows in the cellar which were just large enough to permit access by an enterprising youth and his little sister.

We'd explored the manor, top to bottom. And I'd taken what we'd discovered to the Stoneford Village Library, where I'd done some research, unearthing carefully-preserved documents and diagrams and descriptions, and even some old black and white photographs of the building's interior.

I had no trouble at all imagining how the Great Reception Hall had once looked, decorated for a grand ball with fresh flowers and English ivy and hundreds of beeswax candles burning brightly in chandeliers and silver holders. There would have been elaborate chalk designs on the wood plank floor, put there so that the soles of the attendees' shoes didn't slip as they danced. A small group of musicians would have been installed up at the far end of the room— perhaps a fiddler, a flautist and someone on the pianoforte—to provide live music.

Now, I saw that a portable stage had been erected in exactly the same spot, and it had been decorated with our pale mauve gauzy backdrop curtain and equipped with arrays of lights, mic stands and amps.

"Good morning!" my mum called, cheerfully, from the stage. "Welcome back!"

"'Morning," I said, taking the stairs slowly. I'd pulled the bandages off my hand to try and make the cuts and bruises seem a little less obvious. But my mum's got eyes like an eagle, and she knows me well enough to be able to tell when something's not right.

"What have you been up to?"

"Best not to ask," I replied. "I'll be all right by Friday."

My mother didn't say anything. But I could tell she wasn't impressed. She gave me one of her looks.

Our instruments had been set up exactly as we wanted them arranged onstage. We also had long-legged stools, which all of us could revert to if we needed a rest. I hadn't anticipated requiring mine at all—other than for visual variety—but I was extremely grateful it was there now.

We planned to run through the show exactly as it would be presented on Friday, beginning to end, including the interval, so that Tejo and Dr. Sparks could program their sound and light boards and make sure they had their timings right. Tomorrow we'd be doing it all again in our stage clothes.

Back in the day, the Figs had begun their gigs in total darkness. Five-minute warning…mum and dad standing in the wings with the rest of the band…a pitch-black stage…house lights out. Ten seconds to adjust their eyes, and then each of the Figs had walked on and picked up their instruments and, as the stage lights had come up, they'd started playing.

But when you're travelling with a group of elderlies, and your tour insurance has all kinds of waivers and exclusions regarding safety, liability and risk factors, you'd best not tempt fate. Dr. Sparks had therefore designed some very effective subdued lighting for our entrance, which would grow in intensity as we took our places, and then the full effects would cut in as we began our first song.

We reassembled at the foot of the little portable staircase. Mum had always led the band onstage. As I stood behind her, waiting for our cue, I felt the oddest sensation. Was it my dad? There weren't any storms about. I hadn't seen any clouds, or heard any thunder. But I've always believed that when people die, they never really go away. Their spirit stays close by. And I know my mum had been feeling his presence, on and off, all through our rehearsals. I'd only been aware of him once—during Sunday night's storm—but perhaps I just hadn't been looking for him.

And now, it seemed, I was.

As we climbed the steps and walked onto the stage in a single line, we were greeted by applause and wild cheers thundering through the speakers—courtesy of Tejo, who'd imported the sound effects as a one-time surprise to get us in the right mood.

Mum was laughing as we took our places for "The Gypsy Rover".

But dad wasn't with us.

I glanced over at the staircase.

What was holding him back?

#

I was drained by the time we finished at half past one. I'd dragged my stool around the stage to approximate where I planned to stand on Friday night. I'd managed most of the instrument switch-outs, though I fucked up monumentally with "High Meadows." Just before "High Meadows" we'd done "The Fog's Lament", an old English folk song that featured some intricate fingering on my part. I'd tuned the sixth string of my Strat down a full tone to make it easier to play, and I completely forgot to re-tune, so that when Rolly counted us in for "High Meadows" and I hit my opening chords, it sounded horrible.

Fortunately, I'd moved my pedal board from the front of the stage to where I was sitting, and the digital tuner was easy to get to in a hurry. Literally, and without skipping a beat, I kept singing while I re-tuned the low E string with my foot, and it was fixed.

The good thing about an incident like that is that it's burned into your brain and it will never, ever, be repeated during a performance.

The bad thing is that the band—and especially your mother—will never let you forget it and will bring it up for years afterwards, usually at Christmas dinner.

Everything else went fairly smoothly. Banter (rehearsed and unrehearsed). Last minute changes to the song order. Mic and lighting adjustments.

And I finally met our runner, who'd set up the stage and our instruments that morning, and who would be driving our equipment van. I was quite pleasantly surprised to discover that Kato was female—I'd assumed someone with a name like that would be a burly guy schooled in martial arts with a fondness for superhero cartoons. But our Kato was a very fit young lady with a penchant for biking shorts and sleeveless tops.

Three more people also made themselves known to me that day—Freddie, our tour and merch manager, who was also in charge of our wardrobe. And the two women who'd be providing our pre-show meals and who'd very graciously cooked up a post-rehearsal lunch for us.

I was seriously impressed. Jack and Jill (those were their names, honestly, and their company was called Up the Hill Catering) provided handwritten menus and locally sourced food, and while we were on the road, they planned to visit the markets in each city to buy the ingredients for our meals. That day's lunch featured a lovely choice of sandwiches and wraps with wonderful fillings: curried egg, spicy tuna, mozzarella and tomato, assorted hams, a special something vegetarian for Freddie and another special something with mindful calories for Tejo. There were tins of fizzy soda and little boxes of salad and chocolate and vanilla puddings for afters. They got my thumbs up—and the thumbs up from all of my Instagram followers, who'd begun to panic after not hearing from me for two days.

Where have you been, Jason? We've been worried sick! Are you doing that starvation diet?

I decided to coordinate my menu with yours. I've had to resort to doggie chews and raiding the hummingbird feeder. Don't you dare do this to me again, you selfish bastard.

Typical musician. Leading us on with teaser starters. Half-expected you to have a channel on YouTube demanding payment for access to the entrees.

I assured them I was fine, provided witty, culinarily-themed answers to another three dozen questions, and then sent off a text to Lisa Matthews.

Can you tell me what Elizabeth Foster's married name was?

Lisa wrote back immediately. *It was Scattergood. Why?*

Housekeeping, I messaged back. *Thank you.*

It was an unusual name, which made my job infinitely easier. I popped onto the family tree research site and typed in the details for Elizabeth Scattergood. And there she was. Death date 28 Oct 2015, Southampton, Hampshire. Confirmed.

Whoever had met me for drinks the other night at The Dog's Watch—and it was most definitely not Elizabeth Foster—had been provided with an agenda. And that was to try and convince me that Pippa was dead, and that her parents might have been responsible.

So where did Bernie's manufactured video fit in? What kind of agenda did he have?

I gave him a call.

"Just wondering," I said, "if you could reconfirm Pippa's height to me."

"I told you," he said. "Five foot two."

"I thought she might have been taller," I said.

"What makes you think that?"

"The clothes in her cupboard. They didn't strike me as belonging to someone who was that short."

"Different times," Bernie said. "Different styles. She liked long skirts. Anything else?"

"Nothing," I said. "Thanks."

Bernie was beginning not to like me very much.

The feeling was mutual.

A quick check online told me what young women were wearing in the mid-1970s. Ten years after Mary Quant's miniskirts had turned the fashion world on its head, hemlines were on their way down. The maxi was all the rage. But the mini was still popular. It hadn't gone away. And what I'd seen on the hangers in Pippa's cupboard were dresses and skirts whose hemlines had been designed to end well above the knee.

There was no way on earth that Pippa Gladstone was only five foot two.

CHAPTER FIFTEEN

I was on my second little pot of chocolate pudding when Duncan Stopher finally ended his silence.

I gather Rose and Valerie were not as helpful as you might have hoped. Brilliant deduction, I wrote back. *I know that Ellie Hammond's father was Edward Champion and I know that he had a conversation with Linus Montrose concerning a missing photo. Ellie remembers that, and she remembers Pippa was mentioned, but only in terms of her being "gone". Ellie was told by her father to forget everything she'd seen and heard. So she did.*

That's a shame, said Duncan. *I was expecting more.*

What kind of more?

I cannot reveal who the fuck I am, Duncan said. *Nor can I tell you how the fuck I know so much. But I will confirm what the fuck I want: I want justice for Pippa, the same as you.*

You've got a bizarre way of trying to achieve it, I said. *Tell me something else. To the best of your knowledge, how tall was Pippa?*

All of the press reports from the time stated that her height was sixty-two inches. Five foot two.

That's not what I asked you.

There was a very long silence. And then:

Do you know what Susan Gladstone's maiden name was?

Why? I asked.

Is it your birthday soon?

No, it's in May. May 11, 1968. Why?

For some reason I thought you were born in 1978, Duncan said. *October 23.*

Why would you think that? I asked.

I waited ten minutes for an answer.

But he'd gone again.

Fucktard.

#

My Instagram followers seemed intent on mining me for insider details about the tour, so I posted some photos from our production rehearsal, along with helpful captions.

My fellow chuffer Tejo, sitting at his sound board. The knobs all go up to 11.

Dr. Sparks throwing light shapes around the stage. We've decided to add a laser. Tejo uses it to light his ciggies.

A copy of our set lists. Subject to constant change. Please ignore my Sharpie scribbles and I really didn't mean to swear like that.

And then I went back to the family tree site and searched for Harry and Susan Gladstone's marriage record from 1956.

I found it easily—along with Susan's maiden name: Percy.

But why did Duncan want to know about my birthday?

I had a little think while I finished off my chocolate pudding.

Perhaps it wasn't so much *my* birthday he was interested in…as someone else's.

And it was that someone else that he wanted me to know about—a person who was born on October 23, 1978 and whose last name was Percy.

The General Registry Office had made it exceptionally easy to search online for individual births and deaths, as long as you had a year and a last name. Unfortunately, there were gaps in their still-evolving database and 1978 turned out to be missing. So it was back to the family research site.

I input the details and did a search…and there she was.

Violet Rosemary Percy, born in Hampshire in 4th Quarter 1978. Mother's maiden name…also Percy.

Was she Susan's child?

I wouldn't be able to see her mother's full name or who the father was—if he was shown at all—unless I ordered her birth certificate from the GRO.

I knew a quicker way.

I created a private file for Violet in my personal area on the site and then went looking for as much verifiable information as I could about her. I quickly found a UK Electoral Register entry for 2003-2004 which provided her address. It was The Old Vicarage in Middlehurst.

Pippa's old home.

I brought up the actual document on my screen and made it big so I could read the printed entry. The other occupant of The Old Vicarage—who was also registered as a voter—was Susan Gladstone.

Susan had to be Violet's mum.

I thought it very strange that neither Bernie nor Susan had mentioned Violet to me. A half-sister to Pippa. Born four years after she'd disappeared.

Violet wasn't mentioned anywhere else either—notably absent in the news stories marking the anniversaries of her sister's disappearance and death, no red top gossip, nothing.

So why did Duncan want me to know about her?

A further search informed me that Violet had married Aidan Halliday in 2004 and that she currently lived in Milford-on-Sea and, from that little tidbit of information, I was able to find her contact details, including a phone number.

I gave her my usual introduction—I had it committed to memory. "Do you think we could meet this afternoon?" I asked.

"Yes, certainly," Violet replied. "Where are you?"

"Just along the coast road. See you in…an hour?"

#

Violet Halliday lived in a modern end-of-terrace house in a neighbourhood that would likely be listed in census stats as populated with Rural White-Collar Workers, whose average age was 59.46 years and whose designation was "Affluent Communities". I could see, as I parked my car, that she was about five minutes' walk from the beach, and about the same distance from the centre of the village.

The front of the house was all windows and vertical blinds and there were no trees or fences to speak of—just a brick driveway and an expanse of thirsty lawn.

Violet was unmistakably her mother's daughter. She was 40 years old and she had the same carefully-shaped eyebrows as Susan and the same facial structure, the same cheeks and nose—but not her eyes. Violet's eyes were green.

"Hello," she said, warmly, greeting me at the door and leading me through the front hall and the kitchen. "Do join me in the snug."

The snug looked as if it had been added to the rear of the house as an afterthought. It had pale grey walls, a faux-wood plank floor, two small armchairs, a sofa and an immense TV, and French doors which opened onto a concrete patio with a pebbled glass table, four comfy chairs and a bright orange sun umbrella.

"It's much cooler in here on hot summer days," Violet said. "Have a seat and a biccie." She offered me a plate of ginger snaps. "Tea?"

"Yes, please," I said.

I sat on the sofa and she sat in one of the armchairs.

"The kids are at school," she said. "Hubby's at work. We've got about an hour 'til they come home and all hell breaks loose. Let's get the obvious questions out of the way first. I am the result of an illicit relationship between my mum and a gentleman who shall remain nameless. Mum told me who he was when I was ten. And we're actually good friends. Though, of course, his wife and children must never know."

"Of course," I said.

"I mean, how dare Susan Gladstone besmirch the memory of her dearly departed husband by embarking on a scandalous affair with a married man barely four years after entering widowhood. Bernie hated her for it. And he hated me, too. He couldn't wait to get away from us. He left home as soon as he could."

That was interesting. "So Bernie and his mother—your mother—don't get along."

"They do in public," said Violet. "But otherwise, most definitely not."

"And that would explain why he never mentioned you to me," I said.

"I'm never mentioned to anyone. Which is OK with me. And I'm quite certain Bernie would prefer I met the same fate as Pippa."

"What do you think about that?" I asked. "What was her fate?"

"To be honest, I have no idea. I know she disappeared under very mysterious circumstances. I know there was a police investigation and that it was inconclusive. I know mum had Pippa declared dead. But I've never really questioned any of it."

"Does the name Duncan Stopher mean anything to you?" I asked.

I could tell it did, even before she replied.

"Yes," she said. "Why?"

"He seems particularly keen that I track you down."

"He's a strange man." Violet said, with a laugh. "But I like him a lot."

"He's not by any chance your father…"

Violet laughed again. "No bloody way."

"How did you and Duncan meet?"

"I've never actually 'met' him—not in real terms. We're in touch virtually. On a chat group."

"The Pippa Gladstone Mystery Forum."

"That's the one. I've been a member since it started up. It's highly entertaining."

"So what do you know about Duncan?"

"Not a lot. Never really asked, to be honest. You don't, do you, with chat groups and online forums. So many people prefer to keep their real lives a secret. You never really know who you're dealing with."

"You don't," I agreed. "Do you have any idea at all why Duncan might want me to find you?"

Violet had to think. "It must be the film," she said, at last.

"What film?"

"The film that had Pippa on it. And two of her friends."

"Singing and dancing?"

"I'm not sure. I've never actually watched it. I just know what's on the first few frames."

"Like this?" I played Bernie's video for her on my phone.

"It might be the same, yes," Violet said, thoughtfully.

"You said you only know what's on the first few frames. Is it on a reel?"

"Yes. It's a little home movie. Would you like to see it?"

"Very much."

Violet got up and rummaged through a bright blue fabric drawer in a white IKEA shelf unit under the TV.

"Here you are."

The little plastic reel reminded me of the old audio tapes that fit into portable recorders in the days before cassette players. Except this one contained a length of 8 mm celluloid. I pulled out the first few inches and peered at the tiny series of frames. There they were: Pippa, Elizabeth and Belinda in front of the fireplace in Susan's drawing room. I really couldn't make out a lot of detail because the images were so small. But there was no way that was the source of the digitized video Bernie had given me.

In Bernie's video, all three girls were wearing matching black satin waistcoats. In Violet's film, the three girls were all in skirts and tops. The skirts were short and flared. One of the girls was wearing a white sweater. Another was wearing a black pull-on top with a large ceramic fruity brooch—green leaves and red cherries. Pippa's top was high-necked and striped black and purple and blue and pink.

The other difference that was very apparent was the girls' heights. One of the girls—the one with the fruity brooch—was quite a bit shorter than the other two. I held the film up to the light and took a picture of the frame, and then looked at it on my phone, increasing the size so I could see it properly. That girl's left leg was very definitely smaller than her right leg. And she was wearing a brace.

"How did get this?" I asked.

"I was a very curious child," Violet said, humorously. "I was always investigating the drawers and cupboards in our house. One day when I was about six, I was digging through a suitcase in the loft and that's where I discovered it. I had no idea what it was, but I unwound the first bit and saw it had pictures on it. And then I saw it was Pippa. I mean, I'd seen photos of her. I knew what she looked like. I thought it was a lovely treasure—a keepsake—so I hid it in my bedroom and I never mentioned to my mum or to Bernie that I had it. I thought that if they'd forgotten about it up in a suitcase in the loft, it couldn't have been that important to them. They still have no idea I've got it."

"But Duncan knew?"

"Yes. We were chatting about Pippa—in private messages—and I mentioned it to him."

"When was this?"

"A few years ago. There was a very heated argument on the forum about what Pippa really looked like. The photos that mum and Harry distributed when she went missing showed a much younger Pippa, because it was all they had available to them at the time. There was considerable sentiment on the forum that Harry and mum had deliberately misled the police and the searchers by providing outdated photos. They were trying to argue that Harry had accidentally killed Pippa and he and mum had concealed the crime by making her 'disappear'. There was even a theory that they'd secretly arranged to have Pippa's remains cremated and then they'd taken her ashes with them back to England. There was a newspaper interview with mum when she had Pippa declared legally dead, and there was a photo with the story that showed some brass jug ornaments on the mantle over the fireplace. People were claiming that Pippa's ashes had been hidden inside one of those. Which was nonsense, of course."

"Did you look?" I inquired, not-quite-seriously.

"What do you think?" she said, with a grin. "Anyway, if you search the forum you can find the thread and see what people were accusing mum and Harry of. It was quite an entrenched belief. Their arguments made me angry. I knew I had this home movie that showed Pippa, so I asked Duncan what I ought to do."

"And what did he say?"

"He wanted to know more about the movie."

"So you told him."

"Yes. I described the first few frames to him. And he told me it was Pippa preparing for her school's Christmas show a few months before she'd disappeared."

"Hang on," I said. "How could Duncan possibly know that?"

"I asked him the same thing. And he told me he had a daughter a year younger than Pippa who'd attended Mewbury—that was their school—at the same time as Pippa. He remembered that Christmas show very well. And based on my description—what the three girls were wearing—that's what he thought the film was. Pippa and her friends rehearsing for the show, in the clothes they were going to perform in."

"That seems," I said, "to be an extraordinarily accurate conclusion, based on just your observation of a couple of stills from the beginning of a film."

"I'm telling you exactly what he said," Violet shrugged.

"So what did he advise you to do with the film?"

"He told me it would be wise to keep it to myself. And not to share anything with the group."

"So you followed his advice."

"I did."

I had a thought.

"You said you used to go exploring through drawers and

cupboards in your house. Were you allowed into Pippa's room?"

"Not at all. It was very much off-limits. But the door didn't have a lock on it, so I used to go in there all the time. Mum never knew, of course."

"What do you remember about the room?"

"I remember," said Violet, "that it was almost like a shrine. It was as if mum was trying to hang on to everything she remembered about my sister."

"What did you do when you went inside?"

"I mostly just wandered around and looked. As you do when you're very young and curious. Touched things. You know."

"Did you ever take anything?"

Violet shook her head. And then, she changed her mind.

"I might as well admit to it. Since you already know about the little reel of film. I took Pippa's passport."

"You're kidding."

Violet laughed. "Why do you sound so incredulous?"

"Your mother told me she sent it back to the Passport Office when she had Pippa legally declared dead."

"Well, that's a porky, for a start," Violet said. "No, she hung onto it. She put it away in one of the drawers in Pippa's dressing table. Whereupon it mysteriously disappeared. Roundabout 1988 or 1989, I should think. I was nine or ten at the time. She must have gone looking for it at some point after that and discovered it gone. She asked me if I'd been in Pippa's room, but I vehemently denied everything, so the cleaners got the blame."

"Do you still have it?" I asked. I was literally holding my breath.

Violet smiled, then got up and went back to the IKEA shelves— a different fabric drawer this time—and came back with an old-fashioned hard covered black passport that had been issued in January 1974. It looked brand new. But then it would have been— before her 16th birthday, Pippa would have been travelling on Susan's passport. This was her proof of coming-of-age. She'd have been so proud of it—I knew I was thrilled when I'd turned 16 and could finally have my own passport. I looked at the black and white picture. There she was. Close up and real, smiling a little cheekily at the photographer—it was allowed in those days.

"So," I said. "Pippa really did leave her passport behind when she disappeared."

"She did, yes."

"I'd been wondering if she'd decided to run away. But she wouldn't have got very far without that."

"Bang goes your theory," Violet said.

"Do you mind if I ask you one more thing…when you were in Pippa's bedroom, did you ever go into her bathroom?"

"Of course."

"If this makes you uncomfortable, please say so. In her bathroom…did you ever come across a box of sanitary pads from Spain?"

Violet had to think. "I don't remember seeing anything like that at all. Box of tampons, yes. From England. I might have even helped myself to one or two. Or three. But no sanitary towels at all. Not even from Spain."

#

Back in my room in Stoneford, I called my son, Dom, who was in London doing his university degree in film.

"I don't suppose," I said, "you happen to have access to anything that can play something shot in Super-8?"

"It's not used all that often. But I do, in fact. What's up?"

I told him. Violet had let me borrow the little reel, as long as I promised to return it—and not tell Bernie or Susan. I'd easily agreed to both conditions.

"And I don't suppose you could convert that film into a digital format for me."

"I could," Dom replied. "How quickly do you want it?"

"If you can get here this afternoon to collect it…I'd love to have it by tomorrow."

"Not too urgent, then."

I laughed. "I have utmost faith in you."

"You worry me."

"See you in a couple of hours," I said.

#

I met Dom in The Dog Watch's parking lot. He pulled up beside me on his motorbike. I invited him to join me in my car.

"This is all very cloak and dagger," he said, with a grin. "Are you working on another case?"

"I am," I said. "And it is very cloak and dagger. It has all the hallmarks, anyway. So utmost secrecy, all right?"

"Yes, dad."

I gave him the little reel of film. He pulled it out to have a look. "Strange," he said. "There's no head leader."

"What's that?"

"It's a little white strip of cellulose that protects the beginning of the film and lets you wind it through the projector without missing anything that's on the first frames. It's pretty standard. It looks like this leader's been removed."

"Why would somebody do that?"

Dom shrugged. "Bad editing? Maybe they wanted to cut something out at the start?"

"Interesting," I said. "Guard that with your life. And be careful."

"No worries. I'll get it converted as soon as I can and I'll email you the digital copy. I'll bring the original back when I see you in Middlehurst on Friday."

I was surprised. "You're coming to our opening night?"

"The Figs are my favourite band," Dom replied, with a ridiculously straight face.

CHAPTER SIXTEEN

We had another late start on Thursday, this one to accommodate a second production rehearsal that included us wearing our stage clothes. Mum had scheduled it for the afternoon so we'd have time to work through anything that needed last-minute attention. Though the way we were sounding—the way we'd come together with Beth as our new fiddler—I didn't think we'd have very many problems.

I slept soundly until 9 a.m. and woke up to discover that I was in much less pain than when I'd gone to bed. And that Dom had sent me a message which contained, as an attachment, a two-minute digital conversion of Violet Halliday's Super-8 film.

I watched it as I was drinking my morning cup of tea.

You know those records you used to be able to buy back in the 1980s—the "soundalikes"—where, for a bargain price, you could get all the top hits of the day on one vinyl album, performed by groups that were very good at mimicking the original artists? That's what Bernie's video reminded me of, as I was watching Violet's original.

Bernie's film was the cut-price copy.

Violet's was the authentic real deal.

The song in both versions was the same, and so was the setting— the drawing room in Susan's house. And all three girls were dancing in front of the fireplace. But that was where the similarities ended.

In Violet's version, there was a fourth person: a teenaged boy.

His job was to act as a foil for Pippa. He walked into the shot a few seconds after the girls started miming, and he stayed there, acting and reacting to all of the claims Pippa was tossing at him. He was quite good, and even made me laugh a couple of times. He was wearing an Indian cotton shirt and bell-bottomed denim jeans.

I needed to see the two videos side-by-side. I had Bernie's version on my phone, so I propped it up beside my laptop and ran Violet's original at full screen, so I could compare the two.

It was very evident that Violet's version had come from a real film: there were scratches and bits of debris popping in and out of the frames. Bernie's copy, on the other hand, was "clean".

Aside from the height differences and the change of costumes, the girls in both films looked incredibly similar—but they were most definitely not the same girls. I watched them, beginning to end, three or four times.

The perspective was slightly different in each movie, too. In Bernie's version, the girls were performing a few feet in front of the fireplace, and the camera was static. It never moved. I suspected it had been propped onto a stand or a tripod.

In Violet's film, whoever was behind the camera—Harry, I supposed—was moving around, and at one point he captured Pippa backing up to the fireplace and accidentally bumping into the mantle.

And I could very definitely see, when I froze the two images, that the mantle in Bernie's video was noticeably higher in relation to Pippa's head and shoulders than it was in Violet's film.

I made myself another cup of tea and finished off the last of Tuesday's pizza, which was still sitting in its cardboard box on the writing table. I'd forbidden whoever was cleaning my room to remove it, sticking a large note written in big block letters to the lid of its box. Fresh pizza is delicious. And it's at its absolute indestructible prime two days later, especially when it hasn't been put into a fridge. I was certain my Instagram fans would wholeheartedly agree.

There was something else about the two frozen images that was niggling at my brain. I wasn't sure what it was. I stared at the pictures while I drank my tea. The girls…the fireplace…

And then it became abundantly clear.

I rang my daughter.

"I'm sending you something," I said. "Let me know what you think."

I zoomed in on Violet's film, grabbed a shot of Pippa's top, and attached it to my message.

It took Jenn about thirty seconds.

"That's the source photo for Pippa's head in the folk festival picture," she said. "The neck area of her top's an exact match to the pattern that's hidden in the shadows under her neck. Where did you find it?"

"It's from a Super-8 home movie of Pippa in 1973," I said. "And here's something else."

I sent her a screencap of the boy in Violet's film.

"It's him," said Jenn. "The kid from the folk festival. The one who's standing beside Pippa."

"That's what I thought, too."

"Same home movie?"

"Same home movie," I confirmed.

#

"Sorry," Violet said, apologising for the delay in answering her phone. "Doing my laundry."

"I'm going to send you a digital copy of your Super-8 movie."

"That was quick!"

"Friends in high places," I said. "It's only about two minutes long."

I waited while she watched it.

"That," she said, coming back to me, "is amazing. Thank you."

"You were telling me," I said, "about you and Duncan and the film. And that he'd advised you to keep it to yourself."

"Yes, that's right."

"And did you?"

"Yes."

"I'm going to send you a picture. Let me know when you've looked at it."

I sent her the photo of Pippa at the folk festival.

"Got it," Violet said. "And that's Pippa."

"It is," I confirmed. "The thing is, it's not a real picture. It's been photoshopped. Pippa's head's been stuck onto another girl's body, and the boy she's with was also added in after the fact. He's the same boy who appears in your film, by the way."

"Really?"

"Really," I said. "Have a look."

She did.

"You're absolutely right. He's wearing the same clothes, too."

"He is," I said. "In fact, his image was lifted directly out of your film. As was Pippa's head. And you're the only person I know who could possibly have done something like that."

"No," Violet said. "It very definitely wasn't me. I don't know the first thing about photo editing. Truly, Jason."

Her reaction sounded genuine.

And then: "Oh my God. Duncan."

"I thought you told me you didn't share the film with him."

"I didn't. Not then. But I did…later."

"When later?"

"Last year," Violet said. "You have to remember, he dropped off the grid about two years ago. Completely disappeared. No explanation whatsoever. Then, last September, he popped up. The old conspiracy theories were making the rounds of the forum again. Harry and mum's involvement. The photos that didn't show what my sister really looked like. I lost my temper and posted a public message saying that I owned a home movie that had been made a few months before Pippa disappeared and that if anyone was good at converting a frame from it into a photo, I'd be happy to send it to them. The posting was only up for a few hours, and then I thought the better of it and deleted it. But Duncan had seen it. And he got back in touch with me privately and offered to get a print made if I could post him some frames."

"Didn't he wonder why you'd decided to go public with the film after he'd advised you not to?"

"He didn't say anything at all about it."

"And you didn't think that odd?"

"A little, I suppose. But I didn't mention it either."

"And you've just remembered this now?"

"Sorry," Violet said. "I know it sounds daft. Yes. I've got so many things going on around me—my life is organized chaos. I really only just now remembered."

"So you sent him the frames?"

"Yes. I cut off the white bit at the start of the reel and the first few frames and I mailed them to him."

"By regular post?"

"Yes."

"Where did you send them to—can you remember?"

"It was a post office box."

"In Jamaica?"

"No, not Jamaica. I know that's where he lives. He told me he had a post office box in London, and to send them there, and his daughter would collect them and make sure he got them."

"Sounds like a very roundabout route."

"I thought so too," Violet said. "But that's what he wanted me to do."

"And did he ever post the pictures on the forum?"

"No—he said he never received them. He thought they must have been lost in the post."

"And you didn't send him any more frames?"

"No. Didn't want to risk it. And by then the forum had moved on to other theories anyway. So we just let it drop."

"Did you ever hear from him again?"

"I didn't. That's why I was so surprised when you told me he'd been in touch with you."

#

I rang Dom in London.

"Did you happen to notice any splices in the film when you were converting it?" I asked.

"None at all. And you'd have seen it if there were any because the action would have jumped. You didn't see any jumps, did you?"

"I didn't," I said. "Harry moved the camera around but he never stopped filming. It was all one big take without cuts."

"Why are you looking for splices?" Dom asked.

"Because of this." I sent him the Wiltshire Festival photo. "It's a constructed picture. Both the boy and the girl were lifted from frames of that film. She obviously came from the beginning, but I'm trying to figure out where he could have come from. He's not at the start of the film. He walks into it a few seconds afterwards."

"Why couldn't he have come from a frame at the end of the film?" Dom asked. "It just runs out. There's no tail leader."

"Tail leader?" I said.

"Yeah, a white piece of celluloid like the one that should have been at the beginning of the reel. But this one would have marked the end."

"And it's not there?"

"It's not," Dom said.

"Thank you," I said. "See you tomorrow night."

#

I rang Violet back and told her what Dom had told me.

"You're the only person who could have cut the frames from the end of the film," I said.

Violet was silent for a few seconds.

"You're right," she said, finally. "I pulled out the whole film. I sent Duncan three frames from the beginning and three frames from the end."

"Why didn't you tell me this before?"

"Quite honestly, Jason? I forgot."

"Again," I said.

"Again," she said.

I resisted the impulse to say "conveniently". I liked Violet. I really wanted to believe her.

"I'm really sorry, Jason. It completely slipped my mind until you jogged my memory just now. Please don't think badly of me. I didn't know it was that important."

"No problem," I said. "I'll make sure you get your original film back safely. Thanks."

#

Bernie took his time answering his phone. He could see it was me: I don't shield my name and number.

"What," he said, "do you want now?"

"Could we meet at your mum's house? There are a couple of things I'd like to clear up."

"I don't believe anything useful would be accomplished by my continuing to speak with you," Bernie said.

"On the contrary," I said, "I think you might find what I have to say quite enlightening. Shall we say…half an hour?"

"If you insist."

I still had about two hours until I was needed at the rehearsal. I would have driven faster, but the narrow country lane connecting Stoneford to Middlehurst had been created when horse-drawn carts and peoples' legs were the principal means of getting from A to B. I'd have ended up crashing through one of the tall hedges that lined both sides of the road. Or worse.

I sped through the open gate and tried very hard not to skid to a loud stop next to Bernie's car in the gravel courtyard. I eased myself out of my Volvo and *tat-tatted* the knocker attached to the front door.

Moira answered.

"Please come through," she said. Her demeanour wasn't quite as welcoming as before.

She took me into the drawing room, where Susan was once again sitting in one of the comfortable armchairs, and once again she had a blanket over her legs. Beside her, on the matching sofa, sat Bernie.

"And what 'enlightening' information do you have to share with us this time?" he said, without getting up.

"Nice to see you too," I replied. "Susan, would you mind if I popped upstairs to have another quick look at Pippa's room?"

"I don't know what it will accomplish," Susan said, her voice betraying distress. She was ruckling the edge of her blanket with both hands.

"I'm so sorry, Susan. Please just allow me to do this? I promise I won't bother you again."

Susan looked at Bernie.

Bernie was on his feet. "I'll come with you. But this had better be the last time."

Upstairs, I went straight to Pippa's cupboard and opened the door and looked through all the clothes on the hangers.

Just as I'd thought.

"Thank you," I said. "That's all I need to see."

Back in the drawing room, I took Bernie's seat on the sofa, forcing Bernie to stay standing, or to sit further away.

He decided to stand and hover over me, doing his best to try and make me feel uncomfortable.

I ignored him.

"I wanted to ask you about the field trips your husband made with his students," I said, to Susan. "I understand you and Bernie and Pippa went along with him to Jersey."

"Only on the last two trips," Bernie said, intervening. "Dad went on his own for the first three."

"Do you remember those trips?" I said, to Susan.

"Oh yes," Susan replied. "He went every February for five years. Harry loved to visit the tunnels. I wasn't much interested in them, but he certainly was."

"I know this might be difficult for you," I said, "but do you recall anything unusual happening while you were there on that last trip in February, 1974?"

"You don't expect her to be able to remember the details of anything that far back, do you?" Bernie said, irritably. "You can see how bad her memory is."

"Sometimes," I replied, "our memories can surprise us. We forget ordinary things. But we hang onto other things which cause us great distress or joy. Things that make an impression. Even if we think it's insignificant at the time." I looked at Susan again. "Do you remember anything about the guest house where you stayed?"

"Yes, it was the Gainsbourg," Susan replied. "It was owned by the Champions. A lovely couple."

"Just try and think back, Susan. Did Pippa say anything to you about something that might have happened while you were staying there? Anything at all…?"

"There was a castle you could visit, up high on a hill," Susan said, her eyes remembering, "but only at low tide…I was always afraid we'd be caught out and washed away if the tide came in while we were walking back…" Her voice drifted off.

"There," said Bernie. "You see. She isn't able to concentrate. She just doesn't remember."

I got out my little notebook and pencil and jotted down a couple of things to jog my own memory for later. And then I took out my phone, and cued up Violet's film.

"I've got something to show both of you," I said.

Bernie continued to hover behind me as I ran Violet's film.

"Oh!" said Susan. "I haven't seen that in years. I used to play it, over and over, after Pippa disappeared and after my Harry died. We had a little projector and a screen."

I allowed her to watch it again. Her reaction, as far as I was concerned, was genuine.

On the other hand, I could literally feel the prickle of Bernie's irritation as he stood behind me.

"Where did you get this?" Susan asked, touching my phone as if it was Pippa herself.

"I'd rather not say," I replied. "When was the last time you watched it?"

"I don't remember…I'd put it away. Because I thought, I must move on. Life must move on. So I'd put it away…and then it got lost…and I wasn't ever able to find it again."

"Would you like a copy?" I asked. "I can send it to Bernie and then perhaps Moira can play it for you anytime you feel like looking at it again."

"That would be lovely," Susan said. I could see tears in her eyes. "I don't know how to thank you."

"It'll be my pleasure," I said, meaning it.

I stood up and took my notepad and pencil over to the fireplace, where the little copper jugs were all lined up on the mantle.

"These are from Jersey, aren't they?"

"Yes," said Bernie. "They're handmade. They sold them in all the souvenir shops."

"Still do," I said. I picked up each of them, examining them, turning them upside down, making a point of looking inside.

"Why are you all of a sudden interested in those?"

"There's a thread on the Pippa Mystery Forum," I said, "that mentions a theory that Pippa was killed and her ashes were put into one of these jugs. But I can see that's wrong. They're all empty."

"If my sister had been cremated," Bernie said, "and her ashes had been brought back to England, my parents certainly wouldn't have been stupid enough to leave them somewhere that obvious. Do you have any other questions?"

"I think I'm finished," I replied, going back to my chair and retrieving my phone. "And I'm due at a rehearsal. Thanks for your time."

#

Lunch was catered again, and again, we had a lovely assortment of sandwiches and wraps, salads and puddings. And today Jack and Jill had also included Nanaimo Bars, which I was completely familiar with (courtesy of Jenn, who'd grown up in Vancouver), but which were an absolutely delightful surprise for nearly everyone else.

There's always a little bit of excitement and anticipation surrounding what you're going to wear onstage. It's part of the show. In my mum's case, the Figs' audiences had always looked forward to seeing what new gypsy skirts and tops she'd chosen. And she wasn't going to let them down. For the first set, she'd picked out a beautiful chrome-blue cotton and linen skirt and a loose silk chiffon blouse in the same colour, but a slightly paler hue. For the second set, she had the same skirt, but in a brilliant rust colour, and the same top again, but in the new rusty hue.

My dad had always been known for his brightly-coloured silk shirts—a concept I'd borrowed when I was gigging at sea aboard the *Star Sapphire*. This time 'round, I'd decided to part with his sartorial selection. I was going to wear fashionably faded jeans and a cotton shirt, with rolled up sleeves, that more-or-less matched the colours in my mum's skirts. It's hot on stage under the lights. I was opting for comfort as well as style.

We assembled once again at the foot of the little steps and waited for our cue. And once again, I was aware of my dad's presence.

I was dressed for the show.

And so was he.

But he still wasn't ready to go on.

#

We finished on time. Set 1, interval, change of clothes, Set 2, encores. We'd rehearsed until we were perfect—or as perfect as we could possibly be. Sometimes you need the buzz of a theatre filled with people to work out the kinks. It's one thing to play in a practice room, surrounded by the safety of your fellow bandmates and techies. It's another thing altogether to get out on stage and actually perform. And I knew we'd get better and better as we toured and got used to our audiences.

We made plans for a celebratory dinner in Middlehurst.

"I don't suppose you have a measuring tape," I said, to my mum, as we left the stage.

Mum gave me a look.

And then she went and got her handbag and pulled one out.

"I had an idea you would," I said. My mum's bag is like a surprise treasure chest, filled with all sorts of things you'd never expect but might possibly need in a pinch. A miniature sewing kit, emergency plasters in case you've nearly severed a finger, packets of breath mints and Ibuprofen, a spare pair of tights. In another era she'd probably have had a bottle of smelling salts and two lace handkerchiefs.

"I'd like it back when you're finished, if you don't mind."

"Promise," I said.

While I'd been checking the copper jugs over the fireplace at

Susan's house, I'd smudged my pencil lead onto the front of my shirt. The smudge exactly marked where I'd been standing in relation to the top edge of the mantle.

Back in my room at the inn, I measured the distance from the floor to the grey pencil mark on my shirt. It was exactly 47 inches. An inch short of four feet.

On my laptop, I played the video that Bernie had given me of the three girls miming in front of the fireplace. I paused it and increased its size and measured the distance from the marble hearth floor to the top of the mantle on the screen. Then I measured the distance from the top of the mantle, to the top of the head of the girl purporting to be Pippa. And then I did a little math, converting the image measurements to real ones.

Five feet, two inches.

I did the same things with Violet's film. Hearth to mantle, copper jugs, mantle to the top of the real Pippa's head.

I checked my calculations three times.

The real Pippa Gladstone was five foot seven.

CHAPTER SEVENTEEN

Bernie really wasn't expecting to see me again. And he truly wasn't happy as he opened his front door. But I knew that unhappiness was going to be outweighed by his curiosity about Violet's film. And I'm sure he was dying to know why I'd wanted to have another look in Pippa's cupboard. I'd deliberately left Susan's house before he'd had a chance to ask.

He didn't bother taking me upstairs to his office this time. We sat in his front room.

"Would you like to see that film again?" I inquired. Butter wouldn't melt in my mouth.

"Where did you get it?"

"No comment."

"Is someone trying to pass that off as genuine?"

"I'd say it probably is genuine, wouldn't you? Same drawing room. Same fireplace."

"Dad must have made two films. Two different rehearsals. Two different nights."

I'd been wondering how he was going to try to explain it away.

"Nice try," I said. "But there are a couple of differences between this one and the one you showed me—aside from the change in clothes. As you can see, in my copy there's a young man. It's the same young man, by the way, who's in the photo from the Wiltshire Folk Festival."

Bernie shrugged. "I still have no idea who he is."

"There's also a problem with your sister's height. In your copy, she's 5'2"—the same height everyone reported when she went missing. But in my copy, I'd say Pippa was about 5'7". In fact, if you look closely, you'll see that the three girls in my film aren't the same as the three girls in your film at all. They're very good matches…but they're three entirely different people."

"Then your film must be a fabrication."

"You're suggesting someone stole into your mum's house with three lookalikes and shot the whole thing without her knowing anything about it?"

Bernie didn't say anything.

"If I were to go back to your mum's house tonight, do you think I'd find that black skirt and the striped top hanging in your sister's cupboard?"

"Unlikely."

"Why? Do you know that for a fact?"

I was willing to bet he didn't want to risk it.

"That was exactly what I was looking for earlier when I went up to Pippa's room. And guess what."

"You found the black skirt and striped top."

"I did. Hanging next to her school uniform. What I didn't find was the outfit Pippa's wearing in your film. No black waistcoat and no black trousers. Because the waistcoat would have been too small and the trousers would have been too short."

Bernie was silent. He was out of explanations.

"All of the people who went out searching for your sister when she disappeared in Spain were looking for a 16-year-old girl who was 5'2". Not 5'7". That's quite a discrepancy."

Still nothing.

"But you know what absolutely convinces me that my film's genuine and yours isn't? The copper jugs on the mantle."

I loaded a screen grab from Violet's film and held up my phone so he could see it.

"Four copper jugs," I said. "Because it's Christmas 1973 and your dad hasn't taken his annual field trip to Jersey yet. That doesn't happen until February 1974. But in your copy…"

I replaced the photo with a screen grab from Bernie's video.

"…there are five copper jugs on the mantle. Which is somewhat of an impossibility if it's 1973. If you see the problem."

"My father could have filmed it after we got back from Jersey in February and before we went to Spain in March. Maybe he wanted to send it to someone as a gift. He was always doing things like that. Our gran's birthday was at the end of February."

Why was Bernie so desperate for me to believe in his film and not Violet's? Now he was just being ridiculous.

"That still doesn't explain the discrepancy in Pippa's height. And the fact that it's three completely different girls."

There really wasn't anything else Bernie could say. I'd nailed him.

"Did your parents have something to do with her death? Did they cover it up by claiming she'd gone missing?"

"No no, not at all."

"Did you have something to do with her death, then?"

"I was 13 years old!"

"It wouldn't be the first time parents tried to cover up a murder caused by a sibling. Would it."

I waited.

Perhaps Bernie was hoping I'd just give up and leave.

No chance.

"Look," Bernie said, in exasperation. "It's complicated."

"I'm listening."

"There was an argument the night before we were going to come back to England. Between Pippa and my father. He didn't want her to go to the party. She was adamant that she was going. My mother intervened and told Pippa she'd be allowed to go but she had to promise to be back by 11 p.m. She didn't come back until 1 a.m. and my father was furious. She'd drunk too much and they had a shouting match which escalated when my sister threw a table lamp at him. It missed, and my father leaped forward to grab Pippa to stop her from throwing anything else. But my sister stepped back and lost her balance and fell. She hit her head on the edge of a table. It knocked her unconscious and then she went into convulsions. There was nothing my mother and father could do to save her. She couldn't be revived and she died."

"Did you see this?" I asked.

"No. I was in bed asleep when the shouting started. It woke me up but it was all over very quickly. My parents told me what had happened afterwards."

"Why didn't your parents report it to the police? It was clearly an accident."

"You must remember, Jason, that in 1974 Spain was still under the rule of General Franco. It was still a dictatorship. And my father was afraid he'd be arrested and he wouldn't get a fair trial. He and my mum would be forced to remain in Spain. And he feared what might happen to me."

"What did they do with Pippa's body?"

"They put her into a suitcase and carried her to the beach and found a big boulder they knew was visible at low tide but underwater for most of the rest of the day. They moved the boulder and dug a hole and took Pippa out of the suitcase and put her body into the hole. Then they moved the boulder back on top of the hole."

"Were you with them?"

"I wasn't. My mother and father wanted to keep me safe. I stayed behind at the villa. I knew nothing about what they were doing. Again, they told me the details later, after we were back in England."

"So Pippa's body is still there, under a boulder on a beach near the resort where you were staying?"

"No. We stayed in Malaga for two weeks beyond the date we were supposed to return. My parents were able to move Pippa's body several times before finally leaving her permanently in a crypt in a graveyard. And don't ask me which graveyard because I don't know. And even if I did know, I wouldn't know which crypt."

"Fair enough," I said.

"My father felt a great deal of remorse and guilt after we came back to England. He became very depressed. He committed suicide by jumping in front of a tube train in London."

"What was he doing in London?"

"I have no idea. Perhaps he was obsessed with the idea of jumping in front of a train."

"He could have done that from any platform at any train station in Hampshire," I said.

"So now you're doubting that my father killed himself?" Bernie said, bitterly.

"It's quite a lot of effort and work," I said, "to move the body of someone who's 5'7". Not a small child. A teenager. How much did she weigh? About nine and a half stone? She's not a slender girl in that film. And you want me to believe your parents packed her into a suitcase and carried her—unobserved—to the beach, where they were able to move a large boulder, dig a hole at low tide—with what? Their bare hands? All of this again completely unwitnessed. And then pack her body into it, move the boulder back, and then sometime later go back to the beach, move the boulder again, dig up

Pippa's body—and then drive that body to a crypt in an unnamed graveyard and leave her there—again, all without anyone seeing them or hearing them—or smelling a decomposing body—or suspecting anything at all. Is that what you're asking me to believe?"

"Yes," Bernie replied, looking at me. "It is."

"If that is the truth," I said, "why did you feel the need to make a fake video?"

"In order to protect myself and my mother. Even though I was only 13 at the time, I knew the details about my sister's death. And my mother witnessed it. And assisted my father when they hid her body. So we could have been held accountable. We still can."

"Your mother has dementia," I said. "I doubt any jury would convict her now, even if the police did press charges. And you didn't witness anything. It's all hearsay. I still don't see how a fake video ties into that."

"I remembered watching the home movie my father had made of Pippa's rehearsal. But that had long since gone missing. So, I recreated it from memory as one of the pieces of 'proof' that I had that Pippa was quite short."

"In case her body was ever discovered?" I said. "And you thought you could prove it wasn't her? In spite of her dental records? And her DNA?"

"In case anyone was looking," Bernie said. "And DNA wasn't even a factor until 1986."

"I'm willing to bet," I said, "that you made this film well after 1986. And knew full well that if anyone found Pippa's body, they'd be able to use dental records and familial DNA to confirm her identity. In spite of the height discrepancy."

Bernie shrugged. "Suit yourself."

"Unless you knew," I said, "that there was no chance on earth that her body would ever be found. And that film was just a PR exercise to throw people like me off the scent. To confirm her height as 5'2" and nothing more."

"It is what it is," said Bernie.

"I gather you were behind Elizabeth Foster contacting me?" I guessed.

"I monitor the Facebook group for Pippa's old school, yes. And I knew both Elizabeth and the other girl in the film, Belinda, were dead."

"So who came to meet me at the pub?" I paused. "Your wife?"

Bernie wasn't going to confess to that one. But as I glanced around the front room for family photos I spotted "Elizabeth", wearing the glasses with bright red frames, sitting with a woman who was likely their daughter. She was wearing glasses too.

"Why didn't you include the boy who's in the original film in your remake?"

"I hate to admit it, but I simply forgot he was there. I was working from memory."

"Do you know who Duncan Stopher is?" I asked.

"I'm aware of a Duncan Stopher who used to post messages on the Pippa Gladstone Mystery Forum. He seemed quite obsessed with Pippa's disappearance. More so than most of its members."

"You monitor that group as well, I suppose."

"Of course. Duncan stopped contributing to the group two years ago. And I haven't seen anything from him since."

"Did you know someone made a public posting about a year ago claiming to have a copy of the home movie that your father filmed?"

"I didn't see that, no." Bernie seemed genuinely surprised.

"The message was quickly deleted. You must have missed it."

"Is that how you got that film?"

"Again, no comment."

"Who made the posting?"

I didn't say anything.

"Who hired you to investigate Pippa's disappearance?" Bernie asked. "Was it Duncan Stopher?"

"Why would you think that?"

"He turned up dead, didn't he. Last week. In Stoneford."

"That wasn't Duncan Stopher," I said. "It was someone impersonating him. An actor named Alistair Watford."

"Shame," said Bernie, standing up. He didn't seem the least surprised. "Shall I show you to the door or can you find your own way out?"

#

I was on my way to Curried Flavours for our end-of-rehearsals/pre-tour celebratory dinner when my mobile rang. I glanced at the number. Ellie Hammond. I pulled to the side of the road and took the call.

"I'm sorry for ringing you like this," she said, "but I've just

171

remembered something. I don't know how helpful it will be but I think I heard that student—"

"Linus Montrose," I said.

"Yes, him. I think I heard him saying something along the lines of Harry not being a problem, or not being a problem anymore."

"Not being a problem anymore," I repeated.

"Yes, I'm sure it was that. And something else. When they were talking about Pippa being gone, the student—Linus—said something like, it was nothing to do with him."

"Linus said Pippa being gone was nothing to do with him."

"Yes. That. And that's all I remember. I'm so sorry. I hope it's useful."

"It is," I said. "Thank you."

"And this is a little bit of extra information for you. I'm not sure if this will help with your investigation, either, but you couldn't have known this when you were talking to me the other day. Edward Champion wasn't my father's real name. After he died, mum and I discovered his real name was Aleksandr Kuznetsov. He'd had it legally changed before he married mum. He'd told us both his parents were dead and he was an only child, which explained why we'd never met anyone from his side of the family."

"Aleksandr Kuznetsov," I said, writing it down.

"Yes. Mum and I tried to find out more…but we hit nothing but brick walls. In the end, we just gave up."

#

I had to wait until our pre-tour toasts were finished and the bottles of wine were drained and our celebratory mango and pistachio kulfi's were posted to Instagram before I could race back to my room in Stoneford and go online to look for Aleksandr Kuznetsov.

But there was virtually nothing on the internet about him. For once, Google wasn't my friend at all. I really had to dig. And all I could locate, in the end, was a relatively recent story about a former Soviet spy, Mikhail Yahontov, who'd defected to the UK during the Cold War. The article was in *The Times*, and was actually a review of his just-published autobiography, in which he'd named names, all of whom were now dead.

And there he was: Aleksandr Kuznetsov. A certain gentleman

who'd run a guest house in Jersey and was, for years, used as a courier by the KGB. He was never caught, never unmasked, and he'd died in 2009 without ever being detected.

I went onto Amazon and downloaded Yahontov's book and got it open with the Kindle software on my laptop.

I could have just done a search for mentions of Kuznetsov. But that would have excluded any other background information I might have found useful.

One of the more interesting skills I learned a long time ago was speed-reading. I took a course. Basically, it involved acquainting yourself with whatever was being discussed in a chapter or document, then skimming yours eyes down the centre of the page, and letting your peripheral vision pick up anything of value along the edges while you digested what was in the middle.

I'd never recommend it for fiction, or for anything requiring expert and concise comprehension. But it's a doddle for scanning lengthy documents when you're hunting for key thoughts that you need to extract in a hurry.

Yahontov's biography was a proper spy story—and it was all true, as I was constantly reminded by the author, who, he made very clear, was a Soviet patriot until he'd become disillusioned, whereupon he'd switched loyalties and turned into a double agent for the UK—until it became apparent he was going to be betrayed, at which point he'd officially defected and gone into hiding somewhere in England.

I assumed he was writing from the safety of an assumed identity, given the Russian penchant for hunting down disloyal expats with deadly nerve agents.

In the same chapter that he talked about Aleksandr Kuznetsov, he also mentioned a Brit-born KGB operative who'd fled to Moscow in March, 1974. This fellow, who was only ever referred to by his code-name, Dickens, was a professor of history at a well-known university who also had quite a reputation for seducing attractive young women who worked at assorted western embassies in London. In the process, of course, he learned interesting secrets, which he then passed along to his Soviet masters.

The defection of Dickens, Yahontov wrote, resulted in the several important unnamed British operatives being exposed, with three of them losing their lives.

One of those three British agents was found hanging from the rafters in a barn on his farm in Dorset—a supposed suicide. The

body of the second agent was washed up on the shore in Norfolk—
a victim of drowning. And the third was killed when he was
presumed to have leaped to his death in front of an Underground
train at Holborn tube station in London.

#

Before I went to bed, I composed two private messages to
Duncan. I wasn't naive enough to believe he'd answer me
immediately. I was willing to wait until morning.

Violet Halliday, I wrote. *Maiden name Percy. Daughter of Susan
Gladstone. I've met her. I've seen her film. I have a copy. You know all about
her film as well. In fact, you asked Violet to send you some frames from it.
Which, apparently, you never received. But I don't believe that, Duncan. I think
you did receive them and then you used them to create a new picture of Pippa,
and then I think you hired Alistair Watford to impersonate you to try and
convince me—on the basis of that picture—to try and find Pippa.*

I sent it off, and then wrote the second message.

*Ellie Hammond's father was Aleksandr Kuznetsov. KGB. He liaised with
Linus Montrose, son of Garry Montrose, aka Dickens. Also KGB.*

I paused.

How am I doing so far?

I was so annoyed that Duncan wasn't online.

Dickens defected in March 1974, I wrote. *At the same time that Pippa
and her family were in Spain. Covers were blown. Including Harry Gladstone's.
Pippa went missing. And two weeks after that, Harry ended up dead.*

I paused again, then added a final thought.

*Pippa saw or heard something when she was in Jersey. She might have taken
a picture. And that made her a very dangerous person.*

As I was driving home from Middlehurst it had suddenly become
clear to me. The reason Bernie was positive Pippa's body would
never be found was because she wasn't dead. And he wanted to make
sure that if anyone—like me—went looking for the very much alive
Pippa Gladstone, they'd be searching for someone who was short,
and most decidedly not 5'7".

Is that why you wanted me to find her? I asked Duncan. *Is she still a
danger to someone?*

Is she still a danger to you?

I hit the Send button, and watched the message go.

CHAPTER EIGHTEEN

I woke up on Friday morning with that sense of anticipation you always get when you know it's only "one more sleep" 'til something big happens. Christmas morning. The last day of school before your holidays. The day you're getting on a plane to fly off to a wonderful new adventure. Your opening night concert in Middlehurst.

I stayed in bed, lying on my back, listening to the sparrows.

I don't really get nervous before a performance anymore. I used to, but I've done it so often at the club that it's second nature to me now. What I do get is a little adrenaline kick just before I go on. And I don't mind admitting that I love the attention, the applause, the affection. I love connecting with an audience that I know has come specifically to hear me play. I suppose it all feeds my sense of accomplishment and my ego. I wouldn't go so far as to say I crave their validation. But I grew up in the spotlight. And because I had well-known musical parents, I was always going to be put under the microscope and comparisons were always going to be made.

I long ago gave up trying to compete.

But by the same token, I've always wanted—and needed—to make my own mark.

Which was why I'd deliberated long and hard before I'd finally agreed to take my dad's place on the tour.

I wanted to be remembered as Jason Davey, the wonderful vocalist and lead guitarist. Not as Jason Figgis, Tony's almost-lookalike son.

We had a sound check scheduled for 5 p.m. at the Cottage Theatre in Middlehurst, the first time we'd actually be able to get a feel for our opening night venue. I was looking forward to acquainting myself with its dressing rooms and its stage. It was Grade II listed, built in 1927, one of the first theatres in the country to show films with sound. When it had been turned into a music hall in the 1950s, Eddie Cochran and Buddy Holly had played there. And, in the 1960s, The Searchers, The Dave Clark Five, Gerry and the Pacemakers. But never, alas, the Beatles.

When you do a sound check, you basically run through a few of your songs to test out the venue's PA system and make sure everything's going to run smoothly later that night. It's required before every performance. It's almost a part of the actual gig—except, of course, you don't have an audience in front of you.

After the sound check, Jack and Jill would be serving up dinner and then, at 8 p.m., we'd take to the stage again, this time for real.

Following the concert, we planned to drive back to Stoneford for the night and then, in the morning, check out of The Dog's Watch and board our bus for the next stop—Exeter—which was about two hours away. Our second performance was scheduled for Exeter on Saturday night. We had Sunday off to spend in town, then Sunday night in our hotel, and then we'd check out on Monday, board our bus again and drive to Bristol. We'd have Monday night and Tuesday morning free, and then our third concert would be on Tuesday night. And so on. A gig every few days for the next couple of months.

I got up, made myself a cup of tea, had my morning ciggie, then checked my Instagram comments, my emails and texts. Finally, I had a look at my private messages over on the Pippa forum.

Duncan had sent me a response.

Congratulations, Jason.

However, while I'm well aware the film you refer to exists—I'll freely admit to discussing it with Violet several years ago—I assure you I never requested to see any frames from it. I had nothing to do with the creation of any new picture of Pippa and, furthermore, I most certainly did not hire Alistair Watford. I'm at a loss to explain how you might have arrived at this erroneous conclusion.

I could see that he was still online. I sent him a reply.

Violet told me she cut three frames from the beginning of the film and three frames from the end, and she sent them to you.

I promise you, Duncan said, *she did not.*

Why would she make something like that up?

When was this supposed to have happened?

Last year, I said. *Violet posted a message on the forum saying she owned a home movie of Pippa and if anyone was good at converting a frame into a photo, she'd be happy to provide it.*

I never saw that posting, Duncan replied.

She changed her mind a couple of hours later and deleted the message. But not before it was apparently spotted by you. You offered to get prints made if she could send you some frames.

Again, said Duncan, *it most definitely wasn't me.*

You're suggesting it was someone impersonating you?

I've told you before about that. It wouldn't surprise me in the least.

What did Pippa see in February 1974 while she was staying at the Gainsbourg Guest House in Jersey?

No response.

What did she take a picture of?

Silence.

Who are you? I asked, exasperated.

Do you wear spectacles? he replied.

What the fuck does that have to do with anything?

Well, do you?

Sometimes, I said. *For reading.*

Then I think you should put your spectacles on.

Why?

Nothing.

Why???

But he'd gone.

#

I had lunch at The Four Eyes.

It had turned into a cloudy, hot, humid day. And I could see thunder clouds gathering in the distance, over the Channel. The door to the coffee shop had been propped open to encourage the circulation of fresh air.

I went inside and gave my order to the barista. The young girl who was usually behind the counter wasn't there. Her place had been taken by an older man—perhaps he was her father. The brother of the woman who was the mother of the waitress at Wellers. Our eyes met briefly as he handed over my coffee and a plate with my sandwich and a paper napkin.

I carried my coffee and sandwich over to the buffet where the sugar, milk and cream were kept, along with wooden stir sticks and cinnamon and chocolate sprinkles.

I sat down at my usual table—the table where I'd been sitting when Alistair Watford had first approached me, two weeks earlier. I was going to miss this place, with its vintage photos. One of them was hanging on the wall directly across from me: an exterior shot of the coffee bar from the 1960s, showing off its prominent, hand-painted sign featuring a pair of black framed eyeglasses.

Put your spectacles on.

I paused.

I looked around.

I took my reading glasses out of my jacket pocket and put them on.

Was someone going to come over to my table?

Nobody seemed remotely interested in me.

I sent Instagram a photo that I'd taken during our production rehearsal on Thursday.

Mum standing in front of our little collection of flight cases. Hers is packed with Snoop Dogg albums.

I added a picture of my lunch.

Last full day in Stoneford. We open tonight. Sound check at 5. See you all in Middlehurst.

I drank my coffee and ate my sandwich, which was slightly messier than I'd anticipated. The sliced tomato was a bit drippy.

I reached for my paper napkin. And realized I had two. The guy behind the counter had given me one with my plate and I'd helped myself to another, automatically, at the buffet. Because in the entire two weeks that I'd been going to The Four Eyes for my lunch, I had never been given a paper napkin by anyone serving me sandwiches.

I turned around to have another look at the barista. But he'd disappeared.

Two women at the next table were discussing last night's telly. An older man at another table beside the wall was reading a book. There was a youngish girl in a leather armchair in the corner, doing something with her laptop. But none of them looked up. None of them paid the slightest attention to me.

I finished my sandwich. I stood up and carried my plate and empty mug over to the buffet, where I deposited everything into the grey plastic bin designated for dirty dishes. I dropped one of my paper napkins into the rubbish. I kept the other—the one the guy behind the counter had given me—and went outside.

I crossed the road to the Village Green and sat on the bench underneath the enormous oak tree and turned the paper napkin over and read what had been printed there in neat ballpoint ink:

Beckford Farm.
Two o'clock.
Be careful.

I put the napkin in my pocket. It was still more than three hours until our sound check. My stage clothes were already there in the dressing room. Kato was setting up all my instruments. I had time.

#

I knew where Beckford Farm was. It was to the west of Stoneford, high on a piece of rolling land overlooking the English Channel. Angie and I used to go exploring there when we were kids, clambering over a wooden stile, oblivious to the signs warning us away from the unstable and eroding cliff top. The property had once featured an old farmhouse and some outbuildings, but they'd tumbled into the sea about a century before my sister and I had ever got there.

I drove up a little lane to where I remembered the wooden stile was. In the decades since those idyllic summers, some new buildings had been put up, far enough away from the crumbling cliff edge to never be in any peril. It didn't look much like a working farm—just a house and a garage and a couple of sheds and a very nice garden, proof of what a little bit of wealth and good taste and a hankering to live out in the country could accomplish these days.

I drove my car up the gravelled drive in front of the tidy brick bungalow, out of sight of the tree-lined lane I'd just left. I switched off the engine and wondered what I was expected to do next. I didn't have long to wait. A gentleman came around from the back of the house. He looked about ten years older than me, with greying hair and a tanned face, and he was wearing baggy jeans, a white shirt and a battle-green pullover.

He motioned for me to stay in my car while he walked down to the lane and surveyed it in both directions. After satisfying himself that I hadn't been followed, he walked back to my car. I rolled down the window.

"Hello," he said, leaning down to chat with me. "Please, come inside the house."

I did. And he locked the front door behind me.

We walked through the entrance hall to a comfortable sitting room, with cream walls and an electric fire, a massive flat-screen TV and curtains that were oddly almost the same shade of rusty orange as my mum's post-interval gypsy skirt.

There was a sliding glass door that opened onto a paved patio at the back of the house, after which there was a vast expanse of lawn, and then, at the bottom, a little woodland display of ferns, grasses and wildflowers. I could see another gentleman at work there—a Bohemian-looking man with long white hair and a tanned face, wearing baggy trousers and Wellington boots, and a straw sunhat with a jaunty ribbon around its crown. I recognized him as a gardener I'd spotted on a couple of occasions, tending to the shrubs and plantings on the Village Green, and to a display of boxed flowers outside The Dog's Watch.

"Please, sit," my host suggested.

I did. And so did he.

"My name is John Baumann." He had a German accent. "And you are Jason Figgis."

"That would be me," I said.

"I understand you have a photo that purports to show me and Pippa Gladstone at a music festival in 1974."

"Oh," I said, surprised. "That's you?"

"Yes, it is. I was, you understand, a little bit younger than now."

I smiled. "The photo's a fake."

"Yes, I know that. But it is still me. May I see it?"

I showed him the picture on my phone.

"This is clever," he judged, after studying it at length. "I was never there, of course."

"Of course," I replied.

"And neither was she."

"I understand that, too," I said. "But, if you're the boy in this photo then you must also be the boy who performed with Pippa at her school's Christmas talent show a few months before she disappeared."

John grinned. "Very good," he said. "It's true we rehearsed a song together. But the headmistress of Pippa's school was a dragon and she forbade me to perform with the three girls because I was not a student at Mewbury—I was a student at Shorebridge, along the road. And it was a Christmas show only for the Mewbury girls."

"The witch," I said.

"It would not happen these days, I'm sure. Especially as they've since merged and are now one and the same school."

"Do you remember the name of the song?" I asked.

John was still smiling. "You're trying to verify whether I really am who I say I am."

"I'd be stupid not to."

"'I Can't Stay Mad at You'. I've never forgotten it. But please don't ask me who sang it originally because I truly don't recall. Pippa's father filmed us rehearsing. We were in the drawing room. In front of the fireplace."

"Have you seen the film?"

"I have," John said. "Mr. Gladstone played it for us after he got it back from the processing lab."

"But not since?"

"Not since."

"Do you remember what you were wearing?"

"I was wearing what I'm wearing in your photo at the music festival. The same cotton shirt. The same jeans. But not the baseball cap. Have I convinced you?"

"I can easily check to see if you were registered as a student at Shorebridge in 1973."

"Then please do. My name wasn't John Baumann at that time, however. It was Charles Galpin. I went to live in Germany after Pippa disappeared. My mother's family is from Dusseldorf. I finished my education there. I met my partner, Felix, there. We decided to come back to England five years ago. We bought this land—the land that Beckford Farm had once stood on—and we built our house here. Felix was a landscape gardener in Dusseldorf and he now does similar work in the Stoneford area to supplement our income."

I gathered Felix was the tanned gentleman I could see tidying things up at the bottom of the garden.

"Why did you change your name?" I asked.

"I thought it wise," John replied, "under the circumstances. People who might want to connect me to Pippa might be looking for a very English Charlie Galpin. And most certainly not for one John Baumann, with a strong German accent."

A strong German accent, I noted, which now seemed, almost miraculously, to have disappeared.

"I showed that folk festival photo to Pippa's brother and her mother," I said. "They both claimed not to know who you were."

"They would," John replied. "They were trying to protect me."

"Why?"

"Do you know about Harry Gladstone?"

"That he was working for MI5?" I said.

"Not officially, of course. For all intents and purposes, he was a History professor at Hampshire University."

"Which enabled him to keep an eye on Garry Montrose," I said. "Who reported to Moscow using the code name Dickins. His son Linus, who seems to have shared his father's loyalties, was one of Harry's students."

"Yes. That's exactly right. MI5—and Harry—knew that Garry often used Linus as a courier and a go-between. When they went on their field trip to Jersey in February 1974, Linus did his father's bidding and liaised with a Soviet agent named Aleksandr Kuznetsov."

"Edward Champion," I said. "He ran the Gainsbourg Guest House."

"Which was where Harry and his students always stayed, yes. Quite deliberately. Though it's doubtful Kuznetsov was ever aware he was under any kind of surveillance. Garry Montrose almost certainly knew Harry worked for MI5 but he chose to keep that a secret until he defected to Moscow in March 1974."

"Harry took his family along to Jersey in February 1974," I said. "I believe Pippa saw or heard something during that trip that put her life in danger."

"You're not wrong," John replied. "Pippa overheard a crucial conversation that took place between Champion and Linus and worse, she accidentally took a picture that showed the two of them together, exchanging some documents. She was only trying to use up the roll of film in her camera. She was taking pictures of everything…the guest house, the souvenirs, the Breakfast Room. Linus was foolish, of course. He ought to have used a better method—a dead letter drop, at the very least. But he was brash and overly-confident and very likely poorly-advised and poorly-trained."

The feeling of satisfaction I got from John's confirmation was overwhelming. "How do you know all this?"

"You'll just have to trust me, Jason. Pippa realized what she'd witnessed and told her father. Her father was understandably worried. And his fears played out the very next month, while Pippa and her family were on holiday in Spain, and Garry Montrose crossed over to the Soviet Union. It was then that Harry knew for certain that both he and Pippa were in real danger."

"So Harry was taken care of by the KGB at Holborn tube station in London," I said.

"Harry was indeed killed two weeks after the family returned to England," John confirmed. "But not by the KGB—by Linus Montrose. And very fortunately, before he was killed, Harry had made arrangements in Spain to save Pippa's life."

I knew it. "Pippa's not dead."

John didn't answer.

"How do you know all this?" I asked, again.

Again, John didn't comment. And he held up his hand for silence. I'd heard it too—a car driving onto the gravel in front of the house.

Footsteps…the sound of someone trying the front door handle…

John stood up and motioned me to do the same. I knew he'd locked the front door, but the sliding window in the sitting room was wide open. We both heard whoever it was running around the side of the house but before we could get out of the sitting room, he was standing before us.

It was Bernie Gladstone.

Any relief I might have felt was quickly replaced by certain fear. Bernie was carrying a shotgun. And it was aimed squarely at me.

"Outside!" he shouted, gesturing towards the patio. "*Now!*"

CHAPTER NINETEEN

I'd walked into a trap. Duncan had set me up and I'd fallen for it, spectacles and all.

"There's no need for this, Bernie," John said, calmly. "I have everything under control. Mr. Figgis won't be causing you any more trouble."

If Bernie didn't kill me, I reckoned John would. I should have seen it coming. I'd found out far too much. I thought about making a run for it—straight out through the open sliding door and around the side of the house to my car. But Bernie would blast me to kingdom come before I even got to the patio.

"Too late for that!" he shouted, raising his shotgun.

He was standing with his back to the garden. And I could see that Felix had been alerted by the commotion. He'd dropped his rake and was running towards the house.

"Bernie!" Felix shouted. "No!"

Startled, Bernie swung around and, in that moment, Felix grabbed the rib of his gun. The jarring caused Bernie to pull the trigger, blasting a ragged hole in the wall beside the sliding window. As he lost his balance and staggered back from the recoil, Felix yanked the shotgun away from him and hurled it into the garden. I reckoned my best chance of saving myself was to run. But John and Felix both blocked my way.

"Sit down," John said to me. "Please."

I stayed on my feet. My heart was pounding. They weren't armed. I could get around them.

"I tried to throw this stupid fool off the track," Bernie said, getting to his feet. "But he wouldn't give up and now he's found you. You can't let him go free. He'll betray you."

I thought he was talking to John—but he wasn't.

He was talking to Felix.

"He won't, Bernie," Felix said. He was looking directly at me. "Will you, Jason?"

I stared at his face. At his eyes.

His striking blue-grey eyes.

"I won't betray you," I said. "I promise."

"Everything would have been fine if it hadn't been for that picture," Bernie said, bitterly, to his sister. "I cannot believe you'd risk everything our father did for you by turning up at a bloody music festival. With *you*." He pointed his finger accusingly at John. "Was that your idea?"

"I was never at that music festival," Pippa said. "That picture's not real, Bernie. Someone photoshopped it."

Bernie's face said it all. He'd truly, honestly, had no idea.

"And I told Alistair Watford the picture was a fake," I said, to Bernie. "I was going to drop the whole thing until he turned up dead. That's when I came to see you."

I stopped.

Of course.

"It was you who killed him," I said. "Wasn't it?"

Bernie didn't deny it.

"You assumed that picture was real and that Alistair was trying to get me to investigate Pippa's disappearance and you couldn't let that happen. So you decided to silence him. How did you hear about it?"

"How does anyone hear about anything in a village like Stoneford? Gossip. A friend saw you and Alistair in the coffee shop. Two newcomers, one of them a celebrity. Member of a band rehearsing up the hill. My friend overheard you discussing Pippa. Conversations about Pippa always get back to me."

"I suppose it was you who had me followed when I went to Jersey? And you who arranged to have my daughter's darkroom broken into? And me beaten up? You arranged the helpful 'eyewitnesses' who contacted DS Handsworth? And, of course, you followed me here."

"Someone had to stop you," Bernie said.

"If you'd just left well enough alone," Pippa said, to her brother, "the investigation would have been dropped and none of this would ever have happened."

Nor, indeed, would what happened next…which was that two very intimidating-looking men arrived from the side of the house with extremely intimidating-looking handguns, both of which were squarely aimed at all four of us.

I can only think that Bernie, in that moment, was not entertaining a rational state of mind. There was no other explanation for what he did—which was to try and retrieve his own shotgun from the garden.

One of the men shot him. Twice. In the head.

Without hesitation.

"This way," the other man said to Pippa, John and me, gesturing with his gun.

We complied.

I'd never seen anyone shot. I'd seen the aftermath, yes. But I'd never witnessed the terrible act. I think I went into some kind of shock…you know…when you think, this can't be happening to me. This isn't real. I'm watching a film.

I'd experienced that when the *Sapphire* had gone down in the Gulf of Alaska and I'd nearly died.

I was very close to losing my life now.

It was difficult to think straight. It was difficult to stay calm.

I followed John and Pippa out to the patio and around the side of the house to the gravel driveway. There was a white, windowless delivery van sitting next to my Volvo and the car Bernie had arrived in, a black Kia.

The two men quickly searched us and took away our mobiles.

"Inside," said the one who had blown away Bernie's face.

I climbed into the back of the van after John and Pippa.

The door slammed behind us. I could hear it being locked. We were in total darkness.

The two men got into the front and started the engine and we were thrown to the floor as they sped out of the driveway and onto the road.

"I suspect," said Pippa, "that these two are working for Linus Montrose."

"Now better known as Todd Wolfe," John said. "Ultra-right contender for a high-profile senate seat in California. A frightening possibility for future president. Fell off the grid after his father defected and emerged years later with a completely new identity."

"Linus Montrose," said Pippa, "assassinated my father at Holborn tube station. And I'm the only person who knows about his previous career as a courier for the KGB. I can single-handedly destroy his political trajectory. So now you know why he was trying to find me."

Outside, I could hear distant thunder. The storm I'd seen threatening earlier was upon us.

You're safe, I thought. Best place to be, inside a vehicle. The metal frame's a Faraday cage. If you're struck, the electric current's directed around the outside.

It was a bit of an empty reassurance. We were going to be killed by the guys who were driving the van. Or Linus Montrose.

"He knows I have proof," said Pippa. "The photo I took in the Breakfast Room at the guest house in Jersey. It's fairly damning. You can see the documents he's giving Mr. Champion. And I wrote down everything I overheard him say."

"Where is this proof?" I asked, forcing myself to focus on what she was saying, and not the loud plops of rain that were beginning to assault the van.

"It's with a lawyer in London."

I crawled to the side of the van, where I propped myself up, my back to the hard metal wall, and tried to keep from being thrown about as the driver negotiated twisting lanes and hard turns.

I heard another loud rumble of thunder.

Then, it seemed like we joined a main road, because the twisting and turning stopped, and the van's speed increased.

"I'm guessing we're on our way to meet Mr. Montrose," I said. "I'm also guessing he impersonated Duncan Stopher on the Mystery Forum, created the fake folk festival picture, and hired Alistair—the plan being that I would eventually lead him to you. I'm so sorry."

"Don't be," Pippa replied. "I've stayed hidden long enough. I still have the same scruples and values I had when I was 16. It's time I came out of the shadows and put a stop to Todd Wolfe's rising black star."

I had a horrible feeling this wasn't going to end well for any of us.

"Do either of you know who the real Duncan Stopher is?" I asked.

"Not a clue," said John. "We know he wants justice for Pippa—

he's always been very clear about that. But as to his true identity…"

"We've never met him," Pippa added. "But we've had many conversations. He's been on the Mystery Forum from the beginning. So have we. He's on our side."

"He knows a lot," I said.

"He knows everything."

"He likes to play games," I said.

"One of his more infuriating habits," John agreed. "This afternoon he sent us a message saying he was sending you over to see me. He advised me what he thought I ought to do. If Bernie hadn't shown up just now I would have told you all about Wolfe and given you instructions on how to leak information about him to the press. You would never have found out about Pippa."

"What about Violet? What does she know?"

"The little sister I've never met," said Pippa. "She's completely innocent. She's a little naive…but she really doesn't have any idea about any of this."

I didn't have my mobile but I was wearing my watch. I'd put it on because of that afternoon's sound check. Which I had now officially missed. My watch had a luminous dial. It was half past five.

Our sound check was, at that point, the very least of my worries.

There was a flash of lightning so bright that I saw it through the tiny vertical crack where the two back doors of the van met. I ducked, instinctively. The thunder sounded like an enormous load of hard concrete rubble tumbling down from the sky.

"I reckon," I said, to Pippa, trying to steady my voice, "that Linus Montrose is going to be very nasty to you. If he knows you have that photo, he'll want to know where it is."

"I agree," Pippa replied. "If he was solely interested in killing me—and John—he'd have done it back at the house."

She crawled over to sit beside me, and then she whispered a name in my ear.

"That's my lawyer in London," she said, quietly. "Give him this phrase: 'I left without warning but now I've come home…This morning I'm yours and I'll nevermore roam.' He'll know you're genuine."

It was one of the verses from "Lost Time".

"Catchy code words," I said.

"My second-favourite song by the Figs," Pippa replied, and I knew she was smiling. "I always knew my dad was a spook. It was supposed to be top secret, but I knew. And when he arranged for me to disappear in Spain, he taught me a few tricks of the trade. Just in case."

"And after she disappeared," John added, "the firm continued to look after her. They always do."

Another brilliant flash of lightning, another monumental shitfucking blast of thunder. Pippa must have sensed my fear. She put her hand on my arm, and gave it a squeeze.

"I'm terrified of lightning too," she said. "We'll be brave together. Just for now."

I placed my hand on top of hers, and we sat there, like that, in silence, for a few more moments, listening to the pounding rain and that unceasing cascade of thundering noise from the skies.

And then, Pippa said: "I have a cyanide capsule hidden in one of my teeth. So does John."

"You're kidding," I said. It was a stupid reaction. We weren't acting out a Len Deighton thriller. This was the real thing.

"We've had them for a long time. Maintained regularly by the firm's dentist."

"Just in case," John added.

"And I think, unhappily, that now is the time we're going to need to use them."

"No!" I said. "Please don't…"

"I think we must, Jason. John?"

"Wait!" I shouted. "No! There must be another way—"

But Pippa's hand was going limp on my arm. She slumped over, falling across my lap.

Quick and silent and painless.

And devastating.

I grabbed her. I shook her. I wanted her to live so much.

But there was nothing I could do.

I cradled her in my arms until the last breath left her body and then I pounded on the wall that separated the back of the van from the driver's compartment. I kicked at it and screamed at the two guys on the other side.

The van skidded to a stop.

The back door was unlocked and yanked open.

I glared at the two thugs who were standing in the downpour, staring at the two bodies sprawled on the floor beside me.

One of the guys climbed up and gave John's shoulder a rough

shake. Nothing. He tried the same thing with Pippa.

"They're not breathing," the guy said, to his mate.

Todd Wolfe wasn't going to be happy.

"They had cyanide," I said.

I felt like I wasn't there. I felt like I was watching it all from a seat in a darkened theatre

What happened next on the giant screen in the darkened theatre would have made the audience cheer. Four police cars—lights flashing—appeared on the road. They splashed to a stop, surrounding the van. Four uniformed officers leaped out, taking the two guys completely off-guard and swiftly manhandling them down onto the wet pavement.

Another officer was radioing for paramedics and ambulances.

"Don't arrest me," I said, holding my hands up. "I'm not one of them. I'm a musician."

"It's all right, sir. We're well aware."

I had no idea how they could possibly have been well aware. Nor how they could have known how to find us.

I wasn't going to ask.

Yet another officer helped me out of the van.

There was an immense earth-shattering flash of lightning and a horrendous *BOOM!*

I ducked—again—too late. I could hear my heart thumping in my ears. I couldn't breathe.

"Would you like to wait in one of our cars, sir?"

"Yes," I said. "Now. Please."

"Hell of a night for it," said the officer, opening his passenger door for me.

I dived into the back seat. The officer closed the door and went back to the van.

I was alone. I tried to calm myself. I was safe. I was alive. I was—

There was a hiss and a sizzle and I was simultaneously and momentarily blinded by 300 million volts of focused electricity.

But there was no thunder. Just a deep and penetrating *THUD*, like a solid punch to my chest.

My heart literally jumped.

I saw the police officer running back towards me.

"You alright?" he shouted.

I nodded.

The officer opened the back door, just to reassure himself that I was, indeed, not dead.

"Bloody hell," he said. "Never been that close to a lightning strike before. I reckon you got a direct hit. Thank God for rubber tires."

"Faraday cage," I said. "Nothing to do with the tires."

He didn't know what I was talking about. He went back to his colleagues.

I stared out of the front windscreen at the rain. The air around me smelled like scorched ozone. But I was suddenly aware of the most wonderful sense of green, fresh calm washing over me.

"Look after Pippa for me," I whispered. "Please."

#

We were somewhere near Basingstoke. I spotted a road sign as I climbed into the back of the ambulance.

I'd gone absolutely numb.

They drove me to the nearest hospital where I was taken straight in to the A&E—I had no idea how they'd arranged that. Possibly it was the fact that I had a police officer with me. He waited in a nearby chair while I was checked over and observed and given a cup of tea. And a tiny packet of biscuits.

I finally remembered to look at my watch. It was nearly half past seven. And I was supposed to be onstage at eight.

"I don't suppose you could give me a lift back to Middlehurst," I said.

"We need you for a witness statement, I'm afraid. As soon as you feel able."

"I know. But I'm in a band. Figgis Green. It's our opening night."

"I'm really sorry. I need to follow the process. Two people have died and you were with them when it happened. And, for some reason, the Home Office is involved. They must have been important."

"They were," I said, sadly. "I'll give you my statement on the way. And I promise I'll be available for follow-ups. Please?"

The officer needed to consult a colleague. And then someone else with more authority.

In the end, everyone relented.

A second officer arrived with a car and something to record what I had to say. I got into the back seat with the officer who'd accompanied me to the hospital.

"The guy in the black windbreaker took my mobile. Could I possibly ask one of you to ring my mum and let her know I'm on my way and not to panic?"

"No worries," said the second officer. "Number?"

I had to think. I usually just touched the screen where it said "Mum".

I told him and he keyed it in and then handed the phone to me.

"Where in the withering tits of Nell Gwyn's strumpet arse are you?" my mother demanded.

I could tell she wasn't happy.

#

And that was how I arrived at the Cottage Theatre in Middlehurst, at 8:37 p.m., in the pouring rain, with lights and sirens.

I leaped out of the car and raced inside, explaining who I was to the ticket-taker by the door. I could hear the band onstage. Rather than delay any longer, they'd started without me, completely rearranging the first set list on the fly to buy me a little more time. Beth was improvising my Strat parts on her fiddle. She was singing my lines. She sounded frighteningly fabulous.

Freddie appeared from somewhere and took me down to the dressing room, where my gigging clothes were waiting for me on hangers. I tore off what I was wearing and pulled on the blue shirt and the jeans and tried to calm myself as we sprinted down a long, neon-lit corridor that took us backstage.

I ran up the stairs and waited in the wings 'til the band finished a lead-guitarless version of "What Have They Done to the Rain?"

I caught Mitch's eye. He nudged mum.

I checked I was buttoned and zipped. And then I walked onto the stage to a round of cheers and appreciative applause.

CHAPTER TWENTY

Two weeks later, during the interval in Leeds, I was sneaking a quick ciggie outside our venue's stage door. I'd already had a quick freshen-up and changed my shirt, and I'd drunk most of a bottle of chilled fizzy water.

The concerts were going well. Aside from opening night, there hadn't been any major hitches, and our audiences loved seeing mum, Rolly and Mitch again after such a long absence. They were also extremely appreciative of Beth, Bob and me. Whenever you hear a performer describing an audience as being "warm", they really mean it. It's like a huge wave of love—a generous and welcoming hug. You can feel that energy from the stage—even if you can't see where it's coming from because of the lights.

The one thing that always made me feel a little pang was when we closed each show with "I Can't Stay Mad at You." Every time we sang it, I thought about Pippa.

After all that work I'd put into researching her life, it had been such a wonderful surprise to discover that she wasn't dead, after all. I'd liked her so much. She'd seemed like such a lovely person…and then, for her to have ended it all, so suddenly and for such a horrible reason…

I'd cried about that. Not that night, and not on Saturday. But on Sunday, in Exeter, after wandering around the city on my own…I'd ended up back in my hotel room, feeling completely lost.

I'd laid down on my bed and let it all out. The frustration, the sorrow and the anger. Everything.

I haven't had that much death in my life. My dad, yes. And my wife, Emma. But, by and large, I've managed to avoid the passings that a lot of my friends have dealt with. I haven't lost my sister, or any cousins. All of my good friends are all still with me.

Pippa's death hit home the same way my dad's death had, and Em's.

I felt a little better for letting it go.

But there was still a huge hole in my heart.

I finished my cigarette and got my phone out. The police from Basingstoke had been able to retrieve my mobile from the thug who'd taken it, and had arranged to have it quickly returned to me. I'd got the constables a couple of free tickets to one of our gigs to express my gratitude.

I scanned the news headlines—as I often did during the interval.

My attention was caught by a breaking story—a bombshell report about a document and a photo that had been leaked to the press, alleging that the right-wing conservative U.S. Senatorial candidate Todd Wolfe was both a traitor and murderer.

I'd done what I'd been told. I'd owed that to Pippa and John.

I sent the link to Rolly, who I knew would appreciate it.

As I checked my Instagram, I caught a distant flash in the dark sky. A September storm had been in the weather forecast. I counted the seconds until I heard the thunder. It was still a fair distance away. No need to take cover just yet. But I could smell the approaching rain in the air.

I glanced up from my phone. An attractive-looking woman in her fifties was walking towards me. She had long, wavy, dark blonde hair, and she was wearing minimal makeup. Not your average lady of the night, I mused. The stage door opened onto a back alley that was lit with a single streetlight. It wasn't really the best of places to be hanging around on my own.

"Hello again," the woman said, with a beautiful smile.

"Hello," I said. "Have we met before?"

"We have. About two weeks ago. I looked a bit different."

I saw her eyes.

Blue-grey.

Couldn't be.

"Pippa?"

"I'm sorry about all the trouble. We fell back on an old spy trick. It's a drug that temporarily mimics death. I never really had a chance to test it out before. Thank goodness it worked as advertised."

I wrapped my arms around her and hugged her. I couldn't stop myself. I hung onto her for what seemed like ages.

"I can't believe it," I said.

"I wanted to wait until I was sure the news about Wolfe was out there," she said. "I owe you, Jason."

"I owed you."

"I'm going to have to disappear again while all this is dealt with. But I'll definitely be back in touch"

"Come and see us in London," I said. "Hammersmith Odeon. The Beatles escaped down its back stairs in *A Hard Day's Night*. I'll get you tickets."

"I'm looking forward to singing along to your encore."

"I'll bring you up onstage," I joked. "You can do it live instead of miming."

"I'm going to hold you to that promise."

I still didn't want to let go of her. "One thing," I said. "How did the police know to turn up at just the right time to rescue us?"

"I have absolutely no idea," Pippa replied, amused. "Perhaps it was another spot of tradecraft."

She gently disconnected herself from my arms.

"See you soon, Jason."

I watched as she walked to the end of the alley, where she was met by a woman and a man.

I recognized the woman immediately—it was Andy Escott. And the man was Les Partridge.

They both nodded at me. And then they got into a waiting car with Pippa.

The car sped away.

There was another flash of lightning…and another low rumble of thunder, much closer this time.

"Thanks," I said, lighting a second cigarette. "See you onstage."

ABOUT THE AUTHOR

Winona Kent was born in London, England. She immigrated to Canada with her parents at age three, and grew up in Regina, Saskatchewan, where she received her BA in English from the University of Regina. After settling in Vancouver, she graduated from UBC with an MFA in Creative Writing. More recently, she received her diploma in Writing for Screen and TV from Vancouver Film School.

Winona has been a temporary secretary, a travel agent, the Managing Editor of a literary magazine and, most recently, a Program Assistant at the School of Population and Public Health at UBC. Her writing breakthrough came many years ago when she won First Prize in the Flare Magazine Fiction Contest with her short story about an all-night radio newsman, *Tower of Power*. More short stories followed, and then novels: *Skywatcher, The Cilla Rose Affair, Cold Play, Persistence of Memory, In Loving Memory, Marianne's Memory*, and *Notes on a Missing G-String*, as well as a novella, *Disturbing the Peace.*

Winona lives in New Westminster, British Columbia where she is the BC/YT/NWT Representative for the Crime Writers of Canada as well as an active member of Sisters in Crime.

Please visit her website at www.winonakent.com for more information.

Printed in Great Britain
by Amazon

47324023R00118